CW00867624

# THE KELNARIA CHRONICLES
## BOOK ONE
### THE GREAT SCROLLS

**By: Teresa K Conrado**

# Acknowledgments

DEDICATED TO MY wonderful family: Jason, my loving husband, my beautiful daughter, Kathryn, and, Benjamin, my blessed son. They shall always be what makes life worth living.

And a special thank you goes out to those family and friends that assisted in making this book a realty for me. To the most wonderful parents on all of Earth, Donald and Mona Steck! To the second most wonderful mother on all of Earth, my mother-in-law, Wendy Conrado. To my blessed Aunt Rona Rogers who not only assisted me financially, but also helped check my book. And finally to the best friend a person could ever have, who just so also happens to be my best friend, Vince Hartmann.

Thank you to all of you for everything that have done and will most likely continue to do for me!

# The History of the Prophecy of the Great Scrolls

SINCE THE DAWN of creation, good and evil have warred with one another.

The year was 5001 GW (Gods' War). The evil minions of Kahlrab, called the Fates, and His allies, the Onae, finally defeated the good deities of Mystics. The Fates and Onae also destroyed the Mystics' teachings and prophecies, called the Great Scrolls, which had been meant for the peaceful races of their once tranquil world, Kelnaria. Upon this final destruction, the seven heavens' shattered, the nine abyssal of heaven and hell opened and the scrolls had been scattered to the wisps of time.

Times became evil and dark on the enchanted world of Kelnaria until a small glimmer of hope emerged with the arrival of the goodly races of elves, Sylvan and Forest. For a short time they were able to once again bring peace upon Kelnaria. The elven races were successful in sealing away Kahlrab, his evil Fates, destroyed the High Demons called the Onae and closing the three hells of the Nine Abyssals and bringing peace to the goodly races and truces to most of the other races.

Then, war once again broke out between the elven races and the Draconians employed by the Demon Armies of the three hells from the Nine

Abyssals, once again revived. These demons were lesser demons than their now extinct High Demon cousins. This war continued until the Sylvan Elves were annihilated in 280 EL (Elven Lore) and the world cried in their wake. As the world made way for a new race to emerge as the dominate race, the humans. These beings created two diverse empires; the Kingdom of Cardinia and the Sovereign of Berdinia. The humans of Cardinia reset the world with the birth of the new royal family, the Dagmar Line, and these humans ushered in an era of growth, expansion and peace with both themselves and with other races until the first of an ancient scroll was found ....war began again in 708 DR (Dagmar Royalty).

The Sovereign of Berdinia, found the ancient scrolls of the Onae and became worshippers of the evil god Kahlrab. They waged war with their peaceful neighbors the Kingdom of Cardinia; the banished Mystics' last hope for survival. Their goal was to destroy all goodliness and resurrect their god, Kahlrab, the Fates and perhaps the Onae, if that were possible.

For seven centuries, Cardinia fought valiantly against her stronger, war-faring neighbors. However, the good-hearted Cardinians were losing too many battles...and with them, their land, people, faith and hope. Many people in Cardinia were dying from war, disease, famine and attacks on her poorly defended towns. Those that could no longer be repressed defected to the side of Berdinia. And, sadly as it must be in war, the last humanoid magic wielders, called Telestics, were slaughtered in these battles as they took up their country's battle arms. For the Cardinian people, the future was bleak.

In the winter of 1210 DR, a ray of hope was born into the world of the dying Cardinians. A Zadian Priest named Zaire found a half-burnt, withering parchment in the basement of Cardinia Castle during a renovation to the withering basement. It was the only remainder of the long forgotten prophecy of the Mystics, which had only been touched upon, in the Great Scrolls.

The parchment read:

"It shall come to pass that evil times shall fall upon thy holy kingdom. Great enemies shall fall upon this mighty kingdom with strength given to them by demons. Thine enemies will thus destroy, plunder and pillage with a rage known only to demons. Thus, there will be many moons of unrest and darkness in attempts to destroy this kingdom.

"Thine holy kingdom will turn crimson as the destroyers come. As chaos reigns, the kingdom will fall and its people will be slain. The kingdom will cease all peaceful existence and will take up arms.

"Yet, the lineage that shall come to pass that will birth a child of holy abilities and ancient wisdom. Thus the child shall be born when the kingdom of the

Red Dragon rules. He shall be born in times of great unrest. He shall be born to a people that will know no peace. But, his people will know great hope.

"Thine child shall herald from a family of power and greatness. He shall be destined to restore his people, rescue the Mystics, locate the lost holy kingdom and revive the Crystal Unicorn. He shall be the protector of his people and savior to all the land. Thus, he shall be the ruler when his true birthright has come to pass.

"He shall be known as thy Champion of thy holy Mystics."

# Chapter One

IT WAS A cold, dark night outside with the wind howling, threatening to bring a fierce storm. The moon was all but a tiny thumbnail imprinted into the black and starless night sky. It was almost non-existent in the expanse of that ever-violent growing night sky.

A stranger amongst the quiet little village walked ominously down the road shunned by the good and kindly townsfolk. He was searching for something, but would receive no assistance from the people that inhabited this small village. He slipped back into the shadows and would await a scent, a name, a whisper to come on the wind that would advise him of where his prey could be found.

***

Another stranger sat in the bar listening to the patrons go on about their merriment. He had long stark white hair in which he let flow freely down towards the bottom of his back. His long elfin ears were sticking out from his hair so he could not be mistaken as a short human. His eyes were the color of a grey, cloudy storm and his skin was the palest white, almost iridescent as the moon glows silver in the night sky. He wore a unique set of armor that was a dark red, almost crimson, but almost brown, maroon-like. The armor was tailored to his every curve for full flexibility, comfort and movement. He also had a cloak of deepest black trimmed in silver on his back with the symbol of the full moon with an intricate weave of flowing circles surrounding it on his back, the symbol of his people. He carried a scimitar and dagger on his belt and he had the easy gait of a well-seasoned warrior.

He was nursing his loneliness and wished that he could join them, but he knew that he would not be welcomed here if he revealed himself to them. He was just passing through and did not wish anyone harm. He had gotten the information that he desired and he could move on without any harm coming to anyone over nothing.

Ihoitae Mehadeva Arabus was at the local tavern called The Grenthen Tavern and Inn located in the small forestry village of Grenthen Village just outside of Loralia Forest, the furthest village on the Cardinian border. Ihoitae could disguise himself to look like any humanoid creature of like weight and structure, but humans and kindly folk alike could always sense the presence of the half of his heritage that was demon blood. Therefore, Ihoitae; being of half Sylvan and half demon descent, generally morphed his elfin self over the demon parts and only made quick small talk when necessary to make himself as un-noticeable as possible. It was so that he might enjoy a pleasant hearth cooked meal and bit of mead before the patrons' nerves were too badly frayed and he would kindly be asked to leave the premises and the nice warmth of the glowing hearth, especially on a night like tonight.

"Canni git you anythang' else, Mate?" a burly human male asked the young elven merchant.

"Uh, no thanks, unless you have a room available for a weary traveler to rest the cold night away?" Ihoitae smiled with an expression of desperate hope. Though, Ihoitae looked as a young, elvan male soldier traveling from Loralia Forest to the castle in the Kingdom of Cardinia, his ever-present demonic blood would overshadow his alternate form.

The barkeep adjusted his balance and fidgeted with his hair as he looked around as if trying to search for the right thing to say to avoid a conflict with a hostile humanoid. Ihoitae knew what was going to occur so he smiled at the barkeep to reassure the man that Ihoitae was an innocent lad and wanted an honest answer and nothing more. Ihoitae expected a polite excuse.

"I'm sorry, mate, I'm booked up through 'til affer th' Feast o' th' Moon. Perhaps th' stable warder may have a spare stable fo' ye. It's no th' best room, but a' least it's warm, eh?" The barkeep stammered trying to make his all too obvious lie sound believable so as not to offend this mysterious elfen soldier.

Ihoitae sighed, "T'is ok, noble barkeep. I understand that the festival must be beautiful and that this is the only Inn in this tiny village for all to come and stay at. I also understand that many bandits wander the streets and that you must be careful of your patrons. I shall seek refuge somewhere else." With that, Ihoitae got up from his seat, placed a gold piece on the bar and began to make his way out. "For your trouble, good sir."

Ihoitae stepped outside of the tavern and paused on the porch to acclimatize to the bitter cold and the howling wind. He then began his descent down the stairs and stepped upon the all too quiet of the streets. Was it the bitter cold? Or was it the presence of ill will saturating the wind? It was the dead of the frosting season. The months had just switched from Jan to Frianatte and it would be another 4 weeks before the warm season would start and things would not be so chill. However, there was not one soul, neither man nor dwarf nor elf nor animal, that walked on the street. Though it was bitterly cold, it was odd not to have someone dashing home on the streets or some animal searching for refuge.

Ihoitae realized his answer all too late when suddenly he was surrounded by ten muscle-bound human male warriors with ten very dangerous Dire Tigers chained and held captive by each warrior encircling him so that there was no possible means of escape. Dire Tigers were not easily captured and were very rare in the wild as it was; these men were either very powerful or had some very powerful friends.

"How did humans manage to capture and master ten Dire Tigers?" Ihoitae stated with a cocky smirk. "My guess is that you're either not humans or you're cronies of Lord Mordecai!"

"Not everything revolves around that arrogant, worthless demon, halfling!" one of the men smugly advised. "There are other, more powerful Gods that are interested in you!" The man that spoke, who was obviously the leader, waved his hand and two of the beasts were unleashed and immediately advanced on Ihoitae with snarling jaws and blood-thirsty eyes.

"So, much for the pleasantries! Right to battle, eh?" Ihoitae confirmed, still with his cocky smile, but immediately going into a battle stance drawing his scimitar and dagger. At least he could warm up with battle.

Ihoitae began to calculate all of his enemies, their positions and what spells he had on hand. Upon inspection, the Dire Tigers were actually tigresses, far more formidable than the males of their species. It appeared that he was going to have to pray to the Gods for luck on this one for things did not look good. He could handle between two or three beasts and maybe 5 warriors, but he was by far outnumbered with ten warriors and ten magical Dire Tigers. Ihoitae was going to have a bad fight on his hands and he just hoped that whatever God or Goddess up there that had helped him survive for the last 500 years after he escaped the clutches of Lord Mordecai were still helping him.

"Can we kill 'im, General?" enthusiastically asked one of the other warriors off to Ihoitae's left side, confident that this battle would be quick and in their favor.

The feline tigresses approached and began to slowly turn around Ihoitae in a crouched position, taunting him, toying with him until they could make their deadly strike. Ihoitae had to be careful, as these beasts were deadly with unyielding displacement powers and painfully accurate claws. These beasts were powerful and quick and were magical in nature. Ihoitae needed to be on his toes because he had eight more to beat if he survived these two. The humans did not budge and continued to stay in a tight circle surrounding him and the felines.

"No, we cannot kill him, but we can make him bleed! The Mistress wants the half breed alive!"

Ihoitae now sensed that this was indeed going to be a bad fight and that loosing was not an option. The humans he could handle, but with ten Dire Tigers at their command he would be hard pressed to keep from succumbing to be their prisoner. These humans had a powerful ally and it was one in which he did not want to find out whom. Nor did he wish to know what was desired of him.

Ihoitae ducked as the first feline creature that flanked him on the right pounced, while the left beast ran forward to knock Ihoitae off his feet. Ihoitae made a quick chant and gesture with his hand. As he did so, Ihoitae fell to the side catching his body with his hand and kicking up his legs so the pouncing beast would be kicked back to crash into the warriors and beasts to the right of him. The spell he just cast allowed for a temporary burst of strength to aid in this tactic so he could lift the 600-pound tigress. This now flying feline pounced right on top of the warriors to the left of the now sideways Ihoitae.

Ihoitae was quick to push himself back up onto his feet with a preternatural speed gained from years of internment with his father's army, The Imperial Demon Army. He then immediately began to chant another more powerful spell by falling into combat casting mode. As he did so, he held his first two fingers in front of his nose and mouth with his left hand cupped around his right fist. He closed his eyes and began to feel the spiritual powers of the planet flow through him. He had to cast fast while keeping his concentration. He had little time to cast his spell before the next round occurred.

"Quick!" yelled the leader of the small band, "you fools, don't let him get off that spell!" The warrior band had been distracted by such an unexpected turn of events. They had been warned that their prey was a very capable warrior, but it was not expected of him to be able to beat even half of this little army.

Too late, Ihoitae finished his chant and with a word waved his first two fingers straight in front as the spiritual energy that had been gathered in him was released. "Khelek!" came the fierce cry of a creature fighting for his survival as another one of the warriors succumbed. Ihoitae had unleashed a devastating ice storm down on his opponents. The sky suddenly was filled with giant fist sized hailstones and pounded down all around the wielder of the attack within a twenty-foot radius of its caster. Just out of reach of the buildings on either side of the street.

"Ahhhk," cried one warrior as a hailstone the size of a giant's head came crashing down onto him. Then two more warriors fell to mighty hailstones as the storm raged for another 10 seconds, with severe injuries that took them out of the fight. When the spell had completed, Ihoitae was left with three warriors and four Dire Tigers. It was a powerful spell that had drained him badly, but he knew he could not show that to his opponents.

"Now, the odds are even," gritted Ihoitae as the demon half began to become apparent in his eyes and his voice. His eyes began to glow blood red and his mouth began to show two fangs protruding his lips while his nails grew into short claws. "You better kill me if you can because I have marked all of you for death for this indiscretion!"

"Oh shit," screamed one of the warriors and he ran off. His reward for doing so was to be chased down by his tigress and killed.

"Stand your ground," stated the weary leader, "he cannot possibly get off another spell so powerful, he is weak now! Attack!"

The leader of the warriors unleashed his tigress, which was a beautiful but deadly albino tiger, and so did his remaining underling. The final feline, which no longer had a human holding her tether, followed her other two pride members and began to surround and flank this impudent half-elf, half-demon weakling. One beast went to his right, the other to his left and the third to stand behind him so that the 2 humans could face this whelp of a demon.

Ihoitae realigned his stance and his Moonlight's Dream scimitar and his Moon's Beauty dagger. "Come, then and let us end this. It is cold and I would like a warm fire." He was weak but still confident. Despite the fact that he had sustained a few swipes of cat paws that were not yet seen by his enemies.

Just then the right flanking beast began its pounce as the left one came running low to grapple Ihoitae's legs. Ihoitae did a low sweep with the dagger on the ground to impale the left feline's paw and at the same time did an upward thrust with the scimitar to catch the right beast in the belly. Blood splattered on Ihoitae as the right tiger's belly shredded its intestines. The left feline went limping away with a paw that would no longer support its weight.

"Round three," stated Ihoitae as he was now breathing heavily. Ihoitae's lips began moving as his cold blood red eyes stared down the haggard leader.

"Round three," agreed the leader and he raised his saber and dagger. The other warrior raised his battle-axe.

All combatants were with the knowledge that this would be the end one way or another. However, Ihoitae was slightly overwhelmed with battle rage and battle fatigue, a very deadly combination that could keep a warrior from performing with all his wits and skill. He was also weak from having to cast such a powerful spell and then having to fight with injuries that he hoped his enemies were still not privy too.

In round one, Ihoitae had been raked along his legs by razor sharp claws as the first beast had leapt over him and he had kicked. In the second round he had been unable to stop the beast that had been behind him from using its displaced abilities as its paws racked another fierce attack across his backside as the beast came in and vanished.

Now that last beast from behind, the beautiful white tigress, was crouched for the attack, having stayed to Ihoitae's back and she waited for the two humans to begin their battle cries while rushing in and she would unleash her fury.

"Notherlian      nictieus      protectoranntia spemmeshibia!" finished Ihoitae as he chanted the last of a protection spell in Sylvan. It was an ancient magic lost to Kelnaria with the death of the Sylvan elves, all but the one remaining Half Sylvan Elf that is.

The leader charged first and swords clashed as the two stood face-to-face locked in place. The last feline beast made its move and unleashed a two-pronged attack with its claws and muscular arms. Then, the beast finished it's pounce and landed on Ihoitae's back, breaking the two fighters' lock and dropping Ihoitae to the cold, icy ground. The creature had Ihoitae pinned under 600 pounds of pure muscle and he could no longer move, though he flailed wildly. There was one chance left. He had to pray to whatever God was out there listening and hope they would grant him a victory as he began to chant a teleport spell.

Then, the blackout came as the air was crushed out of his lungs. The tigress, being of a magical being herself, cast her own spell to bring sleep upon her prey. This spell was accomplished by removing enough air from his lungs to make him loose consciousness. Ihoitae knew no more.

# Chapter Two

HE HAD SCENTED his prey on the wind with the smell of blood. There was a battle going on and he followed it. His prey was there and he sensed a chance to snatch it. Upon his arrival, he saw a half demon, half Sylvan Elf battling ten hardened human warriors and ten Dire tigers.

The prey was hurt. The battle was almost over. His prey was severely wounded and now was his chance to strike and take what was his. However, just as he was forming his plan of action, a dwarf, a draconian, a human and a Wood Elf came swooping in.

Frustrated at missing his prey again, he stayed to the shadows, deciding to follow this band and see what they wanted with his prey. They seemed quite abyssal? bent on saving his prey from the clutches of the bungling warriors and tigers. He did not like that his prey was suddenly becoming very popular.

*** 

Ihoitae woke up in a small cell. He was lying face down and the cell was literally long enough to permit a small cot so his five foot six inch frame could lie out. It was only tall and wide enough to allow a person to stand next to the cot to perform ministrations. He was lying on his belly with bandages on his back and wrapped around his legs. Someone was trying to heal his wounds.

From what Ihoitae could see, the cell was in a stark white, warm room. Its walls resembled something similar to a cottage with a plastered texture and wood beams. There was a cozy fireplace on the opposite wall blazing with warmth. The room was bright with lots of windows. The sun was out and apparently had banished the cold, rainy night away. This is not at all what Ihoitae had expected his capturers to have for accommodations. He was somewhat impressed….for demons' minions.

He tried to roll over and immediately winced; deciding that having done so was the worst decision he could have ever made in his more than six centuries of life. However, he was able to move his head around without too much pain, so he continued to look around at his surroundings with this limited movement. As he looked at the cell to study its dimensions he discovered, much to his chagrin, that the bars were magical and designed to keep magical beings in. Damnit, he thought, can't escape that way. Ihoitae's face crinkled up in frustration.

"Aww, poor little demon boy is angry," came a voice from off to his backside. It was a feminine voice that seemed to have a lilting tingle to it, bell like. Must be an elf, thought Ihoitae. "Are you disappointed that you can't escape?", the voice scoffed. There was a mirror on the wall in front of

Ihoitae's cage so he could see behind him, but whomever was speaking was standing just outside of its view. However, this could also permit whoever was behind him to watch him.

Ihoitae tried to speak, but his throat was dry and it didn't do anything but crack when he attempted to speak. He was weak from the blood loss and the cost of the spells he cast. But if he had not cast the very powerful elfin protection spell, he would probably not be breathing right now. So, at least he was not dead and he had definitely been through worse. If he could survive an attack from the Fates, he could survive just about anything. He would escape, especially if it was a silly elf that had him captured. Ihoitae coughed and tried again. Weakly he spoke, "I am a bit impressed at where you are keeping me. I would have thought that cronies of demons would have me in a less than hospitable environment and in chains. Why heal me?"

"Cronies?" the elf voice responded, offended. "Demons?.......Oh no, no, no, no. You have it all wrong there, Mr. Prince Ihoitae Mehadeva Arabus. We are your rescuers, not your capturers. And, we are not cronies of any demon. WE ARE THE GOOD GUYS!!!" With that, he could hear a swish and a stomping sound as the female elf presumably stormed off into the unknown.

"Damn pretentious elves," Ihoitae muttered to himself. Then a little louder so hopefully the she-elf could hear him, "Please come back. Please tell me who you are." Then immediately he winced in pain as he realized too late he was trying to turn over again. Damnit!

"She won' come back, laddie," a gruff, male dwarven accent stated. "Once th' likes of her git angree, it takes jus a wee bit for th' angree to fade away. But I'll answer some questions for ye, if ye like."

In a still weak voice, Ihoitae cleared his throat and began his question and answer session with what he could only assume was a dwarf. "First off, you obviously know who I am, so may I be privy to who are my rescuers?"

The dwarf chuckled as he moved to face Ihoitae. He was pretty tall for a dwarf at four foot five inches but just as burly as any dwarf you have ever seen. He had long orange,- red hair that he wore in a braid down his back. He had a matching orange,- red mustache that flowed down into his beard, which he also wore in three braids down to his ample belly. This dwarf never missed a meal or ale,; that much was obvious. He wore a dark green tunic with rolled up sleeves and brown breeches with knee-high leather boots. He had an axe strapped to his back and he had a network of scars on his arms where his skin was exposed. There was also one large scar on his face that went from the side of his eye to his cheekbone.

"Certainly laddie, me name is Bodolf," he gave a curt little bow. "Bodolf Horsetamer of Clan Horsetamer from the caves of Nedhung. Me be a mercenary wit' this lil band o' mercenaries. We were hir'd ta fin' ye laddie, but fin' ye wit'…….. precautions."

"What is the she-elf's name?"

A hearty laugh issued from this obviously good-natured dwarf. "On no, laddie, I will not raise 'er ere. Ye will have ta ask 'er yerself."

"So, who were the human warriors with the very powerful pets?"

"No, idea, me lad," Bodolf glanced to the side, but whatever he was looking at was out of Ihoitae's view. "Th'mistress tha' hir'd us warned o' 'em. Lookin like we got'ya just in time."

"So, they knocked me out and your mercenary band rescued me," Ihoitae surmised. "How many in your band? And why all the precautions if I am not your captive?"

"There be four o' us," Bodolf replied. "An', our clien' thought ye would be less than cooperative….," he let trail off.

"Hmm,: Ihoitae muttered. "Maybe not, but guess we will never know…..so, how do I get out of this cage?" Ihoitae said with a smile as he tried to switch gears. He wanted to drop the captive versus rescue issue for now. He could tell he was in no clear and present danger for the moment so escape could be postponed.

Bodolf smiled with a glint in his eye that spoke volumes before he even uttered the response Ihoitae already knew he would hear. "I canna do that, me laddie. Only Dean can an' he is no here.

"Besides tha', me laddie, ye is in no condition to move. Ye're safer locked for th' now."

"Alright, then I guess I will have to stay here. However, you know that I can heal myself faster with my magic if you would let me out."

"Aye, maybe, but ye must wait for Dean." However, Bodolf did not look too confident in Ihoitae's ability to heal himself. Powerful magic like that for the goodly folk had not been seen since the days of the Sylvan Elves and now only demons wielded that kind of power. Maybe he canno know how badly he is wounded, Bodolf thought to himself "Dean will see ye when he arrives."

"Ok, then I guess I will rest for now. I am very tired," and so he was. This conversation took more out of him than he realized. Maybe it was due to the powerful anti-magic on the bars combined with his wounds. He truly needed a rest.

# Chapter Three

HE FOLLOWED THE prey's blood to this little cottage on the outskirts of Grethen Village. He found a nice little out of the way set of trees and bushes at the edge of the forest near the cottage from which he could watch his prey and his prey's capturers.

He decided finding out why after 500 years his prey had become much more popular other than "being just the Demon Lord Mordecai's son" had come to pass was an excellent idea. He was going to watch this band of mercenaries to learn as much as he could.

He saw through the windows that his prey was in a cage inside the main room in the small cottage. When the afternoon came, his prey awoke and the she-elf and dwarf both conversed with his prey. Due to his preternatural hearing, he learned some tantalizing details, but not enough to satisfy his curiosity. He would continue to study his hunt, he decided, as he watched the female forest elf stomp off from the cottage. His mistress would need to wait a little longer for her prize.

\*\*\*

As Ihoitae slept, Dean and Diane Moonstone came back to the cottage that they were renting while they were in town. It belonged to the Guild of

Mercenaries that they belonged too and was there for mercenaries to rent as necessary in the area in the event that they needed a safe house. The rental fees helped the guild pay for upkeep and keeping the place well stocked with weapons and food, everything that the mercenaries would need so they could travel lightly, if necessary. The price was steep, but given that everything was at their disposal at no additional cost, it was well worth the price. The guild had many of these safe houses all over Kelnaria for all its members.

Bodolf had filled Dean and Diane in on their conversation earlier. Dean was the leader of this small, but elite band of mercenaries. He was not entirely pleased with all that Bodolf so freely provided to the "package", but was not angry either. He supposed that since they were dealing with a living package, then he must be filled in on some details. Perhaps he would be more cooperative than their client advised.

"He does not look very menacing," Diane stated as she watched Ihoitae sleeping on the cot in the cage. "He actually looks very innocent."

"Diane, my love, looks can be very deceiving, as you should very well know," Dean replied.

"Yes, my husband, but look at him. I do not see the evil in him," she stated as she pointed at Ihoitae. "I see the half demon under his shape shifting, but he is more elf than demon. I sense that he is an innocent soul that has paid dearly for others sins. There is more to our client's story than meets the eye. Let us keep an open mind when speaking with our client and our package."

"Agreed," responded Dean.

At that moment, Ihoitae began to moan a bit as he started to awaken again. Dean and Diane both looked over to him. "Did anyone check his wounds recently?," Diane asked.

"Nay, mi'lady, Aelle was ta have 'em changed out. But th' lassie stormed off when the lad offended 'er," Bodolf chimed in.

"Hmm," murmured Dean unhappily, "the lass gets offended way too easily sometimes." He sighed. "Diane, will you please check his wounds?"

"Yes, my dearest," she replied. "But please try and remember that Aelle has had a difficult life as we all have. She just gets moodier than the rest of us do."

"Me thinks tha' th' lass no likes 'im because o' 'is demon side," stated Bodolf quite matter of factly.

"I do believe you are correct, good dwarf," Dean smiled.

Ihoitae heard the sound of his cage opening and felt someone that smelled of lilacs come into the cage with him. It was definitely female as the hands had a soft touch as they began to remove the soiled bandages, clean the wounds and replace new bandages on his wounds. The pain, however light the touch, was indescribable and succeeded in fully awakening him from his sleep.

"Oh dear," Diane fretted. "It appears I have awakened him."

In his sight, he could see the dwarf, Bodolf was his name I believe, off to one side and a male draconian directly in front of him. The draconian was fairly tall, probably about 6' to 7' tall, which is short for a draconian. It was hard to tell from his angle. The male wore brown leather armor that had metal buttons sequined on it. His skin was a pale green that was patterned like jade scales upon his muscular frame. However, in place of where there should be horns, as was custom of dragons, he had raven, black hair that was long flowing down his back in Dred locks with beads weaved throughout them. The horns that all draconians had, were hidden in his long dreds. His eyes were cat-like in his smooth, lizard like head. The colors of a tiger's eye stone were those eyes and they missed nothing! As Ihoitae looked him over, something in Ihoitae's mind flashed a memory and he knew with a start that he had met this draconian before. Ihoitae's face flashed the recognition and Dean picked up on it but said nothing and showed nothing.

"Well, good afternoon, Prince Ihoitae," Dean said while performing a short bow. "I understand that Bodolf filled you in on our mission very briefly and that you have a request to be released." He definitely spoke with the air of command.

Ihoitae very gruffly and weakly responded, "I did indeed ask to be released and I was very briefly filled in on your mission, but I do have very many more questions." Ihoitae was very surprised at just how weak he still was. How badly did these dire tigers hurt him? Their poison claws were not this dreadful to humanoids. Was it the anti-magic from the bars that was really draining him that badly? If so, that is a very strong anti-magic spell!

"I do understand," Dean replied. "I will consider your request for release, but it will not be granted for now. You are safer in there from your enemies than if we release you. You are also too weak to defend yourself and this anti-magic will keep them out as well as you in.

"Our employer advised us that there were others after you and that they were also very powerful. We were also warned that you were not to be trusted and that you were very powerful as well. So, for our sake and yours, for the moment, your request will be denied, but not as a final decision. Is this accepted?"

Ihoitae weakly replied, "I accept this for now, however, as I advised Bodolf here I could heal myself with my magic if you would let me out."

"While I do believe you have the power to do so on a normal day, you are in no condition to do so now and my instincts tell me that we are........,"

Dean's eyes shifted ever so slightly to the window, "not safe."

Diane sighed, "Oh dear, these wounds are not healing. I believe those Dire tigers you were up against had some anti-healing poison on their claws besides their normal paralyzing poisons. We will need to bring the priest here, Dean, since we cannot transport him."

"Alright," Dean agreed. "Bodolf, please go and fetch Ifem and see if you can't find that surly she elf, too!"

"Aye." Bodolf was off. He was very fast for a rotund dwarf.

Diane had completed the task of cleaning the wounds on his back and legs and changing the bandages so she had closed the cage and went to stand beside her husband. Ihoitae had never seen a more beautiful human woman in all his years than he did right now. She was tall for a human and therefore the right height to match her draconic husband. She stood at six foot four inches with skin as pale and as pure as snow. It glowed with an inner beauty that reminded Ihoitae of his own people. Her eyes were a crystal clear sky blue and her hair was long and raven colored. She wore her hair free flowing down her back that reached her dainty feet. For clothing, she had slippers that were midnight black with silver speckled sequins on them that matched an elegant black maiden's dress trimmed in silver piping. She looked like a princess rather than a mercenary. There was something special about her that Ihoitae could not place, but he would not give up until he learned the secret. She was ethereal while being mortal at the same time. However, Ihoitae felt that she was not aware that she was an ethereal being.

"You are truly breathtaking," Ihoitae stated with great awe. "Dean, please do not misunderstand my words, but she is a rare jewel. Please keep her safe."

Dean blushed a little and was also a little jealous, but remained ever the professional soldier and replied, "I always place her and my comrades above my personal self."

"Well now it seems that the only one you haven't met is Aelle, but you shall soon," Diane replied. "And, Ifem will be here soon to help us heal you."

"Then we will be able to update you more because Ifem has the next part of our mission," Dean advised. "I will also consider your request for freedom more after we speak with the priest. He is our emissary from the mistress that hired us. But be warned," Dean's voice suddenly became very heavy and stern, "you will not be free from us. You are our package and we have a mission that we must fulfill and you are a part of that mission! I will do anything and everything in my power to insure our client that we will complete the mission."

Just as Ihoitae nodded in understanding the door to the cottage opened and Aelle, with a scowl on her face, Bodolf and Ifem all walked into the main room. Greetings were exchanged and Ifem immediately went into the cage once the door was opened. Ifem proceeded to look at Ihoitae's wounds and was not happy. Ihoitae craned his neck back to see the priest. Ifem was also a forest elf. Forest Elves were of human height and stature, though the bloodlines had never mixed, except for a rare half-elf should a match of human and elf ever transpire. Ifem stood at an average height for a forest elf at five foot ten inches. He was lithe but muscular. His hair was as brown as the bark on a tree and he wore this short, cropped to his ears in a disheveled manner. His elfin ears long behind him had piercings all over them to show the mark of a Zadian Priest, a protector of the Great Scrolls. His skin was an olive tan, smooth and his eyes were the deep green of a tree leaf during the heat of the growing season. Ihoitae could tell Ifem was a pure bred.

Ifem did not wear the traditional robes of a Zadian Priest. Instead, he wore a brown Gi fit for a martial artist. His belt was that of a black belt with many ribbons tied on it to convey he was a very high-ranking master in not just one art but several. He had no weapons that Ihoitae could see, but Ihoitae guessed he probably didn't need any. And if he happened to pick one up, he could probably use it as easily and naturally as using one of his own limbs. Ihoitae also noted that his fingers were also very nimble and delicate while he removed the bandages from Ihoitae's back and cleaned the wounds. Ifem then placed a salve on them. It was very cool and soothing and relieved some of the pain. Then, Ifem began to chant.  It was a very ancient spell, a healing spell that only dragons knew. Curious, Ihoitae wondered why this spell would work in an anti-magic environment. This priest was very curious indeed.

Then there was an over whelming pain. Suddenly Ihoiate felt that he was being strangled and could not breath. He began to writhe and squirm as darkness began to over take him.

"Shit!," Dean shouted, "what are you doing to him?"

"It's not me," Ifem replied calmly. "You felt the presence just as much as I did. I cast a spell to see just how strong a hold on Ihoitae it had. Apparently it is a very strong one. And one that I am sure Ihoitae had no clue of. It has been there for a very long time."

"What do we do?" Dean asked.

"Diane, I need you to use your mind reading powers to get into Ihoitae's mind. Try and explain what is going on and to help him back to us. This….thing….will just drag him closer to death if we don't release it now!" Ifem began chanting again as Diane moved closer. "Dean, you will have to remove the anti-magic spell. I need Ihoitae's powers to free him. I am not as strong as he is."

Dean complied, though reluctantly.

Ifem continued chanting.

# Chapter Four

ONE MOMENT IHOITAE was in a cozy, warm room writhing in pain and the next he was in a cold, dark room. When Ihoitae felt the pain subside, he opened his eyes to realize that he was no longer in the realms of reality. The cold, dark room had a mist like quality to it. Though it was dark, he could see using his demon eyes, which allowed him to see everything in the room as shades of gray. The demons called it spectrum seeing because they can alter their eyes to see in any light spectrum they needed too. Sadly, he did have to admit that there were times he appreciated his demon heritage.

Ihoitae could see that the walls were white marble with gray swirls in it and columns lined the room. It was smooth. There were no windows, no doors. It was tomblike. There were sconces on the walls where there should be torches should be burning, but they were dark. In the middle there was a white sarcophagus. Beside it lay a beautiful set of weapons that gleamed brightly in the gloomy room as if a full moon shined upon their silvery, ethereal metal. On the top lay a statue, probably the statue of what the body looked like before it was placed inside the shell. Ihoitae walked towards this sarcophagus.

As he approached and focused on the weapons, the room began to lighten and his spectrum seeing shifted more into normal sight. The weapons were definitely glowing, drawing his attention towards them. He continued to oblige them by gravitating towards their warm glow in the otherwise steely, graveyard feel of this sterile room.

Ihoitae caught the sound of a female crying. It was muffled at first, but gradually grew louder as he approached the sarcophagus. He began to look for its source. Was someone else trapped in this strange hell?

As he drew closer to the sarcophagus, he focused solely on the weapons. They were truly beautiful. A dagger and sword, gleaming in steel as a rune inscribed on the curve of the blade with jewels on its hilt. He then looked upon the sarcophagus. It was a male elf with his arms wrapped on his chest, holding weapons to his breast, two short swords. The elf looked strangely familiar, but Ihoitae didn't want to think about it. In his heart, he knew he was seeing a glimpse of his future.

Then he saw her as he rounded the side of the sarcophagus. Ihoitae rarely ever considered females of any race. His dreams of someday marring and settling down with a young elf-maid died when his people died. He had seen beautiful women in all races, but none had ever stirred his soul. He always assumed it was because no female would ever match his mother in beauty, demeanor and regality. His mother was whom he measured everyone against and since he could never have a normal life, he decided that love and family was something he would do without and his lofty ideals aided him in stopping any endeavors before they began. However, this female caught his breath and for the first time in Ihoitae's life, his heart fluttered at the sight of a female.

She was sitting on the other side of the sarcophagus with her back to it and her legs curled under her. She was an elf-maid and extremely beautiful. Her hair was long and silvery down her back, but was in long, slender braids weaving throughout the loose hair. Her skin was as pale as moonlight. She wore a light white shift and little else and the image under the shift was very appealing. When Ihoitae approached, she turned her head and looked at him with orbs of deep purple, rimmed with red from the crying she had been doing. When she spotted him, she smiled a golden smile of warmth and pure happiness.

"You came!," her voice sounded clear, pure and childlike. It was the sound of pure innocence. "I knew you would! But we don't have much time. The darkness approaches and you must leave soon or you will be dragged to the depths of the Abyss and not even your father will be able to save you from that prison!"

"My father?," Ihoitae inquired. He was still trying to recover from her beauty, let alone her enchanting voice. He was trying to look at her face, but his eyes kept drifting to the shadowy curve under the shift. If she was casting a spell on him, he was entrapped and was in whole hers. "He is the demon lord and rules over all the abysses."

"Not this one," she frowned. "But we need not discuss that. I must tell you this and quickly!"

"I will protect you," Ihoitae said fiercely, feeling a sudden surge of manliness. "There is a set of weapons here. I can protect you with them."

"Aye, you will in time, but not now," she replied. "You must tell my sister that I miss her and she must aid you. Tell her Safiyyah told you this!"

Suddenly and without any warning, the room started to lose its coldness and became rapidly warmer. The mist swirled and had the tinge of red to it as if it were on fire. The room also began to develop a smell of brimstone and it was growing brighter as if the room was catching fire.

"He comes! We must make haste or all will be lost!," Safiyyah spoke swiftly. "Tell Aelle that when the time comes, she must make the ultimate sacrifice an elf can make in order to save our people and our world. She will know when the sacrifice must be made when the time comes. Tell her I am safe and I will guide you and her, but she must be faithful. The day is coming when we must fulfill our promise to our father."

"I will tell her, but how shall I find her?," Ihoitae inquired.

"We are twins, though she wears her hair a bit different and is a bit darker of skin." A wicked laughter began and the room became sweltering hot. "He is here! Oh why does he torture me so? Always he shows me your death and relishes in my anguish! I am already a prisoner with no hope of escape, isn't that enough?!?! But, you must leave......NOW!"

Ihoitae looked at her confused. "But...... how?"

A very tiny voice began to sound in the room, which was now beginning to shake and crack up. As the marble walls crumbled, they were replaced with walls of rock and lava. The voice was calling Ihoitae's name. It was subtle at first but slowly began to gain in volume. The voice sounded slightly familiar; though he could not place it and was sure it was a recent familiarity to him.

"The voice," she pointed up, "follow its call. It is the human maid, Diane. She is special, protect her. You know it already. Trust in your instincts. Time is so very short now. Her voice will guide you back to the surface of consciousness. I will hold off the abyssal demon as long as I can. Now listen!"

"But you are not safe!" Ihoitae replied, that same silly male notion to protect this female that has stirred his soul would not dissipate.

"He cannot harm me physically. His job of entrapment of me has played out. I am on another plain of existence now and he works for one that does not want harm done to me. But you are not and the one that he works for wants great harm done to you. Now you must leave.......she calls, ANSWER IT!" Safiyyah was practically screaming at him with her last couple of words. But she smiled at him and her cheeks flushed. In a softer voice she replied, "my sister is lucky to be able to spend the time with you that I was supposed to have. We have met before. You are even more handsome than what I remember!"

"Ihoitae, please here me," a very small bell-like voice chimed in. "Ihoitae, you must listen to me. You are in danger. Please open your eyes." A smell of lilac began to fill the room around the brimstone smell as Diane's power began to penetrate the demon's magic.

Safiyyah gasped, "That is Diane, close your eyes and shut out all other noise and listen for her voice. Concentrate on the lilac fragrance. Once you can hear nothing and smell nothing but her, open your eyes and you will be back in your realm of existence."

"I AM COMING FOR YOU!" A very dark and sinister voice yelled from somewhere deep and evil as it sprouted through the quickly crumbling tomb. Then wicked laughter followed.

"Diane, call louder!," Safiyyah cried out desperately.

Diane was taken a little off guard by hearing this unknown third voice that sounded a lot like Aelle's own, but performed as it obliged trusting in it.

"IHOITAE!!! Please heed my call! You are in danger! PLEASE COME TO ME!!"

Ihoitae closed his eyes cherishing the last vision he saw of the elfin maid and then followed her advice by shutting out all other distractions. He listened intently for the ever-louder growing voice that was Diane's. He could feel something very evil and very menacing reaching out for him. It was growing very angry because it was sensing that it was going to lose its prize. Ihoitae ignored it and when he opened his eyes, all he saw was a pair of beautiful; clear, sky-blue eyes staring back at him. The eyes were smiling with relief.

# Chapter Five

AS SOON AS Ihoitae opened his eyes, Ifem began chanting, tapping into Ihoitae's own magic using Diane as the bridge. Diane was still holding Ihoitae's hands and staring into his eyes. In his thrashing, he must have rolled over onto his back and thus how he now found himself in his current position. Ifem healed Ihoitae's wounds and placed a basic seal on Ihoitae's mind to help him recuperate. It would be a temporary seal, but one that would hold until they could figure out what it was that was attacking him and why. Dean also decided that Ihoitae could be freed and the tiny cell would be removed from the room. There was little point keeping him caged since the anti-magic spell was now broken and, it seemed, things were going to be a lot more interesting. The team would be able to move a lot more quickly if they were not tied down to transporting a caged person. Ihoitae had also given his word that he would not flee and Dean would have to trust him to keep that word, though doubts lingered.

They had all moved into another room that resembled a dining room. Dean gestured for everyone to sit around the table. They shuffled in one by one and Ifem and Diane helped Ihoitae to a seat opposite from Aelle. As they did so, the surly she-elf from earlier sat across from Ihoitae and glared menacingly at him. He looked up to look at her and gasped.

"What's a matter, half-breed?," Aelle spoke very condescendingly. "Never seen a forest elf before?"

"Ssss-aa-fi-yyahh?," Ihoitae stuttered.

Aelle flashed a look of surprise and then quickly reverted back to her glaring look. She responded very angrily, "How do you know that name?!?!? She would never have mixed company with your kind!"

"That's Aelle, laddie," Bodolf broke in, trying to calm the air and sort out the confusion.

"Oh, that explains the hair and the darker skin," Ihoitae half spoke to himself, then looked up and more pointedly spoke to Aelle by way of explanation, "She said you would have a darker skin tone and you would wear your hair differently. But otherwise you are just as beautiful as she." Ihoitae suddenly blushed, not realizing the words he was uttering until they had already tumbled from his mouth. He was once again caught off guard by how this twin elf maid made his heart flutter, though her appearance did not stir his soul the way Safiyyah had. He realized he was not being himself and looked down. "I am sorry to have offended you."

"How do you know my sister?" Aelle would not let up and asked vehemently, though quietly, demanding. However, she suddenly blushed a little at this half-breed's words not really knowing why they should affect her so. Lots of males of all races found her attractive. She was used to their stare and jeers.

"AELLE!" four voices shouted at once.

Ihoitae looked back up, a bit more composed of himself and advised, "No it's ok. I will explain what happened. If I am to be your package then you will need to know that I am apparently being followed by something very dark and sinister who is employed by something a little darker and sinister than it." Ihoitae told them of his dream turned nightmare and of what Safiyyah said that Aelle must be told.

Aelle was quiet, but the look on her face softened as she began to reflect inward. Something was going on in her mind. That much was clear.

Diane quietly spoke, "I could not see what you saw. But I could hear and feel what you could. It was not something I would ever wish to meet. Though we have only just met and we were hired to find you, please do not think any less of us as companions.

"This elf that was in your mind said that she was on another plain of existence, so I truly believe she was safe from it. However, I feel that both of us were not, which means that this thing is on our realm, our level of consciousness. I also feel that we all have destinies that are somehow intertwined and we need to look upon each other as companion and comrades rather than mission and package. This is why I counseled that we should take on this mission.

"However, I have always felt that you should have your freedom regardless of our mission. As I stated when the avatar told us to imprison, I did not feel that this was the accurate course of action. But I feel that you will soon find that your mission and our mission are going to intertwine very soon as I have just counseled. So, I feel you will be with us regardless of choice."

"My wife is truly wise," Dean spoke up, "Ihoitae, I grant you your freedom. I will deal with our client if you choose to leave us, but I fear that Diane is correct. We have a destiny together that started long ago." Dean glared at Ihoitae with the look of remembrance, though again, he did not speak upon it. Ihoitae knew at that moment, that Dean remembered their long ago encounter in battle, but he was willing to let the past go, for now.

"Aye!" bellowed Bodolf. "Tis good if un we stay together. I feel it in me achin bones."

Ifem cleared his voice. Everyone turned their attention to him. "Well, if we are all in accordance, then may I suggest that we go visit Zaire as soon as possible. The avatar awaits and we must get moving. All signs of the heavens suggest that time is running short."

"That is one thing that Safiyyah said also," chimed in Ihoitae. "Alas, I must agree with Diane due to very recent events. I have always known there was something......um, special for me due to my heritage and my un-naturally long life. But I fear that since some things that were in my past appear to be resurfacing and my instincts tell me that neither Diane, nor Aelle's sister, are wrong in this matter. I will stay with your mission for now. But I must request that at some time, you fill me in on it."

Dean nodded at Ihoitae. "Very well, at this time, there isn't much to it. We were hired by an avatar of a client claiming that you are of great importance to them. We do not know the client's name nor the background of the client. The avatar's name is Shyaralia. She is elfin. She simply said her lady wanted us to find you and bring you to Ifem and the Zadian priesthood. There we would receive our next mission. She also told us that we were to consider you dangerous due to your nomadic and isolated lifestyle. So, we were to take…..precautions. But that you were to be protected at all costs. She warned us that there was a demoness that was also after you that meant nothing but ill will for you and our mission.

"We began tracking you down a fortnight ago and set up shop here as this is where Ifem told us he would be. We were to have brought you here no matter when we were able to have tracked you down and brought you in. However, we were lucky to have found you so close to our base camp. You are very good at making yourself untraceable. I understand why, given the history with your father, but still……" Dean laughed, "I do believe had it not been for the other hunter, we would not have found you at all. For you would have passed by us without our knowledge. You know the rest.

"Now, that task being complete, we will leave at first light." Dean commended with finality and went to make arrangements for their departure. The rest of the group also dispersed to make plans and pack as necessary.

# Chapter Six

HE WAS NOT happy. His mind grip was gone and tracking his prey would become infinitely more difficult now. He had not expected that the human female had such strong powers. What were those powers?

His prey was slipping further and further from his grasp. This group of mercenaries was more than meets the eye and they would protect his prey to the death. He knew it, though they did not as of yet. He sensed his prey was becoming involved in a thought long-dead prophecy. Things had spiraled out of control and he knew he would need to report back to his mistress for his next step. But he would still wait and watch before he consulted her. He needed to know more before he would face her wrath.

***

As Ihoitae and his new companions left the village of Grethen to travel the week's distance to go to Castle Cardinia to meet up with Zaire, the Zadian priest that had the Great Scrolls; there was another tiny village on the other side that were the outskirts of the kingdom of Cardinia that would soon enter into the Great War unwillingly. The little village of Dionness. In this very tiny village lived Faolan Marduu.

Faolan Marduu was sometimes a sad human boy. He had a tough lot in life. He loved his family and he didn't mind his station in life as a peasant farmer. He loved his village and didn't mind assisting anyone in the village when his assistance was needed. But somewhere deep down inside Faolan, he sensed that there was something more than this provincial life. He could not help feel that there was a grander scheme in store for him and his little world.

Of course he knew about the ancient Mystic Gods and the Great Scrolls as well as the prophecy reported by the scrolls and the Zadian Priests, which had been discovered around the time of his birth year. He didn't necessarily believe in Gods and prophecies and scrolls and ancient magics. What he did believe in was the good soil, the weather, the cycles of nature and his people. These were all things that could be observed, worked like clockwork and were reliable. So his sadness grew from his torn happiness and gut feelings.

He thought of these things more and more as he got older. These thoughts grew deeper and stronger when he learned he was adopted by his parents. They were unable to have children and in these dark times, children were always being orphaned. Faolan was no exception. So, when the soldiers brought this wee baby boy into the village from a neighboring village that had been involved in battle, Faolan's parents asked to become his surrogates since they wanted a baby. The village elders discussed it and decided they would be an excellent choice to take in this latest orphaned child. About 3 years later to their great surprise, his parents were blessed with a natural baby of their own, his sister, Fea. But his parents never stopped loving him or caring for him any less. Fea just completed their family is all his mother would say and then hug them all in a giant bear hug.

Faolan was sixteen and tall, at 6 feet five inches, handsome and muscular. His skin was tan from hours working outside in the fields, which is how his large muscles also developed. He had wavy, disheveled black hair and deep brown eyes. He was a hard working boy, but also had an heir of power to him that no one could seem to figure out.

This day, Faolan went to the fields with his dad as he always did with all the men in the village. Some would go to tend the crops, while others would go hunting for meat or others went to go bring back building materials. The women would stay in the village and do the cooking, cleaning, mending and protect the children and elderly. But, Faolan sensed that something was not right this day. There had been war near their tiny village recently and many refugees from surrounding villages had come to his looking for a place to come until they could regroup and head towards Cardinia Castle. The elders knew war would be coming to them soon, but they had no skilled warriors. The inevitable was coming, but no one wanted to desert their homes and move on with the refugees to Cardinia Castle.

The war drums began while Faolan and his dad were in the fields. The time had come and no one was prepared, but the people did what people do when all they have is to protect what is theirs. The farmers and builders picked up their tools and the hunters picked up their bows and daggers and returned to the village. The women moved the children and elderly to as safe as a location as they could and prepared to defend them to the death with whatever they could find for weapons.

The battle was fierce and swift. The villagers put up as valiant as a fight as they could with what little fighting skills farmers, gatherers and hunters have, but the Berdinian soldiers came in and wiped out the village in a matter of hours. They raped, plundered and pillaged. They took a few of the younger lads to press them into their military, but all others lives were forfeit. Faolan's parents being no exception.

One brave attempt was made to spare some of the younger children and Fea. Faolan and two other young men had placed them in a wagon with the swiftest horses the village had. They selected two of the elderly women and told them to make haste to Cardinia. Faolan and the other two lads, with some help from the elderly men, kept the soldiers at bay long enough to give the wagon a lead. The soldiers deemed it not worthy to chase after; it would have been a waste of their time for babies and old women. One of the lads and most of the elder men died in their defense. The other elder men that survived the initial battle were rewarded with death. Faolan and the other lad, however, were rewarded with capture. The Berdinians saw Faolan and the other lad as potential soldiers as long as they could be brainwashed and retrained.

# Chapter Seven

IHOITAE AND HIS new companions traveled a week from Grethen Village to a very small chapel just inside of Cardinia Castle's main walls. This chapel was, in truth, the home of the head priest with a much larger chapel present closer to the castle proper for ceremonies and prayer and housed the majority of the Zadian priests that lived at the chapel. The Zadians were the protectors to the Great Scrolls since their second discovery in 5 DR, However, the head priest called his home a chapel because all were always welcome and was not just his home, but a place of divinity for all to enjoy.

In this smaller chapel, they found the head Zadian priest doing his daily rituals of meditation and prayer. His name was Zaire and he was an ancient human in terms of years. He was well over the average life span of a human by at least a couple of centuries, yet he only appeared to be a man in his middle years of about forty-five.

The head of the Zadian priests is granted a special divine gift of a certain kind of immortality. The head of the Zadian priests earn this right by special training that only one in maybe every three or four generations could pass. Only could the head of the Zadian priests pass on their knowledge and skill and divine gift to the one that was ordained to take his or her place. Zaire had been alive for so much longer than his predecessors because there had not been another ordained born in many centuries, so he continued to protect the Great Scrolls until a suitable gifted child could be found.

The Balasi family had been in the Zadian priesthood for generations and were well trained fighters and magic wielders and chroniclers. They have always been excellent protectors of the scrolls and the head of the Zadian priests. Ifem was Zaire's second. He had taken his father's place as Zaire's second upon his father's retire from protector and fighter to chronicler and archivist. Ifem's mother and sisters were also active in the priesthood as priestesses of lore and magic. Ifem was an elf, and a young one at that, but had been in the priesthood for all his life, which equaled approximately two hundred and thirty years, so Ifem had known Zaire for his entire life. Ifem's father also served the previous head of the Zadian priests as Head Priest of Protection prior to the locating and training of Zaire. Zaire had sent Ifem to locate the mercenaries for the beginning of this mission because he was the best one suited for the task.

Ifem was very knowledgeable in the Great Scrolls religion, the history of Kelnaria and of Prince Ihoitae Mahadeva Arabus. Ifem had also followed in his father's footsteps of martial training and had mastered almost all known weapons and fighting styles known to Kelnaria. Zaire had confided in Ifem that the time of prophecy had come to pass and had Ifem commit to memory all the scrolls that were known and how to seek out any others. Zaire also confided in Ifem that he would need to be the one to travel with the group. Zaire's replacement had been located and soon he would have to pass on his knowledge and gift to the new ordained one and he would soon grow old and too weak to travel. Ifem accepted willingly and eagerly. His family was honored that he had been so chosen.

"Welcome, Ifem, my brother," Zaire greeted in the Zadian priest fashion. "I am glad to see that the rebellious Prince Arabus was willing and did not have to be caged like an animal. Ever was I not pleased to hear Shyaralia advise that we should even do something so vile to one such as Prince Arabus." Zaire bowed to the prince. This took Ihoitae off guard. He was not accustomed to such royal treatment. After all, it had been at least a millennia since his people passed away and almost a millennia since he had been on the run from his father Lord Mordecai. No one had bowed to him recently and he rarely was bowed to at court in the Sylvan kingdom. Only when custom demanded, which was little in his specific case.

Ihoitae politely smiled. "Um, thank you, priest, but your bows are not necessary. I am prince in title only for I do not have a kingdom in either my homeland or in my father's domain. Nor do I lead any peoples. Though your courtesy is welcomed, I beg you to please refrain from them."

"True," replied Zaire, "you do not have a kingdom in either of your homelands at this time. But if all goes as the prophets will it, then you may find a nice reward at the end." Zaire then chuckled. "I also beg to differ on peoples to lead, because you will find that you will be leading soon in some ways."

"I do not take much stalk in prophets nor in Gods and their religions," spoke Ihoitae politely but firmly. "I do not mean any offense to you, the hardworking priests and priestesses or the Great Scrolls, but I have seen many things that would denote that the Gods are nothing more than selfish children using us as their play things. The day my people were destroyed is the day my belief in our Gods, all Gods for that matter, died."

"Ihoitae!" Dean, Ifem and Aelle all snapped at once.

"No, no, do not chastise the wizened," Zaire replied calmly with no feelings of anger, "Prince Arabus has lived for a couple of millennia now and has seen most of the history that only we can read about or that knowledge altogether has been lost to us. Having a firsthand account of things takes the romance out of the history, I should think. Wouldn't you agree, Prince Arabus?"

Ihoitae bowed in respect. "Indeed it does. I thank you for your understanding."

"It is not understanding, it is the correct way to act. The most logical conclusion to your knowledge," Zaire stated. "But we are not here to discuss theological beliefs. What is happening now is very real and happening very fast now that the boy is of age. We do not have much time for the Great Scrolls prophecy was triggered many centuries ago and we have just now caught on and caught up to the brink we are on."

"Um?," asked a puzzled Aelle. Everyone else in the group was thinking it except Ifem, but all were too polite to ask.

Zaire chuckled. "Riddles, that's all we old priests talk in is riddles! Ha!" He then smiled a wide grin. "And though I seem of a middle aged man, I am closer to that age of an old elf! I have lived long and know too much! Not as long as our dear friend Prince Arabus here, but too long indeed. So, riddles is how I speak as that is how the mind perceives with too much knowledge.

"First, I must tell you that Ifem will be accompanying you on your travels. It would have been my job, too, but since the new ordained has been found, then I must give up my gift to him upon completion of his training. With this, I will be too old and weak to travel where a young body must. However, the one who has been ordained does not know his stature yet, so you will all have a great honor in learning who the chosen is. Their ceremony will take place tonight. In it is when the transfer will take place and I require all of you to attend. You will learn many things in this ceremony as well. Maybe even with a few less riddles, eh?

"In the meantime, please take this time to relax and prepare yourselves for many battles that are to come. There are many stores of weapons here in our armory as well as any armor you may need or want. You are welcome to any of it at no cost for the battles you will face; you may need the armor and weapons. Your payment to us will be the fulfillment of the end of the prophecy, in which either way it is meant to go. And soon, there will be very little time to do any shopping or repairing, so take all that is needed or wanted with the blessing of our Priesthood." With that, Zaire turned and walked away leaving the party to speculate just exactly what it was he had been talking about.

***

Later that evening, the party had taken stock of their weapons and armor and re-provisioned anything that was missing or felt that would be needed along with horses, food and equipment. They were ready to go as soon as Zaire gave them leave, but they would all try and enjoy this last evening of rest with the ceremony of the new Head Priest of the Zadian Priests.

As everyone gathered to the great hall of the grand chapel, horns began to blow and gongs were drummed. All the priests, priestesses, their families, the children in training and even King Roland Dagmar and Queen Lyra Wetton-Dagmar of Cardinia were present, along with their son and daughter. The great hall was well decorated with table clothes, fine dining materials and flowers were everywhere. Candles were ablaze on all the tables and torches fluttered bright, beautiful fires in their sconces along the walls. Braziers were placed in the middle of the hall and the tables were in a rectangle around the braziers with the king and queen, Zaire and Ifem at the front table. On one of the side tables off to the left of the king and queen was where Dean and his mercenaries were to sit, with Prince Ihoitae's place being nearest the king and queen per his status. He may not have a kingdom, but he was still a prince and therefore a dignitary.

In rare form, Dean's little band dressed for the occasion with flowering sleeved tunics and breeches for the men and beautiful gowns for Diane and Aelle. Even Ihoitae dressed for the occasion having to have gone into the marketplace to purchase some finery. He had not worn any finery since his days as a prince in the forests of his people. So, he was a little awkward at knowing what to wear. (Fashion had changed a bit since his days at court in the Sylvan kingdom.) But he managed with a beautiful hunter's green tunic covered by a deep brown leather vest, deep green breeches and fine, soft brown leather boots. The ensemble was held together by a studded black belt and a black hair tie that he used to pull his long, silver white hair back at the neck. No weapons were allowed except by the guards that were allowed to accompany the royal family of Cardinia. Protocol dictated this necessity, though the royal house had nothing to fear in their kingdom. They were well loved by their people.

Dean and Diane came matching in purples and blacks, with Dean wearing a noble's outfit and Diane wearing a long, slender slip of a maiden's dress and bodice. Bodolf, being a dwarf, wore his finest armor of soft leather, rather than his usual plate. He even managed to comb out his long fiery red hair and braid his hair and his beard to match. He had one long braid down his back and two long braids down his beard that reached his ample belly.

However, Ihoitae's heart almost stopped when he saw Aelle enter the room. She was truly a rare jewel amongst all the females present. Her tan skin off-set her choice of leaf green dress perfectly. Her brown hair was swept up in a flowing reverse braid on her head and neck. She wore pins of pearl in her hair that glinted in the light of the Great Hall. The leaf green dress was long and flowing from the waist, but the bodice was tight and a pale green color that accented a perfect bosom. The sleeves and hem of the dress were lined with elfin symbols in golden floss. The sleeves were long and flowed down her long arms in the same leaf green color of the skirt. She wore pale green shoes with pearl accents to match the bodice top and her hair. Around her neck, she wore a necklace made of lace and a pendant of a larger white pearl with runes, of a sort, inscribed on it. The pendant looked ancient, but he could not make out the details.

A final gong sounded as everyone that was to attend was finally seated. Head Priest Zaire stood up at this queue and smiled at everyone. He would begin his speech, but his voice was different. Powerful, resonant, not the same voice of the man they met earlier. It was almost as if he spoke with the voice of a God.

"Welcome, everyone," Zaire began in his other worldly voice. "To the King and Queen of the Kingdom of Cardinia, thank you for being able to come on such a short notice. And as an additional blessing, the royal children have also attended." The king tipped his head in a small bow with a smile upon his face.

"And we, of course, welcome all our honored children both of the priesthood and in the training of the priesthood."

The priests, priestesses and the children responded with an ancient greeting, "Siahomdy." It meant 'honored one' in an ancient language, similar to Sylvan.

Zaire continued, "You all know why we have gathered. The time to name my replacement has arrived. I am the only one with this knowledge as it was decreed by the Mystics so many millennia ago. I have chosen today as the day to share my knowledge with the chosen successor as well as with all of the Mystics' children. But, I also have even grander news that I can share on this day and it revolves around our special guests."

Everyone in the room began to whisper in excitement. To have outsiders at the naming of a new ordained was never done before in any documented history of the changing of the Head Priests.

"Our honored guests tonight are General and Mrs. Dean and Diane Moonstone, Lord Bodolf Horsetamer of clan Battle Horse, Lady Aelle Tindonis of the Loralia Forest kingdom and Prince Ihoitae Mahadeva Arabus of the royal houses of the Sylvan and Demon Kingdoms." With that, everyone instantly snapped to look at Ihoitae, including the king and queen. Zaire laughed, "Yes, the last prince of the sylvan elves still lives and has chosen to come out of hiding for soon he will understand why fate has sent him to me!"

Zaire closed his eyes and began to chant silently to himself. His body began to glow with a blue hue as his silent chanting continued. He then opened his eyes and looked around his audience with his glowing body and pupil-less orbs. "I announce Ifem of the House of Balasi of the forest elves of Loralia Forest to be my next successor! He has been chosen by the gods of the Mystics! And for quite some time I might add." Zaire's glowing blue form began to float and his chanting now became louder. Zaire reached out his arm and put his hand out to Ifem to motion Ifem to him. Ifem obeyed.

When Ifem went over to him, he instinctively grabbed Zaire's hand. Then the blue glow slowly went from Zaire, starting at his feet, through his arm into Ifem's arm and slowly down to his feet until the blue glow was transferred completely from Zaire to Ifem. Upon completion of the transfer, Zaire's form was gently, gently transformed and where there had once been a younger human male of about 45 now stood an old human male closer to his 90's. Ifem passed out and some younger priests gently picked him up and moved him to a cot that had been placed in the room for this very reason.

"The transfer is now complete!," Zaire's voice did not match his new, frail body. It was still deep, resonant and other worldly. "But I still have one more thing I must complete before I can..um.. shall we say, retire. While Ifem sleeps and you feast, I will tell you what needs to be told."

At this time, food was brought out to the guests from servers that were not of the priesthood but worked in the temple. Everyone ate, but listened intently as Zaire began a story.

"Everyone in the land that is governed by the Royal House of Dagmar knows of the first scroll of the prophecy of the chosen one, the Child of Light. But they do not know there is actually three parts to the prophecy. I have decided that tonight they shall be known and my brothers will begin to teach the masses. Now is the time of the prophecy and it can now be known throughout the land. As it will undoubtedly fall into the knowledge of the Berdianians shortly after tonight, then this knowledge should too be imparted on to each and every Cardinian and Her allies.

"The child of light's origin and destiny shall be unknown to him and all those around him. However, a seeker will be given to locate the child and help him throughout his journey in choosing the path to his destiny.

"The chosen priest of the Mystics shall ordain when the seeker is to come forth unto him and learn his true destiny. This priest shall be chosen when the heavens crack and shall be blessed with the blessing of immortality so that he may fulfill his role in this destiny.

"The priest shall also be the protector of the scrolls and have the knowledge to safeguard the scrolls, the seeker and the champion child. The seeker must assist in the location of the child.

"The seeker must also assist in the fulfillment of the quest placed upon the child. The child and the seeker must learn the power of the sacred stones, the holy relics and face the three truths. The truth of self, the truth of the Mystics and the truth of choice.

"If the seeker or child cannot or will not accept these truths, the prophecy cannot be fulfilled and the world shall be forever lost."

Zaire paused and looked over his audience. They were listening intently. Someone coughed and asked, "So, do you know who the seeker or the child are? Have they come?"

"Aye," answered Zaire, "They have come. The prophecy is upon us and the seeker is also in this room. But no, I do not know the current identity of the child. That job was ordained to the seeker. However, I do know that the child has come of age as this knowledge has been imparted to me."

"So, pray tell us, who is it?," requested King Roland in good nature.

Zaire smiled and turned to look at Dean and his group. Then he panned over directly to Ihoitae. Ihoitae looked directly at the priest and shook his head 'no,' with anger on his face. "Dear Head Priest, I have been many things in my very long life, but the seeker to a prophecy of a long dead group of gods I am not! I will not disrespect you in your honored halls, but I will not listen to this either." Ihoitae began to stand up.

"Please young elf, sit down and listen!.," commanded Zaire with the voice of a god. Ihoitae had no choice but to obey. "You are the seeker of the prophecy. You will find the child of light. You will assist this child!"

"And just who is going to MAKE ME!," Ihoitae retorted angrily. It suddenly became as if only Zaire and Ihoitae were in the Great Hall all alone.

Zaire smirked and gently replied, "You will."

Ihoitae looked back at Zaire flabbergasted.

"Yes, you will make yourself because deep down inside you will know the truth and you will do what's right. I cannot tell you how the journey will go, but I can tell you that if you search your soul, you will know what to do.

"I will also impart one more bit of knowledge to you, seeker, his old identity was known to you, all of you, as the heir to the throne of Cardinia!"

The king and queen both immediately stood up and looked over at the head priest. The king spoke softly, almost not wanting to know the answer, "Our son Brandon lives?"

"But, we were told that the Fates………," the queen said with tears in her eyes, unable to complete her sentence. She sat back down and the king settled back down beside her to calm her down.

Zaire ignored them and began again, "This story is over and I am tired now. I have performed my last duty as Head Priest and I now must lie down. Please finish your food and I urge Dean and your group to stay the night and leave in the morning.

"My last word to you is that there is a scroll that must be obtained to find the next step in your journey. It is carried by the Marduu family in Dionness Village. Though they do not know the value of what they hold and have hidden it away long ago. And Dean, before I go lay down, can you please accompany me to my chambers?"

"Certainly," Dean replied. With that, he got up and excused himself to escort the now very old and very fragile ex head priest Zaire to his rooms. Also, Ihoitae got up, politely excused himself and went off to the monks' gardens to think. And the king and queen were left pleading to emptiness about the current status of their lost first son.

# Chapter Eight

AFTER THE CREW got their information from Zaire and slept the night, Ifem met up with them and officially joined the group in the morning. However, Ihoitae was missing. His belongings were missing from his room and there was no sign of him anywhere in the temple. They would begin their travels back towards the outskirts of Cardinia but should they wait for the half elf or not? Was he coming or had he backed out of his word?

After waiting for a couple of hours, they decided that he was not coming. Dean would have to explain their failure to their employer, but he would not dishonor himself by taking back his promise to Ihoitae, although he was very angry that Ihoitae had taken his vow carelessly. Damn half demon scum! I knew it! He thought.

They were heading towards the very small farming and fishing village known as Dionness and Ihoitae knew where they were going. If he wanted to join up with them, then he would. It would take about another week to travel to this remote village as it was on a different side of Cardinia Castle's proper. Their trip there was uneventful as they surveyed the war torn land that was once beautiful and serene.

Upon the would-be heroes' arrival to Dionness, they were disheartened to see that the village was just gone. The entire village lay in cinders and was nothing but ash; as the fires the Berdinians had set to it having long since died out. As they entered the village square, a very sad and sickening sight filled their vision when they saw what seemed to be the entire populace of the village piled high so that it resembled a giant funeral pyre. This battle was recent, perhaps about a week or so past. Most likely while they had been travelling from Grethen, this village was sacked.

Aelle cried out when she saw children were also burned on this pyre. Elves revered all life, but the life of a child was the most sacred. Diane openly wept as she could still feel their spirits lingering in what was once their home. Dean seethed in anger and Bodolf shouted a dwarven mourning cry, raising his axe in the air in commemorance of the dead. Ifem began to say prayers to the Gods for the departed.

Ihoitae had a much different reaction...... he laughed.

As he did so, everyone turned around to look behind them and see Ihoitae standing at the gateway to the village. He had tracked them there, unnoticed, quietly. This disturbed Dean just a bit. Some glared and some looked utterly shocked.

Ihoitae could see the dead children. They shifted from sadness and began to play when they saw him enter into their village. They came to dance around him. This is why he laughed. They began to play and dance because they knew Ihoitae for what he was and they knew that their wrongful deaths would be avenged. Ihoitae, however, did not understand it, but he could feel the upset spirits become serene. They laughed and cheered because they knew that when they would be reborn, it would be into a better world. The spirits knew that they could now move on. They had been mourned, they would be avenged, and they would not be forgotten.

He was angry at what befell these innocents, but to see their spirits suddenly go from dismal to happy was a bit disconcerting. So, his reaction was a lot different from everyone else's. Everyone in the party, except Diane, misunderstood this laugh and all turned and glowered at him after the initial shock was over.

"Why do you laugh, you jerk!," shouted Aelle.

"I am sorry," replied a somber Ihoitae. "I do not laugh because of their cruel fate......I laugh because the children's spirits are now free."

"Glad you could join us lad, but what're ye talkin' about?" Boldolf asked confused.

Diane began to respond before Ihoitae could formulate an answer. "The children's spirits stayed behind with their bodies. Ones so young have a hard time releasing to death when it is sudden and not understood.

"These spirits were sad, which is why I was crying, as I could feel their pain and anguish," Diane continued, "but when Ihoitae walked into the circle, their little faces lit up and they began to dance. They became happy and serene. There was peace among them." Diane smiled despite her sadness. "But, I do not understand why."

Ifem turned to Diane and asked, "Why would they light up just because a half demon/half Sylvan Elf walked into the area? He is no sooth sayer, seer or priest." Ifem turned to look at Ihoitae and scrutinized him. "And I doubt this has anything to do with him being the seeker."

"What?" Ihoitae shrugged. He was just as confused as they were. "You're now the Head Priest. Why do you not use your priestly knowledge?," Ihoitae added snidely.

"How many o' ye can see th' dead?" asked Bodolf, a lot concerned. Looking around to see if he could also now see the dead. He was a bit relieved to know he still could not. In dwarven mythology, one usually saw the dead when one was about to move on himself.

Ifem answered as a collective, "I can since I am a priest. I would wager Diane can since she is a seer of sorts, though I am not entirely clear on what her full abilities are. I am assuming Ihoitae can, but maybe only because he is part demon? To my knowledge of Sylvan's, they could never see the dead as a race, correct?"

"I have never had the gift or curse to see or speak with the dead," replied Ihoitae with a baffled look on his face, "until I had that dream with the entity that was trying to steal my soul. And, no, unless you were a priest or a seer, Sylvan's could not see the dead either. Nor can demons, unless you were a demon of the three abyssal hells. Which I am not. Those are lesser demons, subservient to my father. They are usually bringing the dead in for – shall we say – custody. It is helpful if they can see their, um, prey."

Dean began to speak, "Well, regardless, it appears that our presence has made the dead happy. So, we will be glad that whatever we could do for them to ease their suffering has been done. However, our search for the scroll we seek is now ended for the village is destroyed. Ifem, what should be our next step?"

Ifem took a moment to think. The scroll that they needed, and that was held secretly in this village, must still be here. The villagers would not have known anything about it as it had been placed in this village hundreds of years ago when the village was little more than a couple of fishing huts. But, was it burned to ashes having been stored in one of the now torched homes? Or, was it possible that maybe the Zadian priests had hidden it in a protected vault of sorts. The Zadians that had left it here all those years ago did little to make the whereabouts known, in order to further protect its safety. Ifem did not know the answer and expressed his thoughts to Dean and the rest of the group.

As he did so, a little female gnome slipped in behind them. She made a small "ahem" sound as she gingerly approached. As she quietly crept in a little closer and noticed that no one had paid any heed to her, she frowned and very loudly proclaimed, "Hiyas everyone!"

Almost in conjunction, the entire party jumped and turned to look at the little gnome now standing directly behind them. Weapons were brought to bare and battle stances formed. Mercenaries did not like to be caught off guard. None had heard her and all were concerned that they had not. Dean and Boldolf began to make sure she was all that they had to worry about as they scanned the immediate area.

Dean began, "Who ar-"

"My name is Presaya, Presaya Lightfoot. Yes, yes," she waved her hand gingerly in the air not letting Dean complete his thought, "I know I am appropriately named. And treasure hunting is my appropriate game!" She giggled. "I am what most call a thief, quite handy in a dungeon as it were. However, I prefer the term cracksman or plunderer to thief, sooo degrading, if you ask me! But, I guess no one did, so I will get on to why I just so happen to be here in this deserted, eerie village.

"I am here because I was supposed to meet a group of mercenaries that look a lot like the bunch of you, or at least how you were described to me. I was hired to meet you because the one that hired me said you would be in desperate need of someone like me to help you in a quest to find some stones that you would need to appropriate from some dungeons and a sword, also from a said dungeon. This just happens to be my specialty. I was paid quite well, so no need to worry about paying me because my employer will also be paying me even more upon my completion of the dungeon delving." She smiled a grin that went from ear to ear.

Gnomes were well known all throughout Kelnaria as being fast talkers and quick thinkers and clicker tinkers. This gnome definitely talked fast, but not as fast as gnomes that have never left their homeland of Oldverustashnal. The party could tell that this gnome definitely had experience in traveling and dealing with the other races of the world. She had bright green, short-cropped hair pulled back by a cloth bandana dyed the color of her hair to match, which made her hair spike at the back. It was hard to tell if it was her natural color or dyed hair. No one but gnomes truly knew what was normal for a gnome. She was shorter than Boldolf at three foot five inches and she wore light leather that was soft and well-oiled so that it didn't creak as she walked. Her leathers were interesting as they were tooled with all kinds of writings and markings and patterns. These were not magical as far as anyone could tell because they were not imbued with runes or anything of the like. She was a darker tint of gnome, her skin having seen much of the sun, so she was an olive skinned color. She wore shaded round glasses that were common of the gnome folk. She had twin daggers in sheaths on both hips and she moved with an easy swagger that showed she was a formidable opponent as well as a competent dungeon delver.

"Well..........," she began, "you gonna say something or just stare at me? I had fun tracking the silver haired one while he was tracking you. Didn't know I was there the whole time! That's just great! I like to practice my light-footedness because it really helps in the dungeons, ya know? So, but seriously, are you just gonna stand there staring at me or are we gonna get this show on the road?!??!?!?"

Dean was the first to recover and speak, "I am sorry my gnomish friend, but we are not accustomed to being snuck upon as you have done so. And your – um – introduction has taken my comrades and I a moment to comprehend."

"Oh, I totally understand! Please take a moment to ponder what I have said and then please introduce yourselves. My employer did not advise names, only descriptions. Us gnomes are not so good at remembering names though we are excellent at remembering plans and schematics. I would very much like to begin our quest as it seems that I have come right at the exact time in which I was meant too, which is most excellent!"

Boldolf rolled his eyes and grunted and muttered under his breath to Aelle, "Aye, a lil too coincidental, lassie." Aelle nodded in agreement but said nothing. They all knew that it would be Dean's decision if she would be allowed to "tag along".

"I am Dean Moonstone and I am the leader of these mercenaries known as the Lightbringers, though not all are within my main command. I have a couple of extras in my envoy due to a recent assignment we have taken on. However, while I understand that someone may have hired you to come to us, I am not sure that we are indeed on the same mission. Who is your employer and what is your mission? Why should we allow you to accompany us?" Dean stated very diplomatically with very fierce golden eyes.

Presaya began searching through a bag that was on her hip. She pulled out a scroll case and slowly but deliberately began to hand it to Dean. She wanted to make it very clear that she was not hostile and meant no one any danger. "My employer said that you would be leery of me, as you should be, and that I was to give you this so that you would know that I am friend not foe." Presaya smiled her big, toothy grin once again.

Dean carefully took the case while everyone in the group stood rigid on standby, slowly edging into a battle stance. Dean opened the case with care in case there were traps and gently pulled out the scroll. He read it with scrutiny.

"Alright, things seem to be in order, so you may join us on our mission as far as it takes us through the dungeons. Once we have completed that leg of our journey, you are to return to your employer." Dean stated with finality.

A little screech of joy came out of Presaya as she jumped up and down for joy. "YES!!" She exclaimed with the excitement of a child. "Now that we got that all cleared up and we will be dungeon buddies and we are soon to be off, I have one more thing that I must tell you."

"Go on," replied Dean.

"This village was attacked about a week ago, as you can probably guess from the embers and decay," Presaya took a moment to bow her head in reverence to the dead, and then continued as if nothing had happened. "You can also probably assume that Berdinian soldiers were the responsible ones for this destruction and you would be correct. I was here after the attack and saw the soldiers looting and doing whatever it is enemy soldiers do, but I stayed hidden in the forest so I could spy and not be seen. As much as I love a good battle as any other dwarf does, I know that one tiny wee gnome would not have made any difference and I would have ended up burnt to a crisp with the rest of 'em.

"Not everyone in this village was murdered. There were a few boys and old men that had defended a small wagon of some of the children so it could get away. All the old men and most of the boys were slain during that attempt, after all these were farmers and fishermen not soldiers, but the Berdinians did take a couple of the boys with them in capture. Most likely to conscript them. After the battle I left the scene for a bit until I knew you were to come."

"And the remaining children?" Diane had to know, her hopes soaring.

"Fear not, my lady, the wagon escaped. There were two elderly women that carted off the smallest of the small children and a few of the older girls. Sadly, as you can see, the rest did not survive and were brutally slain. However, the soldiers did not bother to chase the wagon. Would not have been worth their time to slaughter them, ya know?"

"Oh praise the Gods!," exclaimed Diane. "At least this village can someday rebuild. Let us just hope they will find refuge with another village or Cardinia herself. The kingdom will surely take them in."

"Well, all'in this be dandy, lads and lasses," spoke up Boldolf, "but we still canna have th'scroll we came h're for. Nor d'we know where ta go next."

"Ah yes, my employer said that you would be seeking the first in two scrolls as well as some jewels and a broken sword. One scroll tells the whereabouts of the five elemental stones - I just mentioned - and the second for the sword – also just mentioned - in which order they need to be placed and how to repair the twain. The second scroll tells you how to repair it. This first will tell you how to find it.

"My employer said that the current scroll you are seeking was on a lad, one of the ones captured by the Berdinian soldiers, which is a good thing because otherwise it would have been burnt to cinders. This lad's family had been protectors of this scroll for many generations and it had just become the lad's responsibility to carry and take care of not but a few days before this tragedy.

"The family doesn't know what it is or why it was given to them, only that it has been in their family for generations and that it is something handed down as an heirloom. Very valuable to the family in the sense that it connects them to ancient times and the royal house of Dagmar, but an old scroll and a useless scroll to the not-so-bright soldiers. So, most likely the Berdinian soldiers won't even take it from him since he nor they won't have any sense of its real value. The boy does not know it is one of the Great Scrolls. It is written in ancient common."

"I see," responded Dean. "Then I guess we now have a new goal, we must rescue this lad to get the scroll. Does he have a name?"

Presaya nodded her head emphatically yes. "Of course he does! Silly that he wouldn't have one. Who doesn't have a name? Well, I guess there are the unknown soldiers that don't have one. And some silly no name wizards that just want to be called silly things like Razzle Dazzle and the like, but I digress. Yes, the lad has a name. And yes, I just happen to know his name as I heard one of his friends call his name before they were slain and he was captured. Faolan Marduu tis the one you seek."

With that Dean nodded and with a motion of his hands the group immediately went into tracking mode trying to pick up the trail of the Berdinian army that came through here. It shouldn't be too difficult given that it was an army and obviously made it no point to hide their actions, but the group had to be sure they were on the right trail. After all, the army had a about a week to two week's time ahead of them and the trail would be cold, but they would find it and then find them.

# Chapter Nine

AS THE PARTY left the ashes of Dionness Village and headed towards the Berdinian army trail, the stranger that was stalking his prey watched. He watched with intense interest as the little female gnome came waltzing into their area without one little sound and startling them. He also watched as his prey was disturbed by the images of the dead in which his prey had never had to encounter before. He was satisfied that this rattled his prey, but knew that now was not the right time to pounce. It would have been so easy to pick him off while he was tracking the others. But he stayed his hand. Instinct told him to do so and now was not the time. Not while his prey was surrounded once again by such powerful allies and such heightened awareness.

This gnome was different somehow and so the gnome would be watched with as much care as his prey.

\*\*\*

The party was able to stumble on the Berdinan's army trail quite easily and quite quickly. The army made no moves to cover its tracks nor suspected that they were being trailed. In fact, the army did not even send out rear scouts to guard. So careless, both Dean and Ihoitae thought. So, the party just made sure to follow at a safe distance until the army decided to make camp for the night. Presaya and Aelle made a quick survey of the camp to see where the prisoners were to be camped and with how much security.

"Well, it seems this army troop is very lax on its prisoners," advised Aelle. "It does not appear that they feel them important at all. Which is good for us, but if they are truly the allies of the Demon Army, then Lord Mordecai must be cringing at his human partners."

"Also looks like they are indeed slated to be conscripted into the troop," added Presaya. "So, they will be decently cared for so they can be trained and brainwashed, but with little security so as to earn their trust."

Dean nodded. "So, this should be an easy in and easy out operation." Dean paused a moment. "Very well then, I want this one quiet. We need to slip in, rescue our lad and slip out undetected. If the others can be freed, then feel free to provide them the opportunity, but we will not risk this mission on the other boys.

"I hate to see our people put into slavery service by these bastards, but our overall mission is far more important to Kelnaria than a few Cardinian boys. Understood?"

"Aye, Aye," came the responses from everyone including the newest member, as Presaya now saw herself.

"Good," stated Dean. "We will wait until just before dawn when the majority of the army should be sleeping and the on-duties should be nodding off from boredom. Presaya and Aelle will sneak in with Diane's add of magical cover. I don't think any army this lazy will have bothered with magic detect spells. If they even have a mage with them.

"Bodolf and I will stay here since we will be the most disadvantaged to this mission. However, if anyone gets into trouble, make the sound and call us to you." Presaya made a face. "Ah yes, since you are sort of conscripted into our little band, you don't know the rules. So, real quick rundown. One, I am the leader and in missions you do as I say, no questions asked. The only time we veer off my command is if I am dead and/or the mission is compromised. Bodolf is my second in command and a warrior. Aelle is our sneak thief," " Dean put a hand up to stop Aelle from protesting, " though she prefers the term treasure hunter and trap detector. Diane is our mage, though this term does not always fit her talents. She is unique, so we give her the blanket term of mage. She is our healer and our wizard and our sorcerer and our summoner when we are not fortunate enough to have these roles with us.

"However, we currently have a warrior priest and a mage of quite some talent currently with us, so we are blessed with extra help in healing and fighting. So, Ihoitae has taken over the role of wizard, summoner and battle mage. And Ifem can assist in healing and melee attack. And now Presaya, you too can assist Aelle in sneak thief abilities. So, now you know the roles..... and now so you can know the code.

"Whenever someone in our party gets into trouble, especially on a mission like this, we each have an animal sound that we make so that if we are in trouble someone else from the team will know who and where to go. We make the animal sounds so that we do not alert our enemy to our numbers or our emergency. However, in the meantime, since you and Aelle will be working as a team, you will both use the same animal code. Understood?"

"Aye Aye," came the replies from the entire party, members and guests.

***

As the pre-dawn light began to loom in the sky, Dean indicated that it was time for the group to get into position and then put their mission into action. It had been a very uneventful night and the camp was soundly sleeping as the alert troops became relaxed and bored on their watch duty.

Aelle whispered to Presaya, "Better than I could have hoped! They are all asleep!"

Presaya nodded as Aelle pointed out the sleeping guards at their posts. "This should be cake," the little gnome quietly, but very excitedly whispered back.

Presaya and Aelle moved as one having gone over their plan of "attack" many times throughout the long, quiet night. Each member wanted to make sure they knew their job, everyone else's job and how to handle any possible scenario as they went over the mission time and again. It also helped keep their minds from getting lethargic as the night crawled on.

Moving swiftly but low to the ground, Presaya was able to reach the tent where Faolan and the other conscripted boys were being held first. She made sure to avoid the front of the flap where the guards would be sleeping and stayed to the back of the tent. The tent itself was surrounded by 4 other soldier tents, but they were occupied by sleep as well and no one else was on guard duty in the camp. The only guards even posted were asleep. Could there be any army lazier than this one troop?

Aelle, being an elf, had a natural ability to move swiftly and quietly as she swept to the opposite side of the camp towards their destination. She was able to disarm the two soldiers that were sleeping on their guard duty posts watching the perimeter of the army camp. She then swiftly maneuvered over to the backside of the tent where Presaya was waiting for her.

Without speaking, Presaya and Aelle made a couple of hand motions so that they would know that each had fulfilled their part in getting to the tent. Now, they were ready to create a backdoor to the tent to allow easy removal of Faolan and, hopefully, the other prisoners. The only sounds that could be heard where the crickets, the guards' snores (and possibly some prisoners' snores) and the small sound of a dagger cutting through canvas. Once the door was large enough to allow entry but small enough to remain unnoticed for the moment, the two thieves worked their way inside to try and locate which boy was Faolan and to remove all the boys' restraints.

Most of the boys were sleeping as the maidens gently, but quickly removed the bondages from their wrists and ankles. Some of the boys were quickly awakened by the sensation and two of the boys were already awake, and looking wearily at these two females drifting in and cutting them loose. Once the awakened boys had their bondages cut, they woke up the other boys and quietly began to sneak out the back door as instructed by Aelle. Presaya was asking each boy who was Faolan before they ran away into the night.

"Who's asking?," a boy with disheveled, wavy black hair stated very firmly, but quietly. He did not want to alert the guards.

"We are here to rescue him for a very important mission for the crown of Cardinia. We can discuss this further once we are out of harm's way, but we need to get out of here before the guards wake up. It's almost dawn!" Aelle responded resolutely.

Another boy of about the same age as the black haired one, looked over at him and whispered, "I think we should go with them."

"Very well, Tian, I will trust your instinct," replied the black haired boy. "I am the one you seek."

"Excellent!", stated Presaya a little too excitedly. A guard grunted and everyone stopped dead in their tracks. After a few more minutes, they heard a snort and then a resumed snoring. Everyone glared menacingly at Presaya and then they very hurriedly, but very quietly moved out with Aelle and Presaya following the fleeing boys into the woods.

\*\*\*

Just as Aelle and Presaya, following the boys, reached the safety of the woods, they began to hear shouts from the army camp. Apparently the mission was discovered and the guards had discovered their conscripted wards were now missing. Aelle and Presaya both hoped that they were not seen fleeing and that just the discovery of an empty tent was made, but not the direction of escape.

"I heard," Dean stated calmly but urgently. "But, I do not think we have been spotted yet. So, let's move quickly and away."

Bodolf grunted his agreement, then added, "But I dunna think all these lads be needin' to come with us."

Dean paused a moment, "Bodolf is right." Dean made a gesture for them to all come around so he would not have to speak too loudly and give away their whereabouts. They were still too close to the edge of the woods to tarry long. Any of the boys that already moved on, Dean did not bother to call back. They were free now and could return to their homes, if there were any homes to return too. "We did not come to rescue all of you, truth be told.

"We came to only rescue one of your number and he has been discovered. Our mission that we are on for now is to protect him and we cannot do that with all of you in our care. However, we did not feel it right to rescue only our mission objective, so we freed all of you. We came to rescue Faolan Marduu."

"What the cap'n is tryn ta say, lads, is that we be needin' for ya ta be headin off in yar own directions," Bodolf said.

"We truly are sorry," added Aelle. "But our mission for the crown of Cardinia is very critical and it cannot allow us to protect all of you and grant you all safe returns to from which you hail."

The boys nodded. Most looked bewildered and some a little afraid but all understood. Some took off with each other, but all went off in different directions. The two that remained behind were Faolan and Tian.

"Is Faolan Marduu a conjoined twin? They don't much look like twins nor do they look attached," Dean inquired, annoyed that two boys stayed behind when only one should have.

Faolan spoke, a little shakily at first, "N-n-n-o s-s-s-ir. I am the one y-y-ou seek-"

He was cut off by Tian whom added a little bit more confidently, "However, captain, we hail from the same village and are like brothers. I am with Faolan wherever he goes because we are all that we have left unless some of our village survived the attack."

"Dean," Diane began sternly, "These boys are fellows at arms and brother villagers. I say they are allowed both to stay with us. We may very well be able to use both of them as it appears that things are happening rapidly and extra man power could be a good thing.

"And as a side note, young lad," Diane added, "Yes, per Presaya here, the old women on the wagon with the children managed to make it safely away. I pray to the Gods for their continued safety and that someday your village will be able to rebuild."

"My name is Tian Rasca and I am so glad to hear it! Faolan and I both had sisters on that wagon, so we are relieved to know that, at least for now, they live," stated Tian excitedly. "We lost a lot over the last week," he added quite somberly.

"Aye, that you have ladies," Bodolf reverently added clasping each one on the back.

"Fantastic! Now let's get the nine hells outta here!," exclaimed a very excited and nervous gnome.

# Chapter Ten

HIS PREY BEGAN to move on through the woods with two new party members. Two boys they rescued from Berdinian soldiers that hailed from the destroyed Dioness Village. He could now confirm that there was more to his prey than his mistress originally let on about and he could sense that something big was stirring in the air.

He knew that the Fates had recently been resurrected by the Berdians and they were trying to raise the demons dead god, Kahlrab. He knew that the Demon Lord Mordecai was after his son for some reason and his mistress had also started hunting his prey after Lord Mordecai's involvement. Also, this mercenary band had secured his prey for someone else who was also a big player in this game. His prey was in very high demand and it frustrated him.

He should kill his prey as his mistress demanded and just end this game of cat and mouse for everyone. But something intrigued him even more than the wrath of his mistress. He could sense this in the air and he desired to see it to the end. So, for now his prey lived and for now he would even protect his prey and this little mercenary band. Something bigger than all these players in this game dictated to him that he was on the right course. He would follow his instinct and he would continue to watch. They didn't call him "The Watcher" for nothing. Patience was a big reason as to how he was very successful at his perfect and completely undetectable assassinations. He has never failed. But that didn't mean he couldn't wait.

\*\*\*

As they travelled through the woods, they questioned Faolan and Tian at length about their village and the scroll. At first, Faolan had no idea what they were talking about but eventually figured out that the tiny case in his tunic pocket that contained some rare paper that no one in the village had the knowledge to read was the scroll that Dean and the band of mercenaries was seeking. Faolan and Tian also explained just how old Dioness Village was and that it was not always called that. They had been told stories as children that the village was once a powerful border town that aided travelers in and out of Cardinia and that it once held a fortress, which was now in ruins, that trained the original Knights of the Horn, the protectorates of the royal family and the Great Scrolls.

Tian and Faolan both admitted that they never really truly believed such stories, but they liked to fantasize that maybe someday they could restore the glory to Dionness Village. Also, as young boys, they fantasized about re-creating the now defunct order of the Knights of the Horn. But, the village was simple farmers and humble fishermen, not trained for battle. The true origins of the village were simple fishing huts that joined farmers to create their village. But because they were not fighters in any sense of the word, this is how it was utterly destroyed.

"So, how is it that if the fortress of the Knights of the Horn was just a legend in your village that your village, and your family more specifically, gained the scroll?," asked Ifem.

Faolan sighed. "I honestly don't know. There are ruins just on the outskirts of the village made of stone and probably wood now long eroded. And many of the homes in the village were made partially from the stones in the ruins. Our people thought that by having at least one of the stones in your walls it would protect you."

"I never believed the stories either," stated Tian. "Even though I was a boy and thought them wondrous, I just thought they were kids' stories made to give us hope in a bleak world. There was never any real evidence. Even the Cardinia royal family denies the existence of the Knights of the Horn."

"I see," replied Ifem. "But back to the scroll, surely your grandfather or father or mother or village elder mentioned something about the scroll and why it was to remain safe?"

"Well, ya, now that I think about it," started Faolan. "Grandpa always used to say that it was our family's heritage to protect the scroll. This honor had been bestowed upon us by Dagmar himself. And that our family was one of the founding families of Dionness Village, before it was known as Dionness Village, and helped build the fortress of the Knights of the Horn. He even showed me some very old papers he thought were once blueprints of the ruins. Though, honestly, they were so old and tattered it could have been anything.

"But grandpa used to tell me a story that none of the other kids got to hear. It was a story that was told in our family only from generation to generation, not even the village chief knew of it."

"Go on," encouraged Ifem.

"Well, he said that when the original fortress town fell during the days of the Demon Wars between 1004 GS and 596 GS, our family was given the scroll to protect it as the knights fought. Only one knight was spared to pull my family away to safety, which at the time consisted of my then pregnant many greats grandmother and many greats grandfather. The knight had instructions on what the Marduus' were to do when the battle was over and the time was safe for them to rebuild. The knight also told him to memorize what the scroll said because in future generations the knowledge to read it would be lost.

"The story was basically about the end of the Knights of the Horn and it continued with what the scroll said," Faolan paused, smacking himself in the head, "ah come on, what did dad say?"

"It's ok Faolan, I can read the scroll," Ifem replied gently and placed his hand on the boy's shoulder. "But why was this entrusted to the Marduu family?"

"You can?!?!?!?," exclaimed Faolan. "But grandfather said……..oh but wait, he also said that if the Marduu of the future meets the one that can read the scroll, he was to be given the scroll! Could you be the one the knight spoke of so many years ago? But how can I trust any of you people?

"Oh, and per my grandfather, the Marduus' were chosen because of our ties that we once had to a race of people called the Telestics. But he never elaborated on that."

"Faolan, surely you know of the Great Scrolls and the prophecy?," Ifem retorted.

"Well, of course we do!," Tian provided. "But we never much took stock in gods and prophecies and all that hocus pocus."

Ihoitae chuckled and then added, "Smart lad."

Ifem sighed and glared at Ihoitae. Then he turned to Faolan and Tian and began to speak gently but with the same other worldly voice that Zaire had used that night of the ceremony. "Faolan, I am now the Head Priest of the Zadian priests. I have been trained in martial arts, the history of the world and the history of the Great Scrolls. Recently I was provided with the knowledge of the ancients, though I do not know how to free its knowledge yet. My master was unable to show me before our quest began. But, I am a proud member of my order and I have faith in the Mystics and the great wisdom they bestowed upon us.

"However, I can understand that some people do not have faith or understanding in my religion," Ifem turned towards both Tian and Ihoitae, "But regardless of whether you believe in gods or prophecies or all that hocus pocus, as your friend here so nicely puts it, you absolutely cannot deny that something in the world is happening. And it is not a weather event or fire or even the Great War. There is something bigger happening that is triggering all these events. You are important somehow and I would like for you to trust me."

Tian frowned. "Hey, what about me?!"

"I am sure you have an importance, too, Tian. Otherwise you would not be here and now with Faolan. We were all brought here for a reason and I have been given the knowledge but I cannot unlock the strings in my head yet.

"So, I am asking both of you to trust me. May I please see the scroll?" Ifem held out his hand.

"Ok, but not here. We should find someplace safe as your dragon/lizard buddy seems to want," Faolan said pointing at Dean.

Bodolf spoke up. "Ahem, the laddie is righ'. Aelle n me been doing perimeter and looks like we been tracked. We gotta move on or be fightin."

Dean looked up, "Quickly, young lad, I am a Draconian. I can see how you're tiny village did not know one of my race. So, I will let the indiscretion pass. However, you speak wisdom." He then turned towards Bodolf and Aelle and asked, " Bodolf? Aelle? How many and how far?"

"Lookin like aboutin a score o soldiers. Perhaps 100 meters," Bodolf responded.

"I say closer," offered Aelle, "but definitely 20 soldiers. And on hot pursuit."

"Ugh, so now they decide to get coordinated......." Dean responded.

Just then there was a cry from the bushes. It was Presaya and she came tumbling into the little clearing they were in with a Berdian soldier hot on her heels. As she ran, the party immediately dropped into battle formation. Weapons ready, they began to square off with the first soldier that came to greet them with clearly more on his heels.

Presaya, Ihoitae and Ifem were left to fend for themselves since the other members had been fighting together for such a long time, their fighting style was well formed and flowed smoothly from one battle after another. It would have resembled a beautiful ballet dance had it not been for the weapons and the blood flying.

Dean yelled out orders to Ifem, Ihoitae and Presaya to protect the boys. But Tian and Faolan did not much like that order. "We can fend for ourselves!" Tian stated firmly.

Ihoitae looked at him and said, "Alright, here is a sword. Stay close to me and you will live. And you will kill if necessary. Don't look your enemy in the eye if you haven't killed before. But never stop looking at your enemy. Lesson one!"

Ifem gave Faolan a sword as well and advised him to stay near him with much the same instruction as Ihoitae had given to Tian. Presaya ran off and did what thief's do best, sneak attacks wherever she could amongst any of the battles going on. She would slip in, slit with her daggers and nimbly dance away to the next unaware enemy. Not to mention the minor little trap here and there to trip or maim them up.

Ihoitae immediately began a chant, ""Notherlian nictieus protectoranntia spemmeshibia!" and cast it on Tian and then Faolan. Ifem heard the words and opened his eyes in amazement. He knew those words as ancient Sylvan magic. He would never underestimate the power of Ihoitae again. He also knew that Ihoitae would be weakened by casting such a powerful spell twice in a row, but understood that Ihoitae wanted to protect the young boys as much as possible. The whole party knew the lads were greenhorns, but lessons would need to be learned swiftly and, hopefully, without deadly repercussions to the boys.

A Berdianian soldier came up to Ihoitae and Tian and sneered. "I see you got stuck with one of the whelps! They have no fighting skill."

"Then why do you want them so bad, I wonder?," replied Ihoitae.

"My business, mate," the soldier replied snottily.

Ihoitae shrugged, "Whichever, but you don't get to have him."

The soldier raised his sword and began to advance. "We will see about that, mate."

Tian raised his sword and parried the soldier's sword thinking he could beat this foe without aid. The soldier quickly dispatched him by knocking him down and his head effectively hit a tree, knocking him out. Then the soldier turned to face Ihoitae. "Just me and you now, mate."

"I am not your mate!" Ihoitae and the soldier engaged in combat.

Meanwhile, two soldiers ambushed Ifem and Faolan. Ifem used his staff and expertly handled both foes so that Faolan mainly just needed to stay on guard and make sure that he kept away from any stray blades. Faolan admired the monk as the monk deftly thwarted blow after parry after thrust after feint from both attackers. Faolan was also amazed that the staff did not get chopped to bits or chip away as it was used to perform the feats its master wielded.

Faolan knew he was severely outmatched in what little sword fighting knowledge he had been given by the hunters of his village. He knew from this moment on that he would need to learn from these men and women rather than think he was their equal.

Suddenly, the sky grew dark and the wind began to pick up. Something ominous was in the air and both soldier and mercenary stopped fighting and began to look around. They looked at each other and then back at the woods and sky. The fear and confusion were evident for both groups. A silent truce was made between the groups when enemy and friend turned to look in the same direction as where a howling had begun. It was not the kind of keening the wind made during a horrible storm, but the baying of a dangerous animal or worse.

Swords, bow, dagger and staff readied themselves as the fierce, ear-piercing howling grew closer and closer to the little circle the soldier and mercenaries were in. The howling grew worse and sounded more demonic the closer it approached. Then one of the Berdians turned to Aelle, whom he had been engaged in battle with, and cried out in fear, "Shit, the Fates! Men, move out!"

"Fates?," Aelle questioned. Many of the other mercenaries also looked confused.

"But I thought they were on your side?," asked Ifem.

One soldier was kind enough to answer Ifem and advised, "Yes, technically they are, but the king is a moron if he thinks he controls them demons! They're just as likely to kill us as they are to kill you. They're here because they are after somethin and we ain't stayin to find out!" With that, he took off running after his comrades.

"Well, now that was just rude, wasn't it? Meany little soldiers. I mean," Presaya continued to babble while Ihoitae picked up Tian and motioned for the group to follow him. Presaya continued ranting. "Really, truly what disgusting individuals to not stay an- HEY, WHERE IS EVERYONE GOING!"

"Shhhhh," Dean, Aelle and Bodolf all spat.

"Follow the Sylvan!, " quietly commanded Dean. "He knows something that I aim to find out later, but for now, we follow in faith. I am hoping he can get these things off our trail! Whatever they are."

The party quickly pulled up behind Ihoitae. He had stopped in another clearing a short distance away. He had put Tian down and placed Tian's limp form up against his legs. He had his eyes closed and was waving his arms in a graceful pattern in front of him. As he did so, he was chanting in the old Sylvan language. At first it just looked like Ihoitae had gone insane, but as he chanted he began to glow a golden color. It came up through the ground and wrapped itself around his legs and slowly crawled its way up his body until it completed him entirely.

"What's he doing?," asked Aelle.

Ifem responded by quickly gesturing for everyone to hurry and gather around Ihoitae. "It's another ancient Sylvan chant. I do not understand the language, but I know the spell. It is a spell of translocation."

"A what?" asked Presaya.

"A spell of translocation, of teleportation," Ifem replied quietly so as not to disturb Ihoitae's concentration. It was probably already growing increasingly difficult with the wind keening and the howling of the Fates got ever so louder and eerier. "It is a very powerful spell and very difficult."

Presaya chuckled, "Tsk tsk silly elf, it's an easy spell. Mages do it all the time. Almost anyone can do it even with a little magical talent."

"Aye, even we non magical dwarves can handle that spell," Bodolf added.

Ifem looked at the both with the look a teacher provides his inept student who thinks he knows everything but really doesn't know anything. "True, however, that spell can only transport either one person at a time or one object at a time in very short distances to a place the mage has previously been and it weakens the mage quite a bit even though it is easy to recite. But you see, this spell can transport many people and objects all at one time to a very far distance – anywhere of the mage's desires, even if the mage has never been there before. It is extremely powerful and can completely drain the mage."

As Ifem spoke, the sound of the Fates were getting dangerously close and had even changed a bit. Almost as if they sensed they were near their prey and they were beginning pack hunting techniques. Their howls changed to whoops as they communicated to one another. Also, Ihoitae's glowing golden body was slowly spreading outwards from his body to create a sphere of golden light that slowly crept over first Tian and then each of the party members as they crowded closer and closer to Ihoitae. They too began to glow in the beautiful golden light that was like a beacon of hope in despair as the Fates approached and the world around them ever darkened.

"OH MY GODS!," cried Aelle, "WHAT IS THAT?!?!?! Hurry, hurry, hurry!!!"

ne of the Fates had broken out of the brush and into the clearing. It was big and solid black. No, not black. More like it was devoid of anything, color or substance. But, it was real, it was tall and it was huge. Its eyes were the color of blood and its teeth the color of stained white, a muddy yellow and brown. It looked as though it was a mixture between a wolf and a bear, a very angry wolf and bear. Its claws were long and talon-like and it crawled on all fours. But even crawling as it was it would tower over Dean, a seven foot tall Draconian. It paced from side to side in front of the party as it yelped a cry to its fellow Fates.

Three more broke free of the brush in flanking positions around the glowing party. Their intentions were clear and they were murderous. If Ihoitae did not finish his spell soon, the party members were all goners. There was nothing but an oppressing feeling of despair and no way to fight these demons. All hope was lost. They began to rear up to pounce. The field finished glowing around the party. The word "miethen" was heard, there was a flash of golden light and then all went dark.

# Chapter Eleven

THE WATCHER CURSED as he came rushing out of his hiding spot. He had to shoo the Fates away before they ruined his chances and kill his prey while the chance presented itself. He also cursed because he had not seen that spell used in millennia, but recognized it for what it was. His prey was going to elude him and he didn't want to have to track him halfway across Kelnaria..... again! Then in a flash, the party was gone and the Watcher was left cursing at the Fates and the spot where his prey had once stood.

\*\*\*

"Ihoitae,?" came the gentle call with a voice as sweet as honey. "Ihoitae? Are you alive?" There was a gentle push from a tender, delicate hand. "Ihoitae, you must stay with me. You cannot let go. They need you more now than ever! You have found him! You have found the child of light!"

The rest of the party slowly started to awaken as Ihoitae continue to lay there, still, motionless. They groaned and moaned and stretched out body parts as they checked for broken bones or wounds or any missing or broken items. All seemed to be in good order with the exception of the soreness from being ripped from one part of the world and magically transported to another in an instant. Even Tian seemed to be no worse for wear despite the bump he took on his noggin. Any cuts, bruises and bumps had been healed in this spell as well and Tian awoke groaning and moaning with the rest of the group.

It appeared that they were in a forest of some sort. A very ancient forest for they could feel the spirits that resided here, though none could be seen. They were watching this group that had just entered their forest. An unwelcome group as all strangers were unwelcomed, but they had been brought here by one of their children, so they would watch and wait. They were concerned for their wayward child for his form was still and lifeless while the others awoke and arose. They protected this forest for time out of mind and would always continue to do so. They would protect these strangers because they had brought a child of the moon with them.

"Oh no!," Aelle said looking at Ihoitae. "Ifem, do something!"

Ifem went over to Ihoitae and began to examine him for vital signs.

"Is he dead?," Aelle asked quietly, scared to know the answer. Despite the fact that Aelle hated this half demon, and even though her twin sister and she had been separated for almost half a century, she could sense her sister's feelings towards this demon/elf. So, her concern for him was genuine.

Ifem shook his head and stated with concern, "I feel no heartbeat and I cannot feel him breathing. But his body is still warm and his limbs still flexible, so I don't think he is dead. Rather in some sort of strange coma. I told you it was a powerful spell. It truly is a miracle he is alive at all. If, indeed, he still lives......."

"Where n th' world ar' we lads n lasses?," questioned Bodolf as he looked around. "Does no' loo' like we ar' even n Kelnaria no more."

"You are still on Kelnaria, but you are not on Kelnaria anymore," came a disembodied voice from the trees. It bounced off the trees so it was hard to tell which direction the voice came from.

Dean spoke up confused, but still trying to sound confident and demanded, "Who are you? Where are we? Show yourself!"

"We are not the ones that need to answer questions. You trespass and are not welcomed. The spirits of the forest wish you gone," retorted the disembodied voice. "The only one welcomed here is the one that is a child of the moon and a resident of this forest. He needs rest, leave him be and we will care for him. You may leave."

"You mean Ihoitae?," Dean asked.

"Aye, we mean Prince Ihoitae. Leave him or face the consequences."

Aelle huffed, "Ifem and I are children of the forest, too. We are Wood Elves!"

"We cannot just leave him," Dean stated. "He is one of our group and he is very important to Kelnaria. He will come with us and you can feel free to fight for him!" Dean jumped up and pulled out his scimitar and readied himself for whatever manner a creature was attached to the disembodied voice. He tried to search the forest for the direction of the voice.

The rest of the group gathered around Ihoitae's prostate form and readied their weapons. They, too, prepared for whatever they were to face.

"I see the Gods have chosen well! You are loyal to a stranger for you recognize his value, though you do not know what that choice means yet," replied the voice almost jovially. "We will let you live and glad that we do not have to fight with ones such as yourselves and destroy you. But we meant it when we said he must rest."

"What do you want us to do?," asked Aelle a lot relieved that they would not need to fight protectors of the forest. They appeared as little spirtes when they were in a good mood. However, to anger a forest spirit was a very bad thing and usually resulted in the death of the antagonizer.

"Take him to the tree in the middle of the woods. This is the heart of the woods. He knows these woods and that tree and that tree knows him. His magic was not strong enough to reach you completely there, but you are not far from it. Follow the light that beams upon it and it will lead you to the tree. Once there, lay him amongst its roots and we, the spirits of the forest, will heal him.

"None of you will have anything to fear while you are in the Forest of Sulilia, home to the lost race of Sylvan Elves. None but Prince Ihoitae could know how to get here as it was the Gods' way to protect it from any more horror. Honor the dead and so you shall be honored. Dishonor the dead and so you shall be dishonored."

The voice ended and a gentle breeze blew. The party turned in the direction that

the breeze urged them and saw that it guided them towards the direction of the beam of light. Dean gently picked Ihoitae up and began to head in that direction. Each member of the group went one by one, single-file after him. Somehow that just seemed the reverent thing to do in the home of the race of elves that had been so brutally slaughtered. Diane, Aelle, then Ifem, Bodolf, the two boys Tian and Faolan and lastly Presaya filed on down the path towards the heart of the forest. Each walked with heads bowed. Some whispered prayers, others walked in silence. Aelle sang a quiet song of elven prayer and peace usually sung at funerals. Ifem joined in with his bartone. Though the song was somber, it was beautiful as only elves could make the song. This seemed to please the spirits as they were joined by many glowing balls of lights on their way to the heart tree.

It was a short walk as the voice had stated and soon Dean was gently and reverently laying Ihoitae down amongst the roots of the great, massive tree that stood at the heart of the forest. It seemed that this tree was not only beaming with life, but with magic as well. This tree was special, but no one could say exactly how special it was, other than the fact it obviously had the power to heal. It had a section of root that look as if it had been made to be a cradle of sorts just for this very occasion.

"Well," started Faolan, "I guess this place is as safe as any to allow you the scroll. I don't think being in a sacred, old forest protected by spirits of a long dead race can get much more safe than this to show it. So, with that, here is the scroll the Marduus' have been protecting for centuries unknown. And myself for a very short period of time." Faolan handed over a very plain, brown box that was about the size of a ring box to Ifem. Faolan looked a little bit depressed, as if he had somehow failed in his duties as its protector.

Faolan stared at it thinking that there is no way that a sacred scroll of the Great Scrolls would surely have been placed in such a tiny, very ordinary box. But this is what was handed down to him from generations of Marduus and so he entrusted to the stories handed down with it.

"It was placed in this box by magic. I assure you that once I pull the scroll out it will look very much the day it did when it was created with no creases. It was placed in a very plain box to keep it from being of interest to anyone but those who knew it for what it was. The Knights of the Horn were very wise, Faolan," Ifem told Faolan seeing the confusion of the box in this boy's eyes.

"Open it already!," shouted an impatient Aelle.

"Ya!," concurred Presaya. "What she said!"

Ifem took the box and chanted some words over the box. He did not know how he knew the words to chant, but he did and knew it to be the correct thing to do. When he opened it, a scroll came out rolled up, but was in one piece and unfolded and very much longer than the box would have appeared. Ifem unrolled it and began to read it silently to himself.

"Faolan, when you didn't refer to yourself as a Marduu just a moment ago, what did you mean by that?," Diane gently asked, sensing there was more to his comment than met the eye.

Faolan, whom still had his head bowed, slowly sat down on one of the roots, which strangely seemed to shift into a stool of sorts. "I am not a true Marduu. I was adopted by my parents when I was a baby. I was orphaned during one of the many battles between the Berdinians and the border towns. My adoptive parents couldn't have children at the time, or at least they didn't think they could, so they asked the soldiers if they could have me. I do not know which town I originally came from or what my real family name is. The soldiers did not say. They probably didn't even know."

"So many have been displaced because of these senseless wars," Diane stated with a gentle tear in her eye. "I am sure your natural parents loved you very much. As I am sure your adoptive parents did. Otherwise, they would never have entrusted you to their family heirloom."

"Oh, I know my adoptive parents did, but I still feel like an outsider sometimes and now I have nothing but Tian and the hope that my half-sister made it." Diane placed her arm caressingly around the young boy, but said no more. She could sense his sorrow at the loss of his village and his family.

"Ifem?," Dean inquired, "What does it say?"

Ifem cleared his throat and began. "It is about the Sacred Stones. 'There shall be five sacred stones that the champion must quest for in order to complete his mission and fulfill the prophecy. These are the mighty stones that were held by the Mystics and thus were scattered after the great shattering of the heavens.'

"'The seeker will be able to search out for the stones and aid the champion in questing for them. They will be all five scattered separately throughout the land, each in their own perilous locations. As they are obtained, the champion will learn the magic held within.'

"'The stones are of the elements of the world: fire, water, land, air and soul. These are the five elements needed to defeat the mortal enemy and save the world and the Mystics' people.'"

Everyone turned and looked towards Ihoitae. Ifem continued, "So, we are reliant on the one reluctant member of our group."

Tian asked, "Now that you have the scroll, are Faolan and I able to find what's left of our village and go home?"

"NO!," boomed yet another disembodied voice that was different from the first.

"Herein we go agin!," stated Bodolf, exasperated.

"LOOK AT ME!," the voice commanded. As it did so, everyone looked around the clearing trying to find out where the voice came from. Then one by one, they all turned to look at Ihoitae's form. It was floating just above the root it had been laying on and it glowed an ethereal white. His pupils were white and his flowing silver, white hair was fanned out in a breeze of its own. The voice did not belong to Ihoitae though the words came from his mouth.

"I AM THE HEART OF THIS FOREST AND I AM AS ANCIENT AS THE WORLD OF KELNARIA ITSELF," the voice continued once it had everyone's attention. It was a deep, resonant voice, powerful and male in structure. "I AM SPEAKING THROUGH THE CHILD OF THIS

WOOD AND I CAN SEE WHAT HE CAN SEE. I
SEE HIS MEMORIES PAST AND PRESENT. HIS
IS A GOOD SOUL THAT HAS HAD A
TROUBLED LIFE AND A TERRIBLE FUTURE,
BUT DO NOT LET THAT DISSUADE YOU
FROM YOUR TRUST OF THIS CHILD. HE
LOVED HIS MOTHER AND HIS PEOPLE
GREATLY AND FOUGHT TO SAVE THEM TO
NO AVAIL.

"HE WILL ALSO FIGHT TO SAVE THIS
WORLD REGARDLESS OF WHAT YOU THINK
OF HIM. BUT YOU ALL HAVE BEEN CHOSEN
ON THE BEHALF OF THE MYSTICS. GODS
THAT HAVE BEEN LONG FORGOTTEN BUT
THEY ARE NOT GONE. THEY CREATED THIS
WORLD AND THEY CREATED THE WORLD
AROUND ME. THEY LOVED THIS WORLD
AND FOUGHT VALIANTLY TO SAVE IT AS
IHOITAE FOUGHT FOR HIS PEOPLE. THE
MYSTICS CHOSE IHOITAE BECAUSE OF HIS
COMPACITY TO LOVE AND BECAUSE HE IS
THE HEIR OF THEIR CHOSEN PEOPLE. HE IS
THE BRIDGE TO UNITE THE GOOD AND THE
EVIL.

"YOU WILL ALL STAY TOGETHER FOR IT
IS WRITTEN THUS AND IN ORDER FOR THE
PROPHECY TO BE FULFILLED YOU MUST. IF
YOU STRAY FROM YOUR PATHS, THEN ALL
WILL FAIL AND THE ONAE, THE EVIL GOD

KHAHLRAB, THE FATES AND THE
BERDINIANS WILL WIN. THERE ARE DIRE
CONSEQUENCES TO THEIR WIN, THOUGH
THE BERDINIANS DO NOT KNOW WHAT FIRE
THEY PLAY WITH. THEY ARE BUT BABIES
PLAYING WITH THE POISONOUS SNAKE
THEY HAVE NO KNOWLEDGE OF.

"THROUGH THIS CHILD'S EYES I CAN SEE
YOU ALL FOR WHAT YOU ARE.

"SO, I TELL YOU THAT, FAOLAN
MARDUU, YOU ARE THE CHILD OF LIGHT,
THE CHAMPION. BUT YOU HAVE A FAR
GREATER FATE THAN THAT OF THE SAVIOR
OF KELNARIA. AS IHOITAE WILL UNITE THE
ELVEN AND DEMON RACES, YOU WILL
UNITE THE HUMAN RACES.  YOU ARE THE
LONG LOST SON OF THE DAGMAR LINE AND
ONLY THROUGH YOU WILL THE POWER TO
RESTORE HUMANITY BE GAINED.

"TIAN HYATTE, YOU ARE HIS FAITHFUL
PROTECTOR. YOUR ROLE AS HIS PROTECTOR
IS INVALUABLE MORE THAN YOU CAN
BELIEVE. YOU WILL FIND YOUR SISTER
AGAIN AND SHE WILL BE IMPORTANT TO
THE KINGDOM UPON HER RETURN TO YOUR
SIDE. YOU WILL UNDERSTAND THIS TRUTH
WHEN FAOLAN CAN TRULY REGAIN HIS
BIRTHRIGHT.

"DEAN MOONSTONE, YOU WILL SOON LEARN YOUR ROLE AND WHY YOU WERE NOT LET YOUR NATURAL COURSE ALL THOSE MILLENIA AGO. BUT IT IS NOT TIME FOR THIS REVELATION. THIS SHALL COME TO PASS WHEN A CHILD IS BORN TO START A NEW RACE FROM ONE THAT WAS ONCE LONG THOUGHT EXTINCT.

"AELLE TINDONIS, YOUR SISTER WILL BE SAVED FROM HER PRISON IN THE OTHER REALM. IHOITAE WILL BE ABLE TO SAVE HER WHEN THE TIME COMES TO PASS, BUT REMEMBER THESE WORDS FOR A TIME WILL COME WHEN YOU MUST SAVE HIS LIFE FIRST OR YOUR SISTER CAN NEVER BE RESCUED.

"DIANE MOONSTONE, YOU WILL CARRY A SPECIAL SEED THAT YOU MUST CHERISH SOON. YOU ARE ONE OF THE LAST OF YOUR PEOPLE, THOUGH YOU DO NOT KNOW WHO AND WHAT YOU ARE, OTHERS SEEK YOU. HOWEVER, IHOITAE KNOWS WHO AND WHAT YOUR PEOPLE WERE AND SO DOES PRINCESS RADON OF THE WHITE DRAGONS. THE TRUTH WILL COME TO YOU WHEN THE PARTY SEEKS THE WHITE WIND.

"BODOLF HORSETAMER, YOUR TIME TO THRONE WILL COME AS YOUR PEOPLE WILL NEED YOU TO LEAD THEM TO THE FINAL

BATTLE. YOU CAN DENY YOUR ROYAL BLOOD FROM ALL THOSE SURROUNDING YOU, BUT YOU CANNOT DENY YOUR BIRTHRIGHT FOREVER. YOU WILL NEED TO TAKE UP YOUR CROWN TO FORGE A MIGHTY WEAPON. FAOLAN WILL NEED YOU AND SO WILL ALL OF KELNARIA. ONLY YOU WILL HAVE THE POWER TO PERSUADE THE CLANS.

"PRESAYA LIGHTFOOT, YOU ARE SURROUNDED IN DARKNESS, THOUGH GOODNESS BLAZES FORTH FROM YOU LIKE A HALO. HOWEVER, YOU WILL HAVE A CHANGE OF HEART ON YOUR CURRENT MISSION. DO NOT DENY YOUR TRUE FEELINGS OR SELF. THE WORLD NEEDS YOU TO REVEAL YOUR TRUE IDENITY AT THE MOMENT OF THE DARKEST HOUR. YOU WILL KNOW WHEN THE TIME IS UPON YOU. IT WILL BE THE ONLY WAY TO SAVE THAT WHICH YOU HAVE GROWN TO LOVE.

"IFEM BALASI, YOUR GIFT BESTOWED UPON YOU BY THE PREVIOUS HEAD PRIEST WILL FULLY AWAKEN AFTER YOUR REST HERE IN MY ROOTS. HOWEVER, LOOK TO MY BRANCHES AND YOU WILL FIND THE SECOND SCROLL THAT WILL TELL YOU OF THE SWORD YOU NEED TO SEEK. THERE IS ALSO A SPECIAL JOURNAL CREATED BY A

MONK OF ONE OF IHOITAE'S PEOPLE WHO WAS A KNIGHT OF THE HORN. IN THAT IT WILL GIVE YOU ASSISTANCE IN THE LOCATION OF THE STONES YOU SEEK. AS WELL AS OTHER GUIDANCE. WHEN ONE IS WAYWARD. YOU WILL NEED TO SHARE THIS GUIDE WITH THIS CHILD.

"AND THE ONE WHO CANNOT HEAR HIS FUTURE, WILL LEARN OF HIS FUTURE UPON THE JOURNEY YOU ARE TO PROCEED. LET HIM REST FOR THE DAY AND SO SHALL YOU REST FOR THE DAY. WHEN THE FULL MOON IS HIGH IN THE SKY, HE WILL AWAKEN AND YOUR JOURNEY MAY CONTINUE. YOU ARE SAFE IN THESE WOODS SO REST FULLY. PLEASE IMPART THIS WISODM UPON HIM, HOWEVER. HIS PEOPLE ARE GONE BUT NOT FORGOTTEN. THE MYSTICS WILL KNOW A WAY.

"THIS IS ALL THE KNOWLEDGE THAT I CAN IMPART." Then a gentle wind blew and Ihoitae's form slowly laid back down into the root it had been cradled in and a deep sleep could be seen upon him. But he was once again breathing and his heart was beating as it does when a man is at peace. Everyone else also began to feel a great calm over take them and, in drowsiness, found places within the roots to settle down and rest in as if the roots created beds for them to sleep upon.

\*\*\*

Many of the party members had started to awaken when the sun began to fade and the stars were beginning to twinkle in the sky. Rested and relaxed, they began to clean armor, clothes, and weapons, re-secure provisions and just mill about. Bodolf and Presaya began to cook when the moon started to climb the spidery web of the glowing stars.

As the other members went about various businesses, Ifem started to look around the tree in the roots and in the branches. He was not entirely sure what he was looking for, so he thoroughly searched all the nooks and crannies and boughs of the gigantic tree. Finally, almost completely on the other side, he saw something twinkling in the moonlight. It appeared to be silver in nature with a tube like structure. It would never have been found during the day and was only noticeabely with the silvery light of the moon. Ifem noticed it was a full moon. As Ifem approached the object, the branch it was dangling on slowly lowered itself so that Ifem would not need to climb for it.

Ifem grasped the tube-like case and pulled easily to remove it from the grasp of the branch. "Thank you, kind tree spirit," Ifem said solemnly as he removed the case. "May this forest once again be blessed by the song of the Sylvans." He bowed and walked back towards the rest of the party members.

Ihoitae was awakening just as Presaya and Bodolf finished cooking their evening meal and calling everyone else to 'grub on'. He was starving and amazed to still be alive after the spell he performed. He was also surprised to find himself in the woods. When he prepared the spell, he had planned to put himself and the party into Cardinia Castle's courtyard. He knew it would probably have been certain death for him due to the extreme distance, but at least everyone else would have been safe. It seemed that the gods were not done with him yet.

"Smells good, I'm starving!," Ihoitae exclaimed as he reached out for a bowl. He was quickly thwarted in his attempts for food when long, slender, feminine arms reach around him and gave him a big hug.

"I am so happy that you are alive!," Aelle cried. "And my sister is happy you are alive as well."

"I know, she is the one that called me back from the Abyss," Ihoitae replied. "I think I know where she is and how she got there. But I don't quite know how we can get her out."

Aelle let go of him and sat down to eat. Before she began to sup, she asked, "Do you remember anything that happened after you teleported us?"

Ihoitae shook his head. "No, not really, other than Safiyyah's voice calling to me that I must stay with her. And I felt a nice warm sensation, as if I was wrapped in my mother's arms once more. Other than that, nope! The next thing I remember is waking up to the smell of food."

"Ah ok, well, let's just say that the Heart of the Tree told us some interesting things and I know that someday, we will figure it out. Ok?" Aelle blushed a little and then smiled.

Ihoitae looked at her a little bewildered but replied, "Sure, ok." As he grabbed his bowl and ate he began to really look around. Everything about this place felt, looked and smelled so familiar. Then realization dawned on him. He was at the Heart Tree in his home forest which was no longer accessible on Kelnaria. The woods had encased itself in a sort of force field when Ihoitae had left his people after the tragedy happened and he was never able to re-enter, but no one else could either. Until today, apparently, thought Ihoitae reflectively. The actual city was gone, but the forest spirits were still here watching and the Heart Tree still lived. Did that mean there was hope?

# Chapter Twelve

THE FULL MOON was still high in the sky when the party began to move on. They were cleaned up, rested and had full bellies. They were following a cluster of glowing little balls of light that looked like fireflies. Ihoitae had told them that they were forest fairies sent by the spirits to assist them on which way was out. They knew which direction to head because of the little book that Ifem found with the second scroll which told about the Sword of Wonders.

The book, a journal, written by the monk of the Knights of the Horn, in the style of a survival guide for the order and it had been placed there by one of the Sylvan Goddesses to help the party on this very journey. It provided clues as to where to find the stones and the pieces of the sword and what to expect in each of the dungeons. It also had directions on who could mend the broken sword and attach the stones to the sword. It had clues and such for other quests that were side notes to the main journey. It was all written in riddles of course, so having a gnome along was wonderful and quite useful!

As they traveled, Ifem read the Great Scroll to the party, "The Sword of Wonders was thus created by Mailicaih, the Blacksmith. The sword's power is unbeknownst to all the planet except when thy five sacred are placed upon its hilt and wielded by the child.

"They powerful sword, deemed Tremblout, shall be well hidden and quiet until the arrival of the champion child. The child must seek the sword out in order to fulfill thine destiny and fulfill thine prophecy.

"They sword's whereabouts shall be unknown but only unto the seeker of the champion be found. Only shall the child be able to wield Tremblout once the ancient weapon is restored to its glory.

"Thy weapon can only be restored by a master blacksmith whom shall be named by the priest upon the sword's founding."

"Hmm, fascinating," stated Dean.

Diane nodded an affirmative while Bodolf replied, "Oh aye! Mailicaih, the Blacksmith, eh. There is a dwarven blacksmith in our myths of that name. Couldn it be the same?"

Faolan walked over to Ifem and asked, "What is the first riddle for the first stone? I mean, I think it only makes sense we find the stones first and then the sword, right?"

"I agree," affirmed Ihoitae. "We cannot forge the sword until we have the stones and the sword pieces. And it seems that everything is leading us in a specific order – stones, then sword, then forge, then battle. Don't ya just love the gods!"

"What order do you think the stones are in?" Ifem asked Ihoitae, trying to ignore his aside. "You are the seeker and I think you have a small intuition with this."

"Well, what are the riddles to the stones written in that little book? Maybe we can figure out a locale and try and work in a pattern," Ihoitae commented, stopping everyone where they were so they could decide their next move. They were now at the edge of the sacred wood to the extinct race of the Sylvan Elves. They knew that they were safe as possible here at the edge, protected as they were by shield and forest spirits.

"Ok, well it's more like one giant riddle and I guess from there you figure out which part belongs to which stone and its location. There even seems to be something about the sword and its forger," Ifem began, "So, here it goes:

By the light and love of the Mystics
You will travel from many cities and into the sticks
The jewels at first is what you must seek
Then to re-forge the sword to heal the world meek

First is the fire that you must claim
And it is a half demon that you must tame
Love will win the day
But only if the elfin maid has her say

Next stop is the white whirls of power ancient
To achieve this goal dirt bound must become
heaven sent
Of scales and honor do abide
Only loyalty will win this side

Travel to the crystal waters for the jewel blue
Only can a fish of man rescue it from the
dune
Let it be known that trust must be gained
From a duel that is a king's bane

Seek out the green jewel which is the heart of
Kelnaria
But you must prove your worth to all of
Centauria
This is done by words of trust
From someone whose people where once
thought dust

The last of the jewels can only be found in
ruins
Yellow is the soul where an extinct race once
has been
To test ones heart is the only way to win
Or all the world will falter to his unforgiven
sin

To find the two pieces of the blade

You will need to travel to cave and glade
Hear the roar of the felines of the forest trees
Prove your warrior soul so the point of the weapon all to see
Deep within the cave the hilt will dwell
Befriend a deep dwarf for only then he will tell

The last clue that this rhyme can provide
Can help locate the forger who is on the Mystic's side
Yet another set of dwarves that reside in Gemeindessal
Will have the ancient power to mend the asundered foresaw"

"Very interesting, the riddles don't seem too tough to figure out, so that will help immensely," Ihoitae pondered. "I think we are finding the red stone first, the stone of fire. And it sounds as if it is located on the isle with Demons, near my father's homeland and the entrance to the nine Abyssal underworlds."

"Yes, Mihak, where the half demons live," interjected Dean.

Bodolf shuddered and said, "Enemy terr'ory, lads an lassies. Its abou' a week's travel, eh?"

"Normally, yes, but it looks like we were provided with a little more help. Look at this,

Ihoitae," Ifem advised while pointing out a page in the book to Ihoitae. "What do you think? Can you pull off this spell without killing yourself?"

Ihoitae gave a sideways glance at Ifem, but responded very positively after reading through the page, "Yes, this spell is very ancient. Even my people did not know it. It is the language of the gods, but yet close enough to Sylvan that I can understand it. So, we are getting some very powerful help from some very powerful people. I would even hedge a bet one of our Elven gods or goddesses, Ifem. But while this spell is ancient and powerful, it actually uses very little magic effort on the mage's part. So, I can use it multiple times before it drains me."

"Excellent!," exclaimed Presaya. "This will save us oodles of time and we should have those stones lickety split!"

"It seems a little too convenient, but since it seems that our fates are currently out of our hands, I guess we will just have to go with it. We are at the mercy of the Gods, of time and of war. But we will stay on alert," Dean surmised while looking out of the forest and into the valley they were about to enter. The spirits had led them to the nearest port town of Maarsis so they could get transport to the island of The Temple of Kahlrab where the city of Mihak was located. They were headed right into enemy territory and needed time to prepare. A warping spell would not be used today. "Let us take passage on a ferry today. We can afford the weeks travel in this instance since we must prepare. And we can discuss this riddle poem more."

"Aye!," went the chorus all around the group.

\*\*\*

While the party booked passage on the fishing vessel that would ferry them over to the island of The Temple of Kahlrab, The Watcher could finally sense his prey. He knew that his prey was now halfway around the world from him and he would have a long travel to get to him. But find him soon he would, but then what? Kill his prey as his mistress had so long ago wanted him to do. Or should he continue to follow his own instincts and leave his prey alive? He could sense his mistress' ire but time was not on neither his nor his mistress' side. He knew a choice would be coming up soon and he had to decide his fate along with his prey's.

# Chapter Thirteen

THE TIME PASSED uneventfully on the ship as Tian, Faolan, Presaya, Ihoitae, Ifem, Aelle, Bodolf, Dean and Diane once again resupplied with food and travelling supplies such as bed rolls, extra clothing, rope, candles, torches and the like, as well as repaired any weapons or armor that had been damaged on their journey so far. They were fortunate that this fishing vessel came equipped with a sort of mini forge and other workstations as they were able to make repairs on the journey. Diane and Aelle assisted in repairing any torn clothing and cloaks as well. They discussed strategy on how they would pass through Mihak without fighting to get to the portals that would lead to the Abyssals. There were two other known cities and the gates to nine Abyssal underworlds also on this island. There was also the ruins of the Onae who were now long extinct. They had been a race of great demons that eventually had banished the Mystics, but the cost was their own lives paving the way for Ihoitae's demon side to become the masters of all other lesser demons.

"Well, at least we won't have to worry about the Gateways," Dean spoke as they strategized. "So, long as your daddy doesn't know you are around, he won't come looking for you and there are only three of the Abyssal worlds that care about you. The other six should leave us alone, the three neutral and the three heavens shouldn't even be concerned."

"Aye, bu' I dona think tha we will be passin by them gates at all," advised Bodolf.

Ihoitae nodded his head in agreement. "And I am quite sure we can avoid the Onari ruins easily enough as they are north of where we need to go. It's the city of the Dijinn's, Defajinn, I am worried about. We will have to pass by very close in order to make it to Waren's Tower and they hate any even semi goodly folk! Heck, anything they perceive even as goodly folk they will tear from limb to bloody limb."

"Yes, and the only way to bring the Dijinn from their homeland unwillingly is if some poor unsuspecting soul summons them from a magic lamp," stated Diane.

"Well, if Ihoitae is powerful enough, I think he and I can devise a way to mask our presence," Ifem offered, "so, long as he is up for the challenge." Ifem smirked.

"Very funny!," Ihoitae replied, "Of course I am up for the challenge, but what did you have in mind?"

They all sat very still for a moment. The members of the party that had any magical ability were deep in thought while the ones that were sans magic kept quiet so the others could concentrate. After what seemed like ages, Presaya finally spoke up, "Though I am a gnome and tinkering is our game, I am thinking that maybe we should get some

Berdinian armor and dress up so. We will have to get a cart so we can haul our regular gear, but we can set it up like we have prisoners or something. This way we look the part. Berdinians are always in cahoots with the evil ones of the half demons, so it won't look odd for us to be traveling there with goodly folk in tow. The Djinn's will leave us alone because even they won't mess with the Fates and Kahlrab's minions and we can exude a persona of evil by our mages projecting an aura of meanness. What cha think? I mean it's not my best work, but I don't have a council and things like this usually take months to plan, but I think it's pretty good for a plan on the fly!"

"I think parts of it could work, but in order to make ourselves unknown, when we get off this ship, we need to disappear from the city so we are not noticed. We will then need to find a group of soldiers to remove their armor from them.....," Dean was devising a plan.

"Um, no," interrupted Ihoiate, " If we bum rush some soldiers and take their armor and gear, we might as well set up a red flag. So, we will need to steal some of their armor from the armory. It will fit us better too because we will have a better choice. Especially for you, Dean. The draconians that travel with the demon army almost always wear their clans own armor, so we won't find many soldiers wearing armor for you."

Dean held his hand to his chin, "Hmmm, yes, I didn't think of that. So, where do you propose we find an armory of the demon army soldiers nearby?"

"That's easy," chuckled Ihoitae, "there is one right here in the city. And I just happen to know a way to get in unnoticed all thanks to my two hundred year conscription into my father's army!"

"Excellent!," exclaimed Presaya.

"Aye, aye, laddie," Bodolf agreed, "so, what being your plan?"

Once they were docked, Ihoitae lead them all to an abandoned warehouse where he could speak freely without eyes or ears watching them in the harbor. His plan would be quick and concise and they would be undetected when they enacted upon it.

\*\*\*

The group of adventurers decided to make the warehouse their base camp. They found a storage room inside the warehouse that looked like it hadn't been used in decades due to the amount of spider webs and rat droppings located inside. It smelled, but it was safe until they could enact their quick but simple plan of minor thievery. Ihoitae assured them that because the island was the Temple of Kahlrab and everything on it was either evil, sinister or just plain chaotic, the guards were very relaxed if even present at all. If they went into the armory in two's, they could easily get in as new recruits, hand over orders, which Presaya would handcraft with Ihoitae's knowledge of the forms, and receive a set of new armor and weapons without any suspicion at all.

So, they decided that Dean, Aelle, Presaya, Ifem, Faolan, and Tian would be the demon soldier guards. Ihoitae, Bodolf and Diane would play the roles of prisoners. As Bodolf put it, no self-respecting hill dwarf would ever follow the ways of evil and Diane was too different to wear armor. Her goodliness would very easily be seen through such a thin disguise. Ihoitae, however, already had his demon armor and would be too obvious a mark if they sent him in anyway. Even after all these centuries, his father would still have everyone on high alert for anyone or anything that looked or sounded even remotely like his wayward son.

Faolan and Tian went in first. Being young humans would make them the least suspicious. They were nervous about going in first, but they went in to the armory and without a hitch got new recruit weapons and armor and given new papers to report to the barracks for green warriors. Next Presaya and Ifem went. They also had no trouble walking up to the clerk that watched the armory. They received slightly different orders of where to report, but other than that all went well.

However, when it was Dean and Aelle's turn, a new clerk had been posted due to a shift change and this clerk was a little more alert. He was a young demon and looking for a promotion out of the armory clerk position. So, he was trying to prove himself to his superiors and he did not approve of the forgeries. He could not completely tell they were fake, but they were in the old style that had not been used for a century or two and so he was wondering if someone was playing a joke on him or if someone was indeed trying to manipulate the system.

"So, you are saying you got these papers from the General?," the young clerk asked.

"Aye, I am," replied Dean trying to snarl a bit as most draconians usually did. "The lass and I were told to report here for armor and weapons then report back to the Hall of Skulls." Aelle kept quiet, preferring to let Dean do all the talking lest she give them away. Plus, elves were commonly known for acting aloof and as if they were the only important creatures on Kelnaria. Letting Dean talk would perpetuate the stereotype of her self-importance.

"Well, that could explain the century old style," sighed the demon. "Those good old boys never change. Traditionalists, prefer the old ways and hate to adopt anything new. Even when they are the ones that created the new policy."

Dean snarled a bit when he laughed and replied, "Aye, this is true."

"Ok," the clerk started as he stamped their papers, "just go right through those doors and find you a set of armor that fits you. Draconian armor is usually to the left and female armor is usually to the right." He pointed the different directions. "And then go through the double doors in the very back to the weapon room. Elves get bow, quiver and rapier. Draconians get whatever in the nine abyssals they want since they can pretty much fight with anything, but max choice is three weapons. When you come back out I will hand you your cloaks, provisions and a small coin pouch. You will also get papers to report you back to the Hall of Skulls." He then waved them off.

Dean and Aelle moved inside quickly, found the items they were told they could procure and quickly walked back. "Efficient! Good choice in you as recruits," he smiled at them. "I guess that is why you two are being escalated to the Hall of Skulls. Here are your papers and on the table over there is the last of your items." Dean and Aelle grabbed them and as they were about to walk out the clerk called to them. "Make sure you give my regards to the General!"

"Aye!," Dean replied with a bit of relief in his tone he hoped the clerk did not pick up. "What is your name so I can tell him?"

"Zandir of the fourth house of the Demon Clans." With that Dean and Aelle saluted walked out and quickly away from the armory.

Geared up in Demon army regalia, supplies and even a wagon to transport the "prisoners of war" the party headed out of Mihak towards Waren's Tower. Ifem and Ihoitae estimated that they would need to start their magic aura of evil within about a day's walk towards Defajinn, the city of the Djinn. It would tax their strength, but it was all they could do to hide their "goodly" presence to that of the Djinn's and their malicious evil magic. Little did the party know that they had a hidden source of godly magic that would also shield them from the eyes and powers of the terrible Genies. In fact, their unknown benefactor was already projecting the aura of malice, just to be on the safe side.

It took about 3 days from the port side of Mihak to travel to Waren's Tower on the tiny island of the Temple of Kahlrab. The Temple itself was a huge city in which the Demon's lived and was where the main seat of their power hailed from. This is where they would travel to once finished at Waren's Tower to search for the red jewel.

While the temple may have resided here, the tomb of Kahlrab did not. The sarcophagus of the undead demon God had been transported to Berdinia where the main temples of the prophet were located. The humans were ever more loving and reverent over the undead god then His children were. The demons had no love loss of their god and many, although they would gladly fight in His name, had no actual desire to resurrect their fallen, undead god. Kahlrab was evil and chaos incarnate and He would pleasure Himself in all manners of torture, love, murder, war, killing and whatever else suited His fancy. He was not a kind God, but He was a powerful God and it had taken all of the Mystics to destroy Him before He could destroy Them. But in the end, He could not be destroyed utterly. His beloved race of Onae, the most powerful demons of their time, intervened, creating the Fates and keeping Kahlrab from total annihiliation. So with Their dying breaths, the Mystics set in motion Their prophecy to attempt to save Their world and placed Kahlrab into a state of unending torpor.

Once the imitation band of Berdinians, the incognito party, arrived at the forest edge close to the village of Waren's Tower, they decided to camp for the night. Their guise had worked well. In all their time travelling, they had come across many check points and they were never questioned more than to state their names, state their business and state their military credentials. After a brief view of the "cargo", the guards were bribed the customary food and coins and the mercenaries were free to travel on their way. Ihoitae always tried to stay in the shadows in the back of the paddy wagon to try and hide who he was. He also used his inherent shape shifting abilities to further disguise himself.   Fortunately, they had not come across any mages or any mages using detect magic to sense the aura of evil or use of detect true to sense Ihoitae's use of his shape shifting ability. As defense had been so many centuries ago, it was the same now, the guards were not on high alert in their own territory. Evil and corruption was a way of life, so no one expended energy to detect it when it was already expected and abundant. However, where the real battles were taking place between the Cardinian and Berdinian lands, the demon army was the finest army in all of Kelnaria.

It was evening and the sun was slowly fading away as they neared the edge of the woods. From the edge, there were about 3 miles of open land surrounding the entire wall structure of the city. It appeared to either be a garden of sorts or farmland as there was vegetation, but it was in lined rows and sculptured with paths leading into the village proper. They decided to stop here and figure out their next step.

"Ok, so we are here and all we know is that there is a half demon we must tame," huffed Aelle. "The only half demon I know is, well you, Ihoitae, and I don't think we are supposed to tame you."

Dean interjected, "Yes, I have known many half demons, at the end of my blades, but I am sure that centuries ago from the Dragon Wars will not count in this case. But we came to Waren's Tower because this is the only place on this rock that has any sort of non-corrupted people living in it."

"So whadda we do?" asked Presaya. "I mean there are no other clues in that book, except that bit about Love will win the day But only if the elfin maid has her say, right?…….. Mr Ifem……… so how are we supposed to know whadda we suppose to do to get the jewel? I mean what does that even mean."

Ifem pulled out the book. He had been reading it almost every waking moment except when "enemies" approached and he was beginning to memorize many of its pages. It did not elaborate on the rhyme that was given them on the scroll and so there were no further hints. He shook his head "no" and sighed. While Ifem looked over the book, Dean was looking over a map of the island and noted just how very small the town called Waren's Tower was compared to all the others on the island. If legend could be believed, this was actually a town of goodly folk that lived on the island unbothered by any of the other inhabitants due to a powerful spell placed on the town. This is why they were headed here rather than any other place on this island.

"Hmmm," Dean scratched under his chin as he reviewed the map. "Ihoitae, what do you know of this little village?" Dean pointed at the dot of Waren's Tower.

Ihoitae looked and pondered a moment. "I remember my father telling all the demons to never go there. It is a few centuries old and a mostly human settlement. It is said that a wizard named Waren came to this island with his family to get away from persecution from the mainlanders. He figured they would not follow him to Kahlrab's island and he was hoping that Kahlrab would take little notice of him.

"And of course, Kahlrab Himself could have cared less, He was/is after all undead and in a state of torpor. However, the demons could not resist the fresh meat and eventually attacked him and his family. They murdered his wife and children. From there, that's when the rumors started of it being haunted and that if demons would go there, they would die. I guess a few humans from the mainland heard these tales and moved in to be free from the political struggles of ......well.....everyone."

"We need to get this stone and move on regardless of ghost stories or not," Dean advised trying to get the group back on track, "We should probably change out of our demon gear, stow it here and be who we are. If this town truly has no love of demons, we would not be well received in this gear. That being said, Ihoitae, can you wear something other than your demon armor?"

"I can wear just my merchant clothes and stow my demon gear. I will not be well protected. Just so you are aware of my ability to defend myself should we come to battle." Ihoitae replied.

The party all agreed and changed back into their normal weapons and armor and attire. They decided to leave the wagon, supplies and demon armor here in the woods in the copse of trees they currently were standing in. Ifem placed a spell on the wagon and its contents to prevent theft. They would walk with the horses to the town and stable them.

They entered the town so aptly named because of the tower that stood tall and erect in the middle of the small, but vibrant community. The town was well kept and beautiful. The citizens here seemed to pride themselves in their homes and their livelihoods, so everything was meticulously maintained, clean and pleasing to the eye. It was a prosperous town, it seemed, and also, per the tales told, also seemed demon free. No war had touched this town or the garden surrounding the town wall.

The town was surrounded by a very tall, very thick stone wall that circled around the tower and was about 7 miles from the tower. The human wizard known as Waren had built this tower and the gardens, but not the wall, and lived there with his family until the demons came and destroyed his family. The party found refuge here as they were welcomed with open arms by the residents. They were welcoming to everyone, although many were apprehensive about Ihoitae giving him strange, uncomfortable looks.

Ihoitae shrugged on one such occasion. "It's the demon blood. No matter how much I try and hide it, they can always sense it. It has been my bane my whole life."

Dean grunted in understanding. "I, too, sometimes get treated unkindly. Because there are both good and bad Draconians and no one ever knows what side you are on. Due to our appearance, we all look fierce and ready to attack. Nature of being related to Dragons, I suppose. So, I wear my armor and my scars with pride because these will always precede my reputation and save me some of the trepidation with people of ill...... most of the time."

The party found an inn and tavern in which they booked a few rooms for a few days. They felt that here is where they could stay, unharrassed, until they could figure a few things out. They found a clean stable and booked the horses for a few days as well. They went around the town and spoke with all the shop keepers and even the mayor of the town, trying to discern anything new in regards to the riddle before them. Their time was uneventful and unfruitful until the third day. On the morning of the third day while breaking their fast, Ihoitae fell terribly ill. He became suddenly dizzy and fell to the floor of the tavern.

"I'm fine, " whispered Ihoiate as he was trying to regain his composure and pick himself up off the floor. "I don't....know.....what happened."

Diane sighed as she reached down to assist him and felt his forehead, "Oh dear, you are not fine! Your head burns blistering with fever. Your skin is sheer with sweat. Yet you are cold and clamy to the touch. Perhaps you have a cold."

"Hmm," Dean responded as he too bent down to help Ihoitae up and touched his forehead. "Well, being I am a Draconian and we are as our kin being cold blooded, I cannot tell your lifeheat, but you do not look so well, my friend. Perhaps let us get you back to your bed."

"Agreed," nodded Ifem, "and perhaps a cleric?"

"On it!" and a streak of gnome went flying out the door.

Aelle and Bodolf went ahead to Ihoitae's room to open the door and get his bed ready for him. Dean and Diane gently carried him back. Ifem went to go pay the barkeep and inquire about the whereabouts of a cleric in case the gnome, in her haste, was unsuccessful.

Ihoitae began to cough in terrible and painful bursts that wracked his entire body causing it to spasm. Upon completion of the spasm, blood and phlegm came up and he shuddered and moaned. Dean flopped him onto his bed as Diane and Aelle began to undress him. "And he calls this fine," Aelle muttered to herself.

Dean went to go change his tunic from the blood and phlegm it so recently acquired. While Bodolf went to inquire about some water and rags. He bumped into Ifem coming back with the very items he sought. "Lad, I not be likin the look of this un," Bodolf told Ifem in the hallway on their way back to

Ihoitae's rooms. "The moons were no' righ'in the sky las night, laddie. Somethin be amiss."

"I agree," Ifem replied. "I sense that something sinister is at work here. Could it be the rumors of the curse are true? But if so, why would they affect him?"

As they entered the room, they could see that Ihoitae's condition was deteriorating rapidly. All were worried, not only for their friend, but also wondering if they caught some strange demon flu and would all soon come down with it. Where was Presaya with the cleric or even a doctor?

Hours passed. There was still no sign of Presaya and a cleric. Dean was getting concerned and frustrated. Ihoitae's fever had deepened and he was sweating profusely, having completely soaked his blankets through. He had fallen into a deep, fitful sleep after he had coughed up what seemed half his lung. Aelle continued to wash his head and body down with cool water, while Diane held his hand and sang soft words to him for comfort. Dean and Ifem paced and Bodolf kept busy by getting fresh water and rags when necessary and honing the weapons of his comrades.

Long after the sun had gone down, the door flung wide open and startled everyone, except Ihoitae who was completely unconscious now. "IIIII'MMMMMM BBBBAAAACCCCCCKKKKK," yelled an excited

Presaya as she escorted a lovely young female human cleric into the room. "And looky, I found one! Took me all the day, but I found one! Those clerics don't like to leave their studies, boy let me tell you! But I told them all about Ihoitae and this one came running all excited like. So, here we are!"

The young woman went immediately to the bed and bent down. She began to feel for his lifebeat, his forehead and she placed her ear down to his chest to listen to his breathing. "Oh dear," she said as she studied him and the sheets and the blood and sputum that covered the area. "Oh dear, I was afraid of that. This is not good." She continued to examine him. She knew exactly what was wrong with him, but was wondering just how an elf could catch the curse. Then, it registered..."You did say his name was Ihoitae, right? As in Prince Ihoitae Mahadeva Arabus, son of the Sylvan elves?"

"Presaya," Dean stated in a warning tone. "What exactly did you tell the cleric to bring her here?"

Presaya took in a deep breath, but before the gnome could begin, the young woman replied instead. "She only told me that her elfin friend was terribly sick and that it wasn't like him to be so sick and that someone needed to help him, please, please, please. Ihoitae really needed my help, so I really needed to come quick.

"I came because many, as the gnome pointed out, will not leave their studies, but I wanted to see if

I could help. The name rang a bell with me, although I could not quite place it at the time. Thought maybe it was a friend of mine. So, I came. And, well, I fear that I cannot help because this is the curse and an elf just cannot catch the curse. It is a curse for demons, but it now dawns on me that if he is who you say he is..."

"Oh my," came the response from Dean.

"Ifem cleared his voice and began to speak as calmly and in as diplomatic of a voice as possible. "Yes, my dear, this is the Prince Ihoitae Mahadeva Arabus of the Sylvan Elves and of the Demon Nation. Please, do not let his heritage alarm you. He is actually one of the good guys."

The young woman giggled as though she were an even younger girl again. "Oh no, he does not alarm me. Actually, he intrigues me. See, I have been studying about the Sylvan Elves for many years now and I know all about them, their wars with the demon nations, their eventual demise and, of course, about their half prince. He is," the woman blushed a deep shade of red, "somewhat of a celebrity to me.

"My name is Arlessa. I am planning my thesis on them, presenting it at the temple for my graduation and.......well, silly as it may sound, I was hoping that maybe I could find a way to save them. I believe that they are not extinct, just simply lost and if I could figure it out, then I would have sought out Prince Arabus to help him locate his people."

"Save... them?" inquired Pesaya.

"I know you all now think I am crazy! Many at the temple think I waste my short human life away on silly fantasies, but I believe they were placed in a time rift, a portal, if you will. It's just this sense in my head that will not stop until I find the answer."

"Quite the contrary," Ifem stated. "We are somewhat on a similar mission, but it would seem that Ihoitae needs some healing before we could complete it."

The young woman looked around at the party and then down at her patient, snapping back into reality. "Yes, so it would seem."

"You said earlier that this was not good. Could you please elaborate?" Dean asked bringing them all back to the matter at hand. "What is this curse you speak of?"

"Oh, right," Arlessa began, "but first I will tell you the full, true story of Waren's Tower before I can explain."

"Very well," nodded Dean, "begin."

The cleric cleared her throat, thought a moment and then began her story as everyone, including Ihoitae, whom no one noticed was quietly awake, listened intently.

"The town is called Waren's Tower because it was built within the walls that were built around the tower itself. The town was built many years after the old wizard died after an unnaturally long life for a human. It is said that Waren was a powerful wizard, whom loved his wife and their two children. They came to this island to get away from the oppression of the mainlanders and had thought it empty of humanoid life. The demons had lived underground mostly, at that time, and the Djinns always kept to themselves in their magical world. They were not interested in one such as Waren.

"The tower was their home and around it they had planted a beautiful garden for food and tranquility. They also hunted the animals of the forest. They were happy until one day the demon armies came through these woods. It is believed that a scouting party had learned of the humans that were living here and were not happy with it. The demons wanted to be sure the trend did not continue. So, the army marched. Waren was away at a magic convention when they came and so, his wife and children were defenseless as the armies marched through the forest and gardens, right to the tower. The wife and children were slaughtered in the gardens right in front of the tower. No one lives in the tower and everyone knows it to be haunted by the spirits of the wife and children. Restless spirits wanting a revenge that can never be despite the curse.

"Upon Waren's return to find his wife and children so brutally slain by the demons and his gardens trampled and forest burned down, went insane. He locked himself in his tower and created a spell so powerful that even after all these centuries it is still very much potent.

"This tower, the town, the gardens and surrounding forest are all encompassed by Waren's Curse. And, if you haven't guessed by now, his curse causes great pain and then death to any demon that enters within the boundaries of the cursed field."

"Waren's Curse....." both Presaya and Ihoitae mumbled to themselves. "I had forgotten about it," Presaya said flatly. But no one heard her speak her whispered words.

The cleric continued. "The demon blood of Ihoitae must have responded to the curse. However, the elven blood must be prolonging its effects, trying to heal him. Usually the few demons that wander this close or are on a suicide mission die within hours. Most never make it to the city walls. I don't think we have ever had any actually make it inside the city."

"This is dire news, indeed," stated Ifem. He looked over to Dean.

Dean looked over to Arlessa and asked, "Is there no cure? Is there nothing that can be done?"

Arlessa shifted her legs with great discomfort. "There is," she began, a little unsure of herself, "but I am not sure that you will be pleased with the cure."

"What is it?!?!" Dean, Alle, Ifem, Diane, Presays, Faolan, Tialan and Bodolf exclaimed almost all in unison.

"Well…….." Arlessa started, "you see, Waren didn't think that anyone could love such a vile creature as the demons, except another demon. So……."

There was a long pause. The party looked at her intently; none wanted to hedge a guess, but all thinking this would not be an answer to save their comrade.

"So, the demon would have to be truly loved in order to be freed of the curse," the young cleric finished. "But, not just any kind of love. True love. Given freely and openly in desire from the lover of the demon that was not another demon."

Dean sighed. "I see what you mean by we would not like the answer. I am not aware of any lovers that Ihoitae may have. Anyone?"

All shook their heads no, including the cleric whom was somewhat a groupie of the Mahadeva and Arabus families and Sylvan elves.

"Then it truly is a dark day," responded Dean. "I want everyone to leave the room………now!" Everyone jumped and began to swiftly file out of the boarding room. The cleric, however, remained at the door, but after everyone had left walked towards Dean.

"I am sorry," she began, "this is not what I would ever have expected for the way of Ihoitae's life to end. If only you knew half of what he has been through……this just seems a cold and stupid end."

"I know more about him than you think, "replied the draconian, lost in thought. "We were once enemies during the draconian wars, when he had been conscripted into his father's military." Dean offered before Arlessa could defend her precious Ihoitae or her expert knowledge on his life.

"My war band went up against his troop. His reputation as an excellent leader preceded him. He did not lose any battles since he had become a lieutenant. I did not know at that time that he was only trying to find a way out from under his father and that he never actually killed anyone in battle. He was also one of the few demon leaders that took prisoners and eventually released them all in various ways. This is how his reputation reached us on the other side. He always treated them well, healed their wounds and fed them. And....eventually.....found a way to free them before they ever reached the intern camps set up by the demons.

"We were trying to protect a small human village from slaughter from the demons. Ihoitae did not know at the time that his people, the Sylvans, had been sacked viciously. They had not been utterly destroyed yet, but the demons were clearly winning on that front. I would be the one to deliver that news to him, trying to measure his, um, humanity. And in his anger towards me and my message, we battled viciously. He trapped me into a magical block of crystal all those centuries ago. I had my answer then.

I suddenly realized that he wanted no part of this war and he only stayed on his father's side to protect his people. All bets were off for him then, I guess.

"I owe him a lot, though I have never told him. I forgive him. If he had not trapped me in that crystal I would have died years ago, my life span spent. Or in battle......"

Arlessa looked long and hard at the scales and horns on Dean trying to imagine so mighty a warrior fighting Ihoitae. She finally replied with, "If he is truly meant to live, the gods will find a way. Maybe the prophecy of the Great Scrolls will kick in. It cannot truly mean that this is the end for his role in our world." With that, she left.

Ihoitae moaned and Dean went over to him. His eyes were open, though barely. In a very tired, quiet, weakened voice, Ihoitae spoke. "Dean, thank you for your kind words. All this time and I thought you despised me."

"Ihoitae.....," Dean began.

"It's ok. I am just glad that you learned the truth about why I did what I did. Why I stayed in my father's army. I thought that as long as I did what he wanted, he would leave the Sylvans alone. And I hoped that while I won battles for him, it would keep his direction focused off them. But I tried to never kill and I tried to save everyone I could. I hated the war. Killing is senseless and stupid."

There was a long silence before Ihoitae spoke again. "I have no one. I have been alone all my life and I have never found anyone that I wanted to be with anyway. There was always a vision of the perfect woman I dreamed of so many times. But, never had I found her in the real world. I figured I had set my standards too high since I was hurt too much growing up. I was never truly a part of the Sylvans nor was I a part of the demons. I was never really anywhere long enough to know anyone anyway after I escaped my father's grasp. So, I do not have anyone that loves me."

"So...... what? We are just supposed to let you die?" Dean angrily replied.

Ihoitae coughed and then spoke again after he spit out more blood. "There is nothing that can be done. I am in pain. Long has my elven blood and demon blood been a curse to me. Well, now they are at war inside me. One is my death and the other is slowly killing me in its intentions to keep me alive. I do not wish to suffer anymore. If there is no hope for me, well, then........please kill me."

The draconian glared at Ihoitae. He was angry and saddened at the same time. He did not want to be placed in this circumstance. He had performed mercy kills for comrades before, but these were almost always on the battlefield with clear measure on the life he was ending.  But, yet, his mission aside, he could not help but feel that there would be something more. There had to be. So, he measured everything before he responded. Solemnly he advised, "If this is your true wish, my friend, then I shall honor it. I do not wish this burden, but nor do I wish this task be thrust upon anyone else. I ask that you give me some time to prepare."

Ihoitae, too weak to speak, just nodded his assent.

# Chapter Fourteen

DEAN BROUGHT THE party together to discuss the events and his recent conversation with Ihoitae. No one was happy about this turn of events, even Aelle whom had always made it very clear her disdain for Ihoitae. However, the party all agreed that since Ihoitae had no one, then there was little point in dragging this to the very end and making him suffer unduly. In the end, it was decided that everyone would be allowed to say goodbye and then Dean and Ifem would carry out the necessary rights. Diane, Boldolf, Faolan, and Tian all went in and said their goodbyes. Next would be Presaya's and then Aelle's turn. Dean and Ifem would go last since they could say their goodbyes before the rights.

Presaya went in to the room and locked the door behind her. She wanted no one to enter without her being aware. She also closed the windows to the room. She hated to shut the windows to the bright, full moon that now shown through, but she needed to be as careful as possible. The future of Kelnaria depended on her carefulness. After she was sure that the doors and windows were locked, the tiny thief went to the middle of the room and began to cast a spell. Around her swelled a white bubble that encompassed all the room. The spell would ensure no one could eavesdrop or use magic to peer in through the mundane construction.

After she had constructed her security, she went to Ihoitae's bedside. "Ihoitae," she called softly in a much different tone than her normally bubbly, jovial tune, "I give you strength. Please open your eyes." A small surge of yellow magic went from Presaya's little gnome hand and went into Ihoitae's larger elfin hand and through his body. His eyes flew open as he felt the energy flow through him.

"Who? What?" the astonished elf asked. "How can you.....?"

"We haven't much time," replied Presaya, her voice deep, serious and almost godlike. "So, I will cut to the chase. I am not who I seem to be. I have watched you for your entire life. I have and always will love your mother as she is a sister to me. Not by blood, but by nature. We were very good friends. As well as I have always cherished your people for your mother loved them as if they were all her children."

Ihoitae looked confused. "But, how?"

"All will be revealed to you in time. There will be a way. I know it not yet, but I trust in the prophecies of my brethren. I just ask that you hope and that you tell Dean and Ifem to wait." Presaya's voice filled with tremendous emotion. "You are my last connection to my brethren and at first I watched you to protect you for only that reason. But I have learned you are truly remarkable. You are akin to my nephew and I cherish you like a son. As I said, I have always watched over you, though you have never known me as the same. But always have I been there. Sometimes as a beloved pet. Sometimes as a rival friend. Sometimes as I am now, the little gnome you know as Presaya. But whatever form I have taken, I have always been with you and kept you safe. I failed you when I let you enter this town. Long is my history and I had forgotten this one's past. But, I feel we are here for a reason and I feel you will not know death this day. So, I ask that you tell Dean to stave off his dagger."

"Presaya, or whatever your real name is, the pain....I cannot endure." Ihoitae said weakly.

"Presaya works fine for now for this is how you will have to know me at present. I have been her for a century or so. I have given you some of my strength. It will sustain you for a little while, my little one. After you wake next, this conversation will be but a fleeting memory, but, please remember you must endure. So much of it rides on you."

"No, Faolan is the prophecy. I have trained him some and Ifem and Dean can complete it. All will be well." Ihoitae responded, but felt very little conviction in it.

"Aelle will be here soon to say her goodbyes, but please, just think what I have said over before it gently fades away from your fore thoughts."

"Who are you?" Ihoitae tried to lift himself up, tried to command the little gnome to tell him the whole truth. But, weak as he was, that would not happen.

Presaya smiled, "I cannot reveal that too you yet, my little warrior, but in time I will. It is not safe for you to know me as me yet. But I promise you will. I have waited for a long time to tell you and to tell the world. So, a few more months will not matter." With that, Presaya kissed him on his hand then stated, "You must sleep now." Then she kissed him on his forehead as a mother would kiss her child and as she did so a blue surge of power went through into Ihoitae, placing him into a deep, restful slumber.

Presaya looked up past the ceiling and into the heavens and said a prayer to all the Elven gods and more directly to the goddess Sohalia. "I beseech you to shine your light on this child. He is the only salvation to this world and to your people. You have the power to save him. Only if I did, I would. Do not let his light dim over some petty foolishness that happened over two million years ago! All life is important, or did you elven fools forget that! Even the demons have their place and their roles in life and nature."

Presaya reopened the windows and to her surprise she could see the moon even more clearly and brightly. It spoke volumes of sadness and Presaya knew her prayer was heard and listened too. She unlocked the door and left with a smile on her face. Ihoitae would rest until Aelle woke him up, but even in that short span of time, he would rest well and feel a bit more refreshed.

Aelle passed Presaya in the hallway on her way to Ihoitae's room. She wondered why the gnome looked so giddy in such a dire time. She also grumbled as to why she had to go and say goodbye. She personally could care less for the half demon. Good riddance to bad rubbish, she thought. However, she had a call from her sister and her sister demanded that she go to him. Aelle would never deny her sister and so she was now walking at her appointed time.

Aelle entered into the room. The room was only lit by a couple of dim candles, but yet the room shown almost as light as day with the way the moonlight poured into the room. Everything was awash within a silver radiance and Ihoitae, being a Sylvan elf, seemed to glow in the light of the moon as his body drank in the power of the moon's light. The full moon had always been a time of celebration for the Sylvans. His white hair was practically gleaming. He looked beautiful to her, all of a sudden, even despite his malady at the moment. He looked at peace as he slumbered.

She came up beside his bed and took his hand. Then the urgent call came. Safiyyah called to her, begged to her, commanded her. Aelle shut her eyes and gave in to the magic call.

"Aelle!" Safiyyah's delicate voice commanded.

"Yes, Safiyyah, I am here and I am in his room. I am holding his hand as you requested," Aelle answered.

The other worldly voice came on strong now. "Aelle, remember when we were children and we would trade places?"

"Yes," came back the hesitant reply.

"We must do so now, tonight. Or all will be lost. If ever you want to save me, then you must do this for me now. Only he can free me from this place, but I must save him first."

Aelle had never heard her sister, whom was normally so demur and polite, was now so commanding and demanding. "But I thought –"

"Aelle, I can save him. But only now and only tonight. The goddess Sohalia is shining the moon especially bright tonight. She has heeded the prayer and She is giving me the strength to leave this realm without danger, but only now and only if you can fool the minotaur while I am away. Are you willing?"

"Who's prayer? What?" Aelle took in a deep breath and sighed in resignation. "Oh it matters not. Alright, let's do this."

Aelle gripped Ihoitae's hand even more tightly than when she had first sat down beside him. He gently moaned at the increase of pressure in his hand. Aelle closed her eyes and let the sensation her sister pulsed her way come freely and completely through her entire being. She had done this switch many times with Safiyyah when they were children. It was dangerous during the actual transfer because either one or both of them could get lost in the void of nothingness that resided between the dimensions. Both sisters could briefly glimpse one another as they passed in the corridors of that void. Both sisters always held tears of joy and sadness as they passed. Both longed to hold each other and be together in the same world again. But the Minotaur's master was very powerful and until the master and the abomination could be defeated, Safiyyah was trapped within that dimension of lost souls. Aelle never truly understood why her sister had been taken from her and her people, until this moment.

Safiyyah had never been ill-treated and never had the Minotaur discovered their switches despite the fact that the twins had completely different coloring. The Minotaur was color blind, so they looked the same to him. Safiyyah, however, had eventually learned from her seer abilities that her imprisonment had been because of the prophecy of the Mystics and for this very moment in which she now defied her captor's prison. She was to save Ihoitae's life and her captor did not want that. Her captor wanted Ihoitae dead and the prophecy to fail. It would seem that the prophecy had other plans. She never told anyone about her role in the prophecy, including Aelle, in order to protect her sister.

She had known Ihoitae since her seer powers kicked in as a child. They had started about two years before Ihoitae's arrival to her kingdom. Ihoitae knew nothing of her, though he dreamed about her on occasion when she was able to visit his dreams. She was also able to physically meet Ihoitae once in their world shortly before she had been captured as a child. Ihoitae had been badly injured by the Fates and he had stumbled into the Wood Elves' forest hoping against hope that they would help him and heal him. The border guards found the elf and the Fates fighting and were able to chase the Fates away as Ihoitae collapsed. Shocked to see a Sylvan Elf still alive, they immediately brought him to their city in the trees. It was in the Wood elves care that the two princesses had their first encounter with the infamous half sylvan, half demon prince. He had been weak, almost dead when he was brought in, but the elves were able to heal him. Ihoitae was able to rest in their lands and heal not only his physical wounds, but also some mental wounds as well. The daughters of the king were always around and always treated him with curiosity and kindness, especially the daughter that soo very much resembled his own people.

In turn, Ihoitae had been a sort of playmate to the princesses. He would entertain them and teach them when no one else in the kingdom had time or care to do it. He was a kind of mentor for them and he was always willing to answer all their questions about their long lost Sylvan cousins. Aelle had felt him a type of brother, but Safiyyah had known from the moment she touched his hand that her role in his life would be very significant when she were older.

Safiyyah now sat where Aelle had sat, holding Ihoitae's hand. She looked upon him and saw the beauty in him that most people could not because most people would not look past his heritage. If only they even knew how important he was to their world! If only he knew how important he was to this world! She was happy to finally be able to touch him as a woman, but she was sad because there was so much more she wanted to share with him. She wanted to heal his heart and mend his wounds because he had had a very rough life and love was never known to him for very long. Thus, it would be so again this night.

Safiyyah began to sing. A bit nervously at first, but gained strength as her resolve solidified. It was the elven song of mating, the ultimate bond between a pair of elves. It was equivalent to the marriage pact that humans make when they desire to spend their lives together forevermore. Especially for elves this was a big step in their lives as elves had very long lives and to choose one mate for that life was very potent. This was not only a song of the declaration of their love for one another, but it was a spell that would bind the pair. They would become one mind, but two souls. Safiyyah could not make a bigger declaration of love than the one she was performing at this time. As she sang, she made love to Ihoitae to complete the consummation of the spell. His body responded to hers as it was not only caught up in the spell, but his subconscious knew this woman. His subconscious knew of her because it had produced the dreams of her to make sure that Ihoitae never mated with anyone else. The prophecy needed this moment to happen.

The song carried through the air and magic swept through the Inn. Elves that were staying at the inn could not help but pick up the song as elves were ever driven by love and magic and nature. An elf couple was committing the ultimate act of love and life and nature and, drawn to this beauty, every elf picked up the song. As the song of life and love continued it became infectious. So much so that eventually every creature began to feel compelled to join in. Many couples renewed their vows and commitment that night to one another as was so strong the spell that Safiyyah started with the power of The Moon Goddess, Sohalia, behind her.

Dean and Ifem were late for their goodbyes and death rights with Ihoitae. However, when the song began to enchant the Inn, Ifem, being an elf and a monk, was immediately swept up in the song and lost all track of time as he sang and added his elfin voice to the power and the melody of the blessing of union. Dean had been in his room with his wife, Diane, when the song began and as it grew in strength he could not help but seduce his lovely wife to the passion of the music. A little while after the song had ended; Ifem and Dean were finally able to compose themselves and met in the appointed hallway.

"What the hell was that?" asked Dean.

"That was the power of the elves, Dean," replied Ifem, calmly and serenely.

Dean grumbled, "I assumed it was elvish in nature by the language of the music, but I mean....what was it for? Why did it enrapture us so?" Dean blushed, if there was such a thing possible for a draconian.

Ifem looked over at Dean perplexed for a moment and then, as it dawned on him, he chuckled a little. "Oh! It was the Song of Life and Love. It is how us elves get married. But I don't think I have ever felt one so very powerful before. It was truly beautiful and I hope to congratulate the couple when I am able to meet them. Their love for one another must indeed be strong to have produced such a strong musical spell."

"Oh, I see," Dean said quietly. At least someone was able to find life and love in these dark times. Ifem, seeing Dean so somber, realized that he should not be so jovial when they had a sad task at hand. "Well, here is the room," Dean continued, "let us get this evil deed done."

Ifem nodded and opened the door. They found Aelle still in the room. Her hand was holding Ihoitae's but she was slumped over in the chair as if sleeping. Ifem walked up to her and gently nudged her awake.

"Oh, spirit walking always makes me so tired!" Aelle blurted. "I meant to leave as soon as they were done!" She began to rise to leave, blushing a bit.

Ifem and Dean both looked at her with sheer confusion on their faces. "Please explain," Dean prompted, blocking Aelle's retreat. Ifem looked over to Ihoitae and noticed a smile on his face and that he was breathing easily. His sleep looked deep and relaxed.

Aelle sighed. "Do I have to? It's gross!"

"Aelle," Dean warned. "I am your commander......" He let the threat hang.

"Oh, alright," Aelle sighed, knowing they needed to know. "My sister and I can switch places, though we haven't for a long time due to the dangers involved in crossing the voids between dimensions. And well, she is a seer, she knew a way to save him and so she did."

Both males still looked utterly confused.

Aelle looked at them incredulously and started to explain again, "You know what has befallen my sister since we were young adults. Well, my sister, Safiyyah, has been in love with Ihoitae since she was a child when we first met him. She knew everything about him the moment she touched him. She knew he would not remember her, but she has never forgotten him and she knew that she was the only one that could save him on this very night. Get it now?" As she stood there she placed her hands on her hips with a look of utter astonishment on her face that these two males didn't get it. "I wish I had remembered him as a child as well."

Ifem was the first to recover, being that he understood the elven way better than Dean. "Are you trying to say that your sister switched places with you and then sang the Song of Life and Love with Ihoitae?"

"That's exactly what I am saying," she replied curtly. She shuddered a little out of revulsion. Even though she did not perform the act, she felt as though she needed a bath.

Dean suddenly beamed at the realization of this turn of events. "I don't have to kill him?"

Aelle smirked, "Not unless you want to murder him, which I won't object too. But, give him a couple of days, he will be just fine. From that smirk on his face, it looks like my sister was good to him. Yuck!"

Dean and Ifem turned to look at each other, such elation on their faces. Ihoitae would live! The curse was broken.....and Ihoitae was now married?!?!?!

"Let us leave him in peace then to rest. I will come by in a few hours to wash him and provide him new linens," Ifem decided.

"No, I will do it now," a male voice from the doorway replied. "He deserves to be cleaned so he can heal properly." All three turned to look at the door and saw Faolan standing there. "I have had plenty of rest and he is my mentor. I will care for him right now. Besides, after that bewitching song, I don't think I could sleep anymore even if I wanted too."

And so, Aelle, Dean and Ifem left to tell Diane, Tian, Bodolf and Presaya the good news and left Faolan to his duties to his mentor.

Faolan first changed Ihoitae's sheets and washed his back from sweat and blood. Then he gently placed the prince down to wash his face, chest and legs. Ihoitae had been left naked, so there were no clothes to change. However, now that the fever had broken, Faolan placed the white linen robes that the cleric had given to them on Ihoitae to prevent chills. Then Faolan placed the fresh blankets on him. Faolan had taken care of many sick people in his village, so this was easy work for him. In such a small village, the young often had to care for the old and infirm. And, sadly, in times of war, anyone living had to care for the dead. Faolan was no stranger to the task of cleaning up a sickly body.

Ihoitae moaned as he turned over into a more comfortable position. Faolan figured Ihoitae was still probably in some pain despite the curse breaking, but hoped that he would heal soon. Faolan sat down next to Ihoitae's bed and watched him while he slept.

Faolan also wondered if Ihoitae knew he was now a married man. He would probably think he had a wonderful dream! Faolan most certainly had had one! However, Faolan knew that most likely Aelle would remind him and not in a very nice way. Faolan frowned at that as he did not see why everyone felt so uncomfortable around him. Ihoitae had a good soul and a good heart. Faolan could never sense the demon blood in Ihoitae.

The moon, though now waning as She went to sleep and the sun began to rise up, was still shining brightly into the room. Ihoitae looked so ethereal, so otherworldly at that moment. Faolan knew at that moment that he was finally on the right path in his life, the one that had nagged him all through his childhood and teenage years. Although he loved his surrogate family, he knew that being in this village as a farmer was not what he was meant to be. He had been happy in the village as a farmer and content with his life, but something always nagged at him that there was something more. Being with Ihoitae and this band of mercenaries, he knew that he was following that path that had nagged at him for so long. He only hoped that as he walked it, he would find his surrogate sister again and she would have a place in whatever his new path had in store for him.

# Chapter Fifteen

THE NEXT DAY Ihoitae was up and moving around, pacing his room like a caged animal. Faolan had fallen asleep on the chair beside his bed. He looked over at the boy and smiled a fatherly smile. He knew that the boy helped clean him up and cared for him last night. He placed a blanket over the sleeping lad.

However, he was starving....no famished, but his armor or weapons were not in the room. He had white linen cleric robes on and didn't want to leave the room in them. He didn't want to wake Faolan either. He knew the boy and everyone went through a lot over the course of his curse. They needed rest. He needed food!

Ihoitae finally gave into the demands of his stomach and left the room. But as he opened the door, there was a thick mist that enveloped him. He stepped into the hallway, fearing fire. But he felt no heat and smelled no smoke. He only saw the mist. He decided it was not fire and that Faolan would most likely be safe in the room.

Then he felt the call. It was weak, but he felt it. It cried out to him, begging him to come. Craving his presence. He walked further down the hallway towards the sound, forgetting his stomach in the process. Suddenly, he was no longer hungry. But he was driven to answer this call.

He continued to walk slowly down the hallway, down the stairs, through the tavern part of the inn and out the door. He hoped that he would not run into anyone as he walked towards the sound calling to him. As he walked, the mist had thinned, but was always present. Everything around him seemed dim, off color, white washed. He thought it odd, but did not stop and ponder it because the call became more and more incessant; more urgent the closer he went. It demanded his presence and stat! He continued down the street. He had no shoes on, but he did not feel anything but the warm mist. There were no temperature changes to his skin or texture to be felt by his feet. He walked almost as if in a trance all the way to the tower, Waren's Tower.

As he approached, he could hear the past, but could not see it. The walls that had been built and the buildings that were the town were not there and he could only see the mist and the white washed tower and gardens that once were. He heard the children as they played. He heard the mom laughing at her children at their play. He heard the approach of the horses that inevitably heralded the troop that would slaughter the family. He heard the battle cries. He heard the screams as the children were butchered and the cries for help as the mother was undoubtedly raped and then murdered. Then he heard the horses and the demons leave. Then there was nothing but blessed silence for a very long time. It seemed as though an eternity of this silence went on. No ambient sounds, nothing. Then, at long last, he heard a wizard's zap as he came home only to be replaced by a desperate cry of outrage, anger and utter sadness. This went on for what seemed as ages. Ihoitae was hearing the sounds of the past - of that fateful day that had prompted the wizard to destroy all demons. More silence passed and then he heard the casting and the spell. A beautiful rainbow array of colors obliterated the white washed world that Ihoitae had come to know this morning. All went dark leaving Ihoitae to wonder if maybe he finally had died and that was his last dream, a last retribution of Waren to all those that died of the curse so that they could feel his pain before they succumbed.

Just as Ihoitae was accepting that he was dead, the voice came to him. It was soft, male, and omnipotent. "Who goes there?," came the challenge.

Ihoitae blinked and in that flash the world came back. It was not the white washed world, but the real living one. He found himself completely back into the living world and all around him townsfolk had begun to gather. He was standing barefoot and white robed in front of the tower's door. He looked as a ghost himself with his white, long flowing hair, his white robes and his alabaster skin. No one had been inside the tower since Waren himself barred it shut. They had all heard the voice too and more and more gathered leaving a wide semi-circle around Ihoitae and the door. Word was getting around town that the half elf, half demon was walking as if possessed and straight to the tower door. Many thought that the half demon, half elf had died and his possessed body was being dragged to Waren's door for vengeance. Word had gotten to the inn as well and so his companions were also scrambling to reach the tower door.

Ihoitae blushed a little to be so bare to the world around him and so many gawking at him, but the call would take no brooking and he remained at the door. Once again, the challenge came, "Who goes there?"

"I...I am.....This... This is Prince Ihoitae Mahadeva Arabus, son to Queen Mylayleriannias Mahadeva of the Sylvan Elves and son of Lord General Mordecai of the demons," Ihoitae stammered, not sure what he was supposed to do here. "I am heir to the throne of the Sylvan Kingdom as I am the last living known Sylvan and second in line to the Demon Nation throne."

"You speak truth to what is in your heart, but not truth as you are not aware of the truth. I will permit you to continue speaking. What is it you seek?"

Ihoitae was taken slightly off guard with that, but tried not to let it faze him. The entity, however, could sense his apprehension. "I am not sure what it is I seek of you. I heard a call and I came. It was not a call that I could ignore." Ihoitae replied only the truth.

In the background, his party finally arrived and wound their way up to the front through the crowd, but stayed back. No one, it seemed, was allowed to approach the elf or door. Ifem realized this was the doorway of truth and the first gateway to the first jewel they sought. Ifem tried to verbalize as much, but Ihoitae could not hear him. They could hear, but he could not.

First is the fire that you must claim
And it is a half demon that you must tame
Love will win the day
But only if the elfin maid has her say

"Search your heart and mind, Prince Ihoitae Mahadeva Arabus, son to Queen Mylayeriannia of the Sylvan Elves and son of Lord General Mordecai of the demons, you will know the answer to that which was asked."

Ihoitae stood a moment, thinking. He looked out at the crowd and saw Ifem and it clicked. The gems, the sword, the prophecy. He was here to seek one of the items. But which one........demons.....the land of fire and brimstone........ hell fire........the ruby! Yes, it was the ruby! First is the fire that you must claim.

"What is it you seek?" the entity asked once more. It was not urgent, it was not anything. No thought, no emotion, it seemed almost surreal.

"I, um, I seek," Ihoitae started, a lot nervous. He knew he was on a trial here, but for what exactly? "I seek the ruby gemstone for the sword hilt of Tremblout so that I may help Kelnaria heal the wounds of this land."

"So it would seem," the entity began, again emotionless, "your heart once again speaks the truth, Prince Ihoitae Mahadeva Arabus, son to Queen Mylayeriannia of the Sylvan Elves and son of Lord General Mordecai of the demons. And, you have answered my third question as to why you seek the stone. So, my final question: are you worthy of it?" And it is a half demon that you must tame.

"Um, please, just call me Ihoitae," Ihoitae replied as he tried to think if he was truly and without a doubt worthy of the stone. He frowned. He felt that Ifem or Faolan or even Dean would be more worthy than he. And it is a half demon that you must tame. Suddenly the answer came to him.

"Very well, Ihoitae, I shall call you what you ask, but you are both your blood and you most honor both as you did so by speaking the truth known to you. Are you worthy of the ruby?"

Ihoitae nodded, finally gaining the confidence in knowing his answer to be the correct one. He answered, strongly, finally accepting his fate, to tame the half demon, "I know not whether I am worthy of it or not. Personally, I don't think so. I don't think I am worthy of a lot of things. But what I do know is that Kelnaria is worthy of it. I know that doing what is in my heart is worthy of it and I know that without it, then we will fail."

A long silence ensued. Finally the entity spoke again. "You are worthy of it. I shall open my door so that you may retrieve it. But beware, the Tower of Waren is filled with traps and puzzles. You must go in with nothing but your true heart and you shall find what you seek. If you do not go in with your true heart, then you will be subject to all the devious traps and puzzles and will forevermore wander the tower's maze. Do you except this condition?"

Without hesitation, Ihoitae responded, "Yes!"

The door opened. "Then go in knowing that you have my approval young son, Prince Ihoitae Mahadeva Arabus, son to Queen Mylayeriannia of the Sylvan Elves and son of Lord General Mordecai of the demons, for your heart is pure even and your soul has now accepted its fate."

Ihoitae closed his eyes and stepped in. There was a collective holding of breath as he entered in. Everyone expected the half elf, half demon to finally meet his demise. The door slammed shut and the bubble that had kept everyone back seemingly vanished as the townsfolk that were leaning against it almost fell over from the release of this force field. The party once again tried to go to where Ihoitae had stood. Arlessa also went, too. Ifem attempted to open the door and was zapped for his efforts.

"This is not for you to complete, worthy monk. He must find a piece of himself. If he is ever to heal the land, he must heal himself. He has tamed the demon. Now he must gain the love of his fair maid. Faolan's reign will be all the stronger for it. Let it pass."

They all looked to and from each other, utterly lost and confused. Faolan's reign? Ihoitae heal the land? Too much was too confusing and even Ifem did not have the answers. So, they sat and camped the door, waiting.........

***

Ihoitae walked into a mist filled, round room at the base of the tower. The room was bare except for the stairs that led up and a few broken pieces of furniture covered in spider webs and dust. Compelled, Ihoitae went up those stairs. Round and round and up and up they went for what seemed ages. Ihoitae felt along the walls with his hands to see if there were any doors, crevices or hidden devices. There would be a landing every flight. Some opened up into other round rooms, sparsely decorated, thick with cobwebs, but absolutely nothing of import. He felt only the urge to go up, up, up! So, again, compelled, he would continue this climb and search and climb and search. He felt that to veer off into any of the corridors would place him with the traps mentioned. He was not here to pillage. He was here to gain the stone of fire. At last, he reached the top of the tower.

At the top of the tower was the wizard's room. It seemed unnaturally large for a room that was at the narrowest point of the round tower. Here he had all his potions, components, books, a desk, scrying devices and mirrors of all shapes and sizes. In the very middle of the room stood a fire pit blazing. The room looked clean and had no spider webs or any other debris. It looked as though the wizard Waren were still living in this very room.  However, the room was completely empty of living souls except for Ihoitae himself.

"Why am I here? What am I supposed to do?" Ihoitae muttered to himself. He knew he was here for the ruby of fire, but how was he supposed to get it?

"I am Waren," the disembodied voice began again. "When I cast my curse, I did not die, though I very much wanted too. I was absorbed into the very tower I called home. And thus, the tower has become a living, breathing entity, protecting this town with my final spell."

"And that is why the curse is still so very potent today! Its creator still lives, albeit not in a living body."

"Correct, young demon," the voice finally had emotion and it sounded very tired, very old and very defeated. "I would that I would have died as I wish to join my Marlee and Cinda and Louc in death. I miss them terribly and I forever hear their terror. They are trapped here and I cannot free them. I hear that fateful day every day at the time that it happened all those years ago, though no one in town, except you, has. My spell had a terrible side effect."

"You did not know that at the time you cast the curse," Ihoitae guessed.

"Correct. At the very moment I cast the curse, I knew that their souls were not at peace. They were forever more trapped on that fateful day as it is now I am trapped in this tower. The ones you heard when you arrived at my tower, were my wife and children and the monstrous demons that did the terrible deed."

"And thus, the tower trapped you."

"Correct again. I cannot be free until they are free and, also, I cannot free them in my...... immortal form," Waren snorted. "I was to be taught a lesson it seemed. Karma, as it were."

"I guess I am here to help you and help you I shall, but what is it that I can do?"

Waren snorted again seeming to go from tired to angry and cynically replied, "Help me? Help them? What does a demon cares to do but slaughter and maim and destroy? You are a demon, go away!"

Ihoitae did not flinch. He had been told that so many times during his years at the court of the elves it did not faze him anymore. His very nature was a constant threat to their way of life. 'He could have snapped at any minute' is what they would say. Yet, he had never shown any anger tendencies towards anyone, even when he had been punished or beaten up or berated by any elf. Even when he had been conscripted into his father's army, he found ways to earn the trust of his comrades by compassion, not by fear, and learned that demons had compassion and love. They must have just forgotten those traits along the way. However, he had been able to bring them out, which is why his troops always worked so well together.

"You are still here, demon scum."

Ihoitae snapped out of his thoughts. Fire.......fire was always tempered by water and caressed by air. So too Waren needed to be tempered by the very thing he hated. Ihoitae would have to show him compassion and then we would win the ruby! Yes, that was the riddle. Love will win the day, But only if the elfin maid has her say. Oh, but who was the elfin maid?

"Ok, I see, so you desire all demons dead. I am but a half demon and not a very common one at that," Ihoitae began gaining confidence as he spoke. "You are mad because I did not die. Because I am loved and you feel no demon deserves love, even a half mongrel like me."

"Go on," Waren replied, defensiveness in his voice.

"Well, I am truly sorry for what happened to your family. I would be just as devastated as you were and I was when the demons killed my entire nation!" Ihoitae snapped, overwhelming anger coming into his voice. "I held my mother as she lay dying on a pile of her dead kin. Everyone of them murdered from very old to......." Ihoitae paused, reliving the memories. "T – t- to very young. Babies! They murdered the elven babies!" Ihoitae began to cry as the memories of that horrific day swept up in him. "I have every right to hate demons the same as you, nay more than you, for what they did to an entire nation of peoples. Slaughtered, wiped out, obliterated! I hated the half of me that is demon, but does that mean that I deserve to die because half of me is demon?

"If my death would bring back your wife and children and restore your life to you, then know that I would forfeit it in a moment! Know that I would lay my life down for anyone in my family and my mother's kingdom, though not many deserve it of me due to their ill treatment of me. Also know that I would gladly give my life to any of those people down there to know they were safe and happy and that my father could not harm nor touch them. I have sacrificed much and will sacrifice more. All in the name of love. I am a half demon, but that does not make me incapable of love or compassion!"

The voice sniffled and answered, "Demon you have moved me. I knew that others felt my pain. Other humans, elves and other various races, but I did not believe that demons could have such emotion, even if you are only a half one."

"I can and I do, everyday. I have lived for two millennia now and you cannot know the amount of suffering I have known in my very long life. I have yet to let that stop me from living, from trying to make a difference, to right the wrongs of my father or his people! I believe that they can be saved as I have seen in them compassion and love. It just got lost somewhere along the way."

"You are sincere in your conviction," Waren replied with no emotion once again.

"I am," Ihoitae replied though the sentence was not a question but a fact. "If you can truly see into my heart, then you can see the depths of my soul. You should know who I am and what I am. I cannot hide myself from you, not that I have any reason to deceive you. I know you have suffered at the hands of my ill-gotten people and I would that I could ease that suffering in the only way that I can now. I cannot asunder what once has been done, but I can bring peace to all four of your souls." Ihoitae paused then and when no response came he inquired, "May I?"

There was a flash of light that blinded Ihoitae. He blinked his eyes and upon opening them again, he was once again in the white washed, misty world and he was outside at the bottom of the tower. This time, he was completely dressed in his demon armor and had all of his weapons. He could not only hear the voices, but this time he could see the characters of the drama that had played out day after day, year after year under this tower unbeknownst to the living that surrounded it. He knew once he placed their souls at rest, the spell would vanish and fade, but he knew that this must be done. He must right the wrong and he must make peace with who he is.

The scene played out. There was nothing that Ihoitae could do to change the events of the past, nor should he. So, as a spectator, he watched the senseless slaughter of the two beautiful children and the rape and slaughter of Marlee. But once the slaughter occurred and Waren cast his curse, Ihoitae went to find the spirits of Cinda and Louc first. The two children's ethereal bodies sat over where their living bodies had once lain, slain, though they had long since disintegrated away. They were crying and calling for their father to save them still and their mother to comfort them in their pain.

"Hark children," Ihoitae called to them, trying to remember the old speech so they would understand him better. "Why dost thou weep?"

For the first time in centuries, a living being recognized them, spoke to them and addressed them as if they were once more living. "You doth see us?, " Louc asked.

"Aye, that I do," Ihoitae replied and continued. "I have come from thine father. He doth wish thee to join him so that ye will knoweth peace."

Both their little eyes widened and happiness once more shown on their faces. Their father did not forget them and he wanted them. They were loved. They were needed and they were called. Although Ihoitae could not hear their call, they did and they answered it with gladness. Ihoitae heard nothing from the little spirits, but saw a bright light shine around them and he could see they knew peace. They would go to the heavenly abyss where they would meet their parents shortly. So, then Ihoitae went to go look for Marlee's spirit.

Marlee was a little more aware than her young ones as to what had happened and that she was now a spirit. So, she wandered around the tower, wailing, looking for her wee ones. She saw Ihoitae and scowled. "What do thee want, demon?" Her speech was more modern which only proved to Ihoitae how much of her surroundings that she was aware of.

"Please, mine lady, I come in peace."

"Fine, what do ye want?," she spat at him. "I must find my babes. I have to bring them home or they will never know peace. They were just children!"

"I have come to free you," Ihoitae changed his speech pattern to meet hers. "I was sent by Waren to free your children and your souls."

The wisp that had once been Marlee stopped short from her wandering and looked directly into Ihoitae's eyes. She nodded once after a few minutes of what felt like her boring into his own soul. Then she smiled. "I can hear them laughing. They have moved on and so must I. Please bid my husband to join us shortly. He must let go his hatred. We miss him so." With that, she faded away.

Ihoitae went back into the tower and up the ever winding stairs until he came to the very top. He went straight for the desk where now sat what could only be the apparition of Waren himself. "They are freed. Please join your family and be at peace. I bid you. Only once you let go your hatred, can you join them. Will you do so now?"

Waren, with tears in his eyes, spoke with pure happiness, "You are the only creature that cared enough to help. All these townspeople ever wanted was for me to stay and protect them with my curse. No one came to ask why or how. You have restored my faith in Kelnaria and......and even demons can love. I wish you well upon your journey, light bringer." With that, he stood up and then faded away the same as his wife had did. As he did so, the room became dim and no longer looked recently cleaned, but rather as if it had sat with the rest of the tower for centuries with cobwebs, dust and decaying books and furniture.

However, one thing stood out now. Ihoitae heard a crackling sound coming from the brazier. He knew this is where the ruby would be. Without a second thought, he stuck his hand right into the hot coals and reached for the only cool stone in the brazier. Out he pulled the shining, bright fire red ruby and marveled at its beauty and the fact that he did not get burned. That, however, was his last conscious thought as he fell into a deep, heavy sleep and crumbled to the floor.

\*\*\*

The doors to the tower opened and there was a wave of magic that swept the town and the surrounding forest. The tower suddenly faded and looked its age. It leaned heavily to one side with stones crumbled along the ground and around the tower walls as if they had always been there. Missing from parts of the tower wall were blocks of stones as well and the shingled, wooden roof was completely gone with only a few rotted timbers still poking up to show that there had ever been a roof attached. The wooden door was worn and planks were missing and bolts were rusted out. The town knew something profound had happened and somehow the magic curse that protected them was fading fast with the change of the tower. It no longer seemed…..alive.

Ifem and Arlessa were the first two to enter through the rotted door. There they found Ihoitae, in full armor and all his weapons, peacefully asleep on a bench in the rough round room. The bench seemed to have been the only thing in the entire tower to still hold some of the old magic and was whole, intact. In his hands he cupped a small red jewel in the shape of a fire blazing in a hearth. Surrounding him were Crimson Glow Flowers which had once bloomed all throughout the forest when Waren and his family lived in the tower, but had long since died off once the horrific events had occurred to Waren, Marlee, Cinda and Louc. The tower was at peace once more and could join time once again. The first jewel was found. But more importantly, Ihoitae learned that even hatred could be defeated if someone took the time to care despite differences. Ihoitae was only able to show his love because Safiyyah was able to convince Aelle to allow her to come and rescue Ihoitae from demise. Safiyyah had shown him that sacrifice sometimes meant love.

# Chapter Sixteen

THE BAND LEFT the town of Waren's Tower grateful that they would not have to travel to any of the demon cities for the fire jewel. They were sad because of the cost to the townsfolk that the retrieval required. There would be no more peace or protection for the town once the demons learned the curse was no more. But Ifem and Ihoitae hoped that once all was said and done, the curse would no longer be needed and everyone on Kelnaria would once again know the peace that had been long lost.

However, they did not tarry long. They did not want the townspeople to come to the realization that the loss of their precious curse was related to the removal of the jewel in which they had no idea existed and had even been there. So, they quickly gathered their gear and their supplies and left that very morning. Their new course, they decided was to get the jewel of wind, the diamond.

Next stop is the white whirls of power ancient

To achieve this goal dirt bound must become heaven sent

Of scales and honor do abide

Only loyalty will win this side

Ifem believed this jewel to be somewhere on the continent of Delphenia and he thought maybe either in the Tauschug mountains where the Gold Dragons lived or in the Lahartden Mountains where the White

Dragons lived. Fortunately, both the gold and white dragons were on Cardinia's side. Unfortunately, dragons could be temperamental at best and may not provide any help at all. But even with assistance from the dragons, should it be provided, searching for the jewel would prove highly difficult even in the most ideal situation. Being dragons, their kingdoms were vast and they nested high up on the cliffs of the mountains. Not an easy feat for creatures that could not fly. They had to depend on the dragons' kindness and hoped that flattery would be all they needed to get the vain giant wyrms to assist them.

They were unable to use the teleportation spell so close to the Djinn whom would sense the magic immediately, so they walked across the island and hoped to find a small fishing village that they could pay transport across the straight or, depending on distance from the Defajinn Kingdom, possibly attempt the teleportation spell there.

They reached the other side of the island without much mishap having resorted back to their old plan by wearing the procured demon army armor, wagon and using the masking spells. They searched up and down the coast looking for any kind of small fishing village or even a lone survivor on the shores but had not any luck. When they reached the Onari Ruins, they decided that they would have to risk the use of the magic transportation spell after all and hope that they were far enough away from the Djinn that those malicious Genies would either not sense the magic or would not be able to stop them in time from using it. The Djinns could travel instantly anywhere, but their magic was much more complicated. Djinns were magic and Ihoitae was a being trying to use magic. Even though elves and demons were of magic, it was decidedly not the same as being magic.

However, before they would attempt the spell, they decided to camp there in the ruins for the night. They all wanted to have energy if they would be facing the wrath of Djinns. Presaya scouted the ruins and could not find anything dangerous except the occasional falling stone or staircase or wall. This was the home of the first demons called the Onae. They were an older clan that had arrived on Kelnaria before any other demon clan did and they are what started the Gods War. They were also the first children of Khalrab and extremely powerful, almost omnipotent in their own right. Possibly even equivalent to demi-gods. However, when the Mystics destroyed the first children - as Kahlrab referred to them, Khalrab obliterated them for their trouble. Fortunately, not before they could seed their world with the Great Scrolls and the prophecy.

All in the party could still feel the maliciousness of the Onae demons. It was so ingrained in the walls and the ground itself. They were uneasy, but no one, not even the Clan of Arabus knew of any souls, demon or no, that would stay in the forsaken ruins.

They would suffice for a temporary place of shelter and probably a relatively safe one at that. Presaya was able to locate one building that still had three sides and most of its ceiling. It appeared to have been a great hall or throne room or some such thing when it existed many millennia ago, but now made a large lean to for the group to shelter in. Faolan and Tian worked on creating a small cook fire while Aelle and Boldolf prepared an area for sleeping and to feed and brush down the horses. Ihoitae and Dean and Presaya patrolled to secure the area.

"This will not be an easy night," Dean stated matter-of-factly after their last circuit.

Presaya and Ihoitae both nodded. Ihoitae added, "No, but it is better to deal with an uneasy night than to be completely vulnerable to the Djinns. Not even the vile genies would suffer this place; the evil is so permeated into the very heart of this land."

"Aye, aye!" Presaya seconded. "The air of evil is strong in this place and there are too many memories here. Not good ones at that. But suffice it to say, I think we are relatively safe due to that very presence here." Presaya looked off almost as if she were remembering when the battles happened here and the Mystics themselves were banished.

"May this night pass quickly and quietly," Dean concurred, but then added, "Are we sure it will be safe to try the spell?"

"Yes," Ihoitae began his reply. "I am worried, of course, but I cannot sense the Djinns at all anymore. So, I am pretty confident we will be safe enough from them. This place will cover my spell casting."

"Unless it is just this vile and evil place that you are now sensing and it is covering up your other senses for the Djinn," Presaya interjected.

"Well, there is that," Ihoitae chuckled, "but no, I am sure we are not close enough to them anymore. And, if we can't sense them because of the evil that still protrudes this place, then I assure you they also cannot sense us. Regardless of how well their good seeking radar is. We are covered."

"Ihoitae is right, my love," interjected Diane. "I no longer sense the Djinns either and I could sense them and this place as we approached. But as we got nearer, the Djinns faded and this place took over. But it is an empty evil. The voices of the dead cry out and the very death of this place permeates it. But there is no other living evil creature here. Yet its very aura of death and hatred and evil will protect us from everything else. Ironic, isn't it?"

Dean nodded, "Well, then let us hope it is only the stone and dirt that remember the vileness and nothing more."

They ate and they slept. They took turns at watch. Nothing of consequence happened though the feeling of unease never left any of them. They could all sense a perverseness of voyeurism, as if being watched. Perhaps it was just the ghosts of the dead.......

***

At long last he had found his prey once more. How silly of his prey to come back to such a dangerous area for himself. He knew his prey was responsible for the removal of the curse at Waren's Tower. The shock wave of Waren's soul leaving the tower rippled throughout the land. How funny it was that after all these years it was the wizard's soul and his hatred that it kept which kept the spell curse so devastatingly strong. How happy that news will make his mistress....and many others besides her. But that news had to wait. Either they would figure it out soon enough, as surely the Djinns felt the magic release and may even tell Mordecai, or his mistress would bear the great news to her father and grandfather once he told her. The changing of the wind was occurring faster now, he could sense it, but what did it mean. For him? For his mistress? For the demons? For the world?

He could kill his prey now and be done with it. But once again, instinct told him to belay his hand and so he did. Ever was he a creature of mischief and he ever followed his instincts. He knew it would enrage her, his mistress, but his instincts were telling him that this one needed to live. Being a creature that revered his instincts above all else, would soon find him at a crossroads at which he did not wish to tarry. However, it was inevitable and once the inevitable occurred, he would once again listen to his instincts..... even if that meant killing his beloved mistress instead of his prey.

# Chapter Seventeen

WHEN THE PARTY awoke, the feeling of unrequited spirits had not dissipated and the evil still permeated the very air they breathed, but the party still felt a bit more refreshed than they had in days and their spirits were a little bit higher than before because they had gotten the rest. They stumbled, quite literally, on their first stone and had achieved its obtainment without little fuss, despite that it almost killed Ihoitae in the process. And, now, they were on their way in the direction of their next stone, the White, the diamond, the jewel of air and wind. After re-consulting the scrolls given to them by the "Great Tree" in the lost elvin kingdom, they deemed that they should try the home of the Silver Dragons first, Lahrtden. These dragons were friendly and possibly allied to their sovereign nation, so they figured that the dragons may even help them search for it if asked. If it could not be found, then they would travel to the Tauschung and deal with the Gold dragons. These dragons were also friendly to their sovereign nation, but were known to be a bit over full of themselves and looked down at every other race; seeing them as inconsequential as a human might an ant. Allies or not, they did not feel they would get much assistance from the golds, maybe even resistance.

The party went through their morning routines of dress, food and preparing to travel. Once they were completed and camp was broken, Dean called them altogether.

"We are finally moving towards the second goal that our employer had set out for us after we had," Dean paused and looked reflectively at Ihoitae, "shall we say, detained, our newest member."

Everyone looked shocked at that. Dean never so easily allowed a being to enter the ranks of his mercenary band without years of training, trials, missions and just plain grunt work. Ihoitae was stunned because he wasn't exactly officially asked to join, but felt that these people were more than friends after all they had been through over the last few weeks;, they had become a sort of family to him. Besides him now being married to her sister, even Aelle seemed to be a little nicer to him. I guess near death and quest success brings people together, he thought.

Dean continued after he gave enough pause to allow all of them to reflect. "I would recruit Ihoitae to our ranks, if he so chooses to join us officially. He has earned it. And, regardless of his rank in our band, he is with us on this mission as he is as much a part of this mission as each of us is…… maybe even more so.

"I would also like to request that Faolan and Tian formally join us as trainees. They are young, but they show a great will and a great prowess for fighting. And, like Ihoitae, they are as much a part or maybe even more so of our mission. However, we are a band of brothers, and though I am your leader, as always, I will listen to objections now or forever hold your peace."

Ihoitae realized this was a formal ritual among the team members in inducting new teammates. He also sensed it was a little outside normal customs, but given the extraordinary circumstances of their recent excursions, he could not fault Dean for from his impromptu ritual. It would bring the team together in a way it hadn't been before. The cohesion was needed to survive the trials to come and Dean knew that and, on some levels, so did everyone else. Ihoitae found new respect for his one-time rival during the Demon Wars so many centuries ago. Dean was an excellent leader and had all the qualities of a good man. No wonder his team, even surely Aelle, respected and obeyed him without question.

Bodolf was the first to respond. "Aye, laddie, fine choices ya make in our new recruits. I accept them as me brothers in arms. To die by their side or to save their skins from harm as it may be. My blood bein their blood. In all honor for life an' death."

"I accept them as my brothers at arms," began Aelle, "To die by their side or to save them from harm as it may be. Even the stinking half demon."

She stuck out her tongue but she had a huge grin on her face and winked at Ihoitae. It had been a gesture of good will he supposed. She had completely went from hating him to feeling a camaraderie with him that he supposed no one else would, seeing how they were now family. "My blood being of their blood. In honor for life and death.'

Diane nodded her assent and then spoke her oath, 'I accept them as my brothers at arms. To die by their side or to save them from harm as it may be My blood being of their blood. In honor for life and death."

"Then it is done," replied Dean. "You are inducted unless you object. Ihoitae, I will not require you to meet the requirements of those of a new recruit. I know you are older and more experienced than many of us. I have seen you in battle both by your side and against you. You should not suffer the shame of an underling but rather as my equal. But know that I am the leader and we defer to my final say in all things. Will you accept these terms?"

"I will accept these terms and I will join you," Ihoitae replied. After all, it had been a long time since he was a part of anything other than pure survival. It felt good to be accepted again, to once again to be a part of something.

Dean looked to Faolan and Tian. "Boys, I will ask of you to suffer the shame of being a new recruit. It is not for us to abuse you or harass you. We do not require silly things of our new recruits in order to prove your worth. Quality of self always will prove or disprove itself both on the battlefield and off. It is to teach you the ways of both a warrior and of a team member and all that is asked is absolute obedience. I, however, will listen to anything you have to say willingly and objectively. But as I have advised Ihoitae, know that I am the leader and that we defer to my final say in all things. Will you accept these terms?"

Faolan nodded without any hesitation. "I will accept your terms and I am already humbled by your offer and faith in me." He bowed.

Tian hesitated a moment. Then he looked at everyone else, sighed and answered, "I will accept your terms, but know that my loyalty is and always will be to my countrymen and to Faolan as he is already a brother to me. Can you accept that of me?"

Dean nodded. "Yes. If there comes a time that I must release you to aid your village or release you and Faolan for the greater good of Cardinia, then know in good faith you follow a leader who would honor that request. Cardinia is our sovereign nation and we honor her people first and foremost and our King and Queen second most. The good of the many always precede the needs of the few."

"Then, I will follow you every step of the way and honor your teaching," Tian replied. "I, however, am confused on the order of obedience."

Dean smiled. "Good lad! Lesson one, there is never anything wrong with questioning your leader should the information not be clear. I will qualify your question with this response. Leaders of anything, whether it be a country, a mercenary band or even a tiny village, can be good and great and tyrannical and merciless. But the will of the people are the heart of everything. If the people deem the leadership good, then they will rule just and fair and so there is no loyalty questions and the people are happy. If the people deem their leaders as evil, then they will rule with corruption and deception and then it is the people's faith that must come first and the people will know fear and hate. Do you understand?"

Tian nodded, "Aye, I think so." He felt happy to know that Dean was an honorable leader. It had been a test.

Dean turned to Ifem and Presaya and began to speak, "Ifem, I cannot ask you to formally join as you are already a monk of the Zadian Priests. I regret that I cannot have you officially join our ranks, but I am glad that you serve our sovereign nation and that you are willing to defer to my orders. But, I would make you an honorary member while we are on this dire mission."

Ifem bowed and smiled. "Of course, Dean, as you pointed out, we are all on this crazy ride together so we must band together. But long has the Zadian Priests worked side by side with the different militaries and mercenary bands loyal to Cardinia. I will defer to your leadership as is necessary. I know you will defer to me for the wisdom I carry."

"So, that leaves me........" Presaya stated a little heavily as if she were a bit hurt by all this not being accepted thing.

"So it does, little one," Dean started. "I respect you greatly, Presaya. I was wary of you when you first entered our little group so suddenly and so out of the blue. It was....a bit.....suspicious. But I feel that you have proven yourself, your loyalty in the short time we have known you. But I can't help but sense that there is more to you than you lead us to believe and I feel that making you a member of our band would be a petty thing to you. I do not understand why."

Presaya smiled a mischievously wicked smile and said, "You may be right more than you know or you may just be thinking that I am mightier than I am. I do tend to carry myself as large as a dragon though I am as wee as a mouse. There are things that are brewing that I know that I cannot reveal at this time. Just as there are things Ifem knows that he can't tell us at this time. Or Saffiyah.... or Diane... Some of us know things that they can't reveal at this time because they don't know that they know it themselves in some instances. But, know that I will follow Ihoitae to the ends of Kelnaria and into the Abyssal Plains. The reasons why, I will not reveal at this time, are simply that I would put myself and your band at more danger should my true identity come to pass. However, because of this, I would be honored to join your group until all can be revealed. I would defer to your leadership while I am a part of your group and, if permitted, to be an honorary member. This would not bring me displeasure."

Everyone in the group looked at her a bit strange. She did not normally speak this way and it almost had an ethereal quality to it. Her voice had an edge that was extremely unseemly from the ever energetic gnome.

Dean thought this over. Then he looked at each one of the group. It was either a nod or shake for the vote. Each member and Ifem nodded their ascent to allow the stealthy gnome to join their band as an honorary member. All felt compelled too. "Then it has been decided. You are allowed to officially join the band and not just as an envoy to Ihoitae. You should not suffer the shame of an underling but rather as my equal. However, as previously stated to Ihoitae, Faolan and Tian, know that I am the leader and we defer to my final say in all things. Will you accept these terms?"

"Accepted," the gnome replied excitedly, practically squealing. Everyone relaxed as this was more normal for the wee gnome.

"Now the final pledge of blood brothers," Dean took his dagger from his sheath as he began to speak.

Then he cut open his palm with a small cut so as just to have a little blood trickle out. He let it spill to the ground below him. Then each member, full, honorary and fledgling, followed his lead likewise. "How fitting that it should be on this foul ground that we now consecrate our bond as blood brothers."

Everyone nodded an ascent.

"Now that this is out of the way, and probably a bit overdue," Dean started, "let us get to our next destination. I feel that we have grown stronger this day, which is odd considering where we are."

"The ancients are here, nothing more and nothing less. This place, though it was an evil realm, is sacred and it was a solemn place despite our location. The choice will empower us." Diane smiled at her new band of brothers in arms. She could feel hope blossoming into this evil place, but she did not understand why. If she had looked upon the blood that had joined on the ground, she would have seen the symbol of the dragon and the unicorn form on the ground. The unicorn's shape resembled that of Cardinia's Banner.

Ihoitae looked at everyone, "Right? Well, so now we try the spell. I think I am strong enough for it, but we might only get one shot a day. Or, at the very least, one shot today due to my recent, um, infirm. So, we need to all hold hands. It will make it easier on me if we all stay connected. I can feel your flow of life connected to me easier and therefore, hopefully, transport us all a little easier. Except the two on my sides. You will have to hold my shoulders or something as I need my hands to articulate the spell. But do not disconnect, please."

Everyone circled around. Presaya was on one side of Ihoitae, so she held his leg instead and Aelle stood on the other side of him and firmly grasped his shoulder. Everyone else held hands and all watched Ihoitae as he closed his eyes and began to chant and wave his arms in specific circular patterns, almost as if he was willing a vortex to open. The words he spoke were ancient and not known to anyone in the group. Although, Presaya, had a smile on her face as though she understood every word. He slowly began to glow green as the flow of land magic pulled up through the ground and flooded through his body. Then, it slowly reached out to each and every member of the party through Ihoitae until the whole group glowed a leafy green of land magic. As the magic cascaded over and through them, they began to feel compelled to close their eyes and concentrate on nothing but Ihoitae's smooth voice.

He performed the spell flawlessly and within a few minutes of the bathing of the green land magic, the group vanished and travelled the corridors of space and time to reach across the ocean, beaches, forests and finally the mountains that they sought within minutes versus days. Ihoitae concentrated fully on the mouth of the mother cave of the White

Dragons. He had been there once in his life when he was hiding from his father. The dragons allowed the son of the Queen of Sylvans to stay and learn with them as the dragons had loved the Sylvans more than any other race on Kelnaria and were greatly saddened by the loss of such a wondrous race. The Whites did not accuse Ihoitae at all and helped him learn to deal with his pain and misgivings in ways he desperately needed. This was where Ihoitae had learned most of his magic and he learned the most about his people despite having lived with them for more than a century. He also learned the history of Kelnaria, not just of the Sylvans and Wood Elvces, and just how important his Sylvan people had been to the Goddess Selunia. He had felt a peace there and hoped that once again, the Whites of Lahrtden would be able to aid him.

He knew that Queen Zinc of the majestic White Dragons was a noble creature, divine in both her wisdom and her exceeding kindness. He also knew that the dragons were fierce fighters and greater mages and had a shield of protection on their mountain home. So, he would not be able to breach their magic and land right inside the Throne Cave. However, little did he know of the ancient dragons and the ancient spells of the elder mages. The party landed right in front of the Great Queen's dais and right in the middle of court, it seemed. It was a bit of a shock to the dragons and the mercenary band alike.

"Io be blessed!" exclaimed the queen using common versus dragon instantly recognizing the beings as humanoids. "What foul creature has wormed its way into our holy cave?"

Ihoitae blinked and everyone else gasped. Ifem recognizing their immediate danger quickly bent a knee and bowed, using his hands to urge the rest of the party to do so. One by one, each one did so as they came to the realization of where they were and Ifem spoke, "My great queen, please do not harm us. We truly are sorry that we came crashing into your most holy of sanctums. We are humbled by the great and mighty Queen Zinc."

The dragon blinked and then sniffed the air. She growled back the other dragons that had quickly recovered from the shock and were about to pounce. Then the queen laughed a hearty laugh and a white glow caressed her and she transformed into a beautiful elfin maid with lovely white hair that trailed behind her. Her skin as pure as alabaster and her eyes shown the deepest blue of the ocean depths, she swiftly ran down the steps of her dais and bent down to Ihoiate and picked up his head.

"It is you!" Her voice had gone from a deep thunderous voice to a lilting, tinkling voice. "Oh, my blessed boy, stand up and let me look at you!"

Ihoitae stood up, a little embarrassed. The queen looked him over, up and down and around.

"Oh my, I guess you are a full grown elf now, my sweet one," she replied. "Then she turned to her court and let the guardians know they could stand down. It was their Sylvan elf ward, Ihoitae, come home. There was a collective sigh from both the dragons and the humanoids.

"Aye, my queen, it is I, Ihoitae. I am sorry that we so rudely arrived. Our intent had been to land outside your barrier and request audience. But it was a new spell and I was not sure of the effects."

She laughed a silvery laugh. "Oh my silly boy, tis not a new spell you used. Tis a very ancient spell you used created by blessed Io Himself! Of course His magic would bring you straight to me! Tis a blessed day! Come, my sweet boy, introduce me to your friends and pray have them lift their heads. No friends to our Sylvarrius shall bend knee in my court!"

Ihoitae introduced them one by one and one by one they all looked at the magnificent queen in her elfin form. So radiant and lovely, she looked like a goddess to them. They all curtsied deeply upon standing up. Ihoitae ended by addressing the party. "Queen Zinc, as all dragons, can shape shift into any form or any size or shape, unlike demons who can only take on forms within their own mass. It is inherent to them as the sun is to the day time. If a dragon truly likes you, they will transform into a likeness of your being to honor you, to be on your level. Queen Zinc has afforded all of us a great honor."

"You speak with great knowledge," Dean inquired, "care to explain?"

Ihoitae started but Queen Zince broke in and informed Dean of the centuries that Ihoitae stayed with the white dragons. She told them how they had taught him his true Sylvan heritage and that of the history of Kelnaria and helped him come into most of his magical abilities. "His father had done such a terrible job at that and wasted his demon talent on war and strategy. At least Queen Mylayeriannia had some sense to teach the boy some of his elvin abilities. But Ihoitae is a light unknown to this world. I bless the Mystics and Their wisdom in his creation."

Ifem choked a little at that statement. "You know of the prophecy?"

"Oh yes my revered one. My people know so much about Kelnaria, its gods, races, history and, of course, the Mystics and the Great Scrolls. Some of us have been here since the beginning and knew the Mystics themselves," She smiled.

Presaya's eyes got very wide at that and looked a bit nervous, but quickly tried to hide her astonishment.

"Oh don't worry little gnome, I am not that old," laughed Queen Zinc. "I was but a youngling newly hatched when the Gods War started. But come, let us celebrate and I will speak more with you. I know why you are here, Sylvarrius. We have all known for so long, but were unable to tell you until the time was true. And I feel the red stone upon your person, so I know the time is true. The ancients will visit you as well as a special surprise."

The queen led them off down a cavernous hallway, which to an ancient dragon would be a snug fit. As she passed by, other dragons also transformed into elfin forms, if their queen thought to honor these beings then they would honor her and change as well. She knew that the guardians would stay dragons to protect the mountains and the hatcheries. Some of the dragons knew Ihoitae personally as they had either helped "rear" him or became his playmates. Some knew of Ihoitae because he was well known throughout their kingdom. All came to the gathering hall, all in elfin forms to honor their queen and to honor their guests. Ihoitae could not understand why he was so honored, but he would very soon, he wagered.

The news had preceded them into the gathering hall and it had been magically decorated. All the dragons looked so godlike in their elfin forms that the humanoids could not help but blush at their beauty. Although the white dragons lived in the ice caverns on the highest peaks of Lahrtden, the caves were warm and glowed a beautiful blue in the misty shards of the ice crystals that formed there. They had set up humanoid sized tables and chairs and food for humanoids was being quickly prepared, all magically induced the group gathered. A dragon band in elfin form began to strike up music as the queen led them to the table of honor.

The entire mercenary band except Ihoitae and Presaya looked around in complete awe and overwhelming dumbfoundness of the caverns and the dragons themselves. Ihoitae had gotten used to this in his time living with the Whites. Presaysa once again had that smile on her face of showing a knowledge that could not yet be shared. No one noticed, except of course, the queen.

"Little one," she began as they all sat and food and drink were brought to them. "You are, hmmm, shall we say, different."

Presaya looked over at the queen with a look that said, yes, but not yet.

"I see," she replied. "You have not been in Radon's visions. But yet, I sense etherealness about you. I feel as if we have met before. However, I hope you will tell all to me, so until then, I will speak of it no more."

Presaya nodded hoping no one else in the party heard her, which they all seemed oblivious too, and said "I shall come to you when the party has time to rest, my queen, if you allow it."

She laughed her glowing, tinkling laugh and replied, "But of course I shall! I love my fellow beings from ancient wyrmling to egglings, but us dragons can be quite droll in our vanity at times! I would welcome a change of chatter from some other being."

With that, another elfin dragon came to sit down beside the queen. She was just as radiant and was almost identical to the queen, almost a younger version of the queen. "Ah, Radon, so glad of you to join us."

"I came, mother, as soon as the guards informed me it was safe to attend and that it was Ihoitae whom had intruded," answered the beautiful, younger elfin maiden, her voice serene and in no way showing frustration to the groups sudden appearance.

"This is Princess Radon," the queen began as she introduced her daughter with such reverence. "She is heir to the throne of the Whites. She is also a truly special dragon. She is a true seer, very rare these days and so she will be a great queen, greater than me, when the time comes. She is truly treasured and severely protected."

"We are doubly honored, then, my queen," Ifem stated reverently. "And, please, do not think we are not grateful for the hospitality, but –"

"You are here for the white stone of wind and air magic," cut off Radon, very timidly.

"Yes, my princess," Ihoitae began. "If you know of our mission, and it seems you know it better than we do, then you know we seek to complete Tremblount."

"Oh I know everything, my lord," Radon sounded far away, lost, but with such authority, it could not be taken as fright anymore. "Mother, may I?" She looked up to her mother, startled, as if she had already said too much.

Queen Zinc nodded her head and smiled at her daughter. The party crowded around her so they could all hear her soft voice over the loud music being played and the merriment of the other dragons.

"Well," she softly began, speaking a little louder understanding that she had a larger audience to address. However, her voice was still misty and distant, as if she were always seeing as the seer. "In case you are not aware of the seer's power, we can see the past, present and future at all times. For some of us it comes as children. Others do not gain the wisdom of their gift until they are much older. It is best if you get the gift as a child because it is easier to learn to cope with it. I gained mine as a human would call a teenager, but in dragon years we are known as juveniles.

"It was a very strange occurrence. Literally, I was what you would call normal from one moment and then to the next moment I was seeing.......how do I explain.........visions. But of historical events as well as current events and future events. They were all over laid on top of one another. It was a bit…..hmm….disconcerting. But being a mystical creature, I was adept enough to at least know what had occurred to me and was able to adapt with a little help of my fellow ancients.

"I am currently a young adult, so I know you all too well Prince Ihoitae Mahadeva Arabus, even though we have never met. I was an eggling when you had arrived and not yet ready to enter the world. I know everything about everyone that I have ever met or ever will meet in my days. This is how a seer's power is limited. We are limited by what was once, what is and what will be as long as it is an occurrence to our beings. I was to meet all of you on this day, so therefore I saw visions of all of your pasts, present and futures. I can also see what revolves around you because I am and was to meet you, so your immediate past, present and futures with those of your knowledge will also come to me, though very limited since it is gained through you rather than directly connected. Do you understand so far?"

Everyone nodded, though many faces were dumbfounded by the knowledge of why a seer could know so much about some things and so little about others. Aelle, having had a sister as a seer for many years understood this far greater than anyone else, though it was still frustrating to her as well at times.

Princess Radon took a sip of wine and began again. "I have met all of you as mere babes in the womb all the way until today. I knew you would arrive as you did, but I did not think to warn my mother. I am humbly apologetic."

"Oh, my dear, no harm no foul," the queen replied.

"I am here to protect my people and, it seems, Kelnaria. I was born under the wishing star when the moons glowed high in the sky, the very same night that you were born Ihoitae, except many centuries later, so in that, you and I are tied by the Silver Moon. I am the protector of the white stone. It actually hatched with me, so it has grown to be a part of me. It speaks to all the other stones and once you received the red, I knew you were coming. The stone was very excited!

"However, as you must be aware by now, there is a test, but we shall come to that by the end of the night. I first must tell you a few things before we commence with business.

"Diane, I can no longer suffer the knowledge of who and what you are without letting you know, my dear. You are one of the last of a people long thought extinct. However, your people, though no longer as populated as you once were, are in hiding and do still exist despite what the history texts believe. You are of the lost peoples the Telestics."

Diane gasped. "What? How? My mother? She died saving our village…….."

"Yes, she did, but she was not human. She was hiding in the human village with your father and brother. The Telestic people had to scatter out in the world and blend in with other races in order to avoid extinction by the Onae. If they were ever discovered, they would be killed or exiled by the race's village they inhabited. As time progressed and the Onae themselves were made extinct, the Telestics were able to recover a bit. But many would live in the same village and not even know another was present unless they were family. Thus was their ability to survive throughout the ages under the cover of extinction.

"The village your parents were in was attacked by the Shadow of the Onae and she hid you away, a little too well it seems, to protect you. Your brother and father still live, though they are heartbroken. They could not find you when they were able to come back to the village after the battle had been done."

"Did they flee? Did they leave my mother alone to defend she and I?" asked Diane a bit angrily.

"No, dear one, they fought with the men in the fields. Your brother is much older than you. You were, shall we say, a surprise to your parents. A happy surprise, but one none the less. And, they did not flee they were already engaged in battle as the Onae had routed the men outside the village while a group of the foul demons went into the village to attack the women, elderly and children."

"Oh, I see," Diane said, afraid of her own voice. Dean took her hand and held it softly. "Can you......can you tell me where they are now?"

"I can, but they will find you, so I will not disturb fate and time. I must only say what the weavers permit."

"Very well," Diane said a little disheartened but understanding. She was so full of questions. Of course she had heard of the Telestics through school and priests, but no one knew much about them since they were thought to be extinct and none of their culture could be found. They were a people of mystery, but now Diane understood exactly why they had effectively erased themselves.

Radon smiled warmly and tenderly laughed. "Oh dear one, do not despair. They will know you and you will know them and they will answer all the questions buzzing through your head. Telestics have a family bond that cannot be undone. Your mother was only able to save your life by severing the family bond, which is how you faded to them. However, they already know of your wee one and they are coming to find you and bless the coming new life. Your wee one is the rebirth of that strong signal that allowed them to finally sense you after all these years. You will be reunited when the time is right!"

Diane instinctively placed a protective hand over her flat belly and looked at Radon unknowing what to say or think. She had an inkling that she might be with child, but until this moment, had been unsure.

"What?" Dean, Aelle, Ifem and Bodolf all stated together emphatically, confused.

Radon smiled again and gently giggled, then replied, "She has not told anyone of her impending new life for fear that others would try to harm her or the baby, or that you would force her away. She was also unsure if she was until I spilled the news on her!" Radon giggled, but quickly changed her attitude and spoke very seriously in the next moment. "But, she cannot leave your party now. She is an important part as well as your unborn. Ihoitae and Presaya have protected her."

Dean looked angry and nearly shouted at Presaya and Ihoitae flatly saying, "You both knew and you could not see fit to tell me?!?!?! I am her husband! And……..I……….am" Dean deflated a little bit as it began to sink in, "going to be a father!"

Ihoitae looked directly at Dean and said, "I knew only because she and I had a connection. The connection that she created with me back in the cage has never severed and her wee one has been adamant about keeping that bond with me. I heard her baby and the baby asked me not to tell you yet. I was bound to my word, but I had also vowed to protect the child as if he were my own. Forgive me, please."

Dean sighed. "Oh alright, Princess Radon is right, I would have tried to send her away had I known, but how far along? And....a boy?"

"Not very long, my love," gently replied Princess Radon. "Diane just confirmed her suspicions just now as I have now told you all."

"Why would my baby ask you not to tell.....his father .......that he was present. I need to protect him and Diane! We all do! And, Presaya, how could you have known?" Dean asked, flabbergasted.

"Oh my," Presaya began. "This is not the right time for me. All I ask is that you trust me at this time and know that I would never have allowed any harm to come to mother or baby. Just as I have pledged my life to Ihoitae I also pledged my life to you all back at the ruins and this includes your unborn, Dean. You will all learn why soon enough, but please take my word for now just a little longer that I can and will protect them and I meant no harm." Again, Presaya spoke in that strange ethereal voice that was not Presaya.

Radon looked to the party and once again began to speak. "Dean, I can attest to Presaya's validity. But she is right, she cannot reveal the full truth to you at this time, though I know who and what she represents. She will prove to be one of your best allies, if she hasn't already done so. She will protect all of you as long as it is within her powers to do so. And she will willingly do so without a second thought to her person or identity. But, if her identity can be protected at this time, then it must be preserved at all costs. Can you please be satisfied with what I tell you?"

"Aye, for the sake of the mission, the world, my wife and everything I hold dear, I will trust your wisdom my mentallius," Dean answered bowing his head slightly in the dragon way of respect.

"Oh Dean!" giggled Radon, "what great respect you show me, though you are my elder! But I thank you in your wisdom, my mentallius!

"So, now I shall continue as our time is growing short and soon the trial will begin. Dean, Diane is a Telestic, That means your child is a one of a kind, half Draconic and half Telestic. I will reassure you that your baby will survive the pregnancy despite the trials all of you will face on this prophetic mission, but still show some caution towards Diane and your wee one as Fate can always change its mind. However, I reiterate that she must stay with the party in order for the prophecy to work. You are all an integral part and must be present from start to end.

"Your roles have been in question at best since the beginning. So, I will remove some of the veil of mists in this regard. Ihoitae and Faolan are the centralized figures in this prophecy. You will learn how and why as time progresses. Each of you is the pillar onto which each other stands on. Should one fall, the whole will fall and the prophecy will fail. This is what the Shadow of the Onae want.

"Ifem is your guide. Dean your mentor. Aelle, I believe you already know part of the role you played."

"Yea, match maker," Aelle snidely, but jokingly replied.

Radon laughed. "A bit of that was indeed match maker, but you and Safiyyah have known Ihoitae far longer than you are willing to admit to yourself. If you will open your heart, you will remember the time when you were children and your people rescued a Sylvan Elf from certain death at the hands of the Fates."

Aelle gasped. Her eyes grew wide and she placed her hand over her mouth with a very barely audible "no!" came forth.

Ihoitae looked over at Aelle and realization had smacked him as well as he suddenly realized just how much he actually knew Aelle. He always had felt that he had met her before, though he could never place where. Now, he could. "You are Princess Aelle? Daughter of Lord and Lady Oakhaven of the wood elf clan? That means your sister is also a princess! But they were young girls that ..........!"

Now everyone gasped at that. No one knew of Aelle's royal background and she had preferred it that way. The group all stated that question "Princess?" in various terms, loudness and confusion.

The only one who did not gasp was Ifem. The Balasi's were of the Wood Elf Clan hailing from the same woods as Aelle. Although they did not visit court often due to their obligations to the Zadian priests, Ifem had thought that Aelle was familiar as he would have recognized the Oakhaven family relation.

"Ugh," Aelle began, "well, I guess since it seems we are having confession time, yes, I am the bloody princess of the wood elf clan, cousins to the Sylvan elves. Daughter to Lord Aileron and Lady Mehdianious Oakhaven. I go by Aelle Tindonis when I wish no one to know my royal person. Tindonis is an old family of heroes that perished fighting during the Demon Wars. It is my way of honoring them and their sacrifice."

"I thought you looked familiar!" exclaimed Ifem. Then he bowed. "My Lady."

Aelle cringed. "Oh stop it. That's exactly why I didn't want anyone to know who I was. My father, shall we say nicely, does not approve."

Radon gently cleared her throat. "I am sorry to be rude, but you will have to reminisce later. As I said before, I am the keeper of the wind stone and as all keepers must, there is a trial that must be won in order to obtain its uses. I am no longer free to express anymore to you and I am now bound by the rules of the prophecy. The trial will begin now."

As she said this, the room blacked out for a moment and when the lights returned, the room was completely empty of everyone and everything except the little mercenary band. They were all in the same spots they had been except now standing as the table and chairs were also removed.

"Damnit!" exclaimed Aelle. "We were learning so much and now we are still lost because of a time frame we weren't even aware of!" Her voice sounded distant and hollow in the cavernous, empty cave. The party all nodded and came closer together, though now they all turned around so each could be facing out of their tight circle.

There was a long silence and there were no sounds except the breathing of the party members along with their beating hearts. Finally, Ihoitae decided to speak. In a loud, clear voice he said, "Please Princess Radon, please show us the doorway to the trial and tell us the rules oh great gatekeeper and let the trial begin."

"Very well," Princess Radon's voice came to them powerfully, clear and surrounding them. No longer did it seem lost or distant. "Prince Ihoitae Mahadeva Arabus, you will each be measured and weighed. Only if your hearts are true will you be able to obtain the Diamond of Wind and Air. If any one of you shall fail, then you will all be found wanting. Are the rules clear?"

Ihoitae replied, "Aye, a test of loyalty and love. Let it begin."

The party was placed on a pillar as the floor fell away from their feet. Below them was flowing lava and above them were sharp, jagged stalagmites from the ceiling that looked dangerously about to fall. From the ground also came up other pillars. Though smaller, these looked spaced enough for most people to jump across and provided a way for crossing the chasm of lava.

"So, it is a gauntlet," stated Ifem. As he spoke, the stalagmites began to gently rock back and forth.

"Oh aye, lad," chimed in Bodolf a bit too loudly. "And me guess is tha' we canno make it through 'less we each help within our special talents." One stalagmite fell into the lava.

"Agreed," stated Dean very quietly catching on to the deadly significance of the stalagmites. "These pillars are fine for human, or larger, sized creatures to cross, but Presaya and Bodolf will have difficulty. I fear those shards of ice will start to rain down on us soon lest we stall in our action or perform any loud incantations or speak too loudly."

Aelle sighed. "So, no magic. This one is all brawn." She was almost inaudible in her speaking.

"Well," began Ihoitae in a loud whisper, "I have a suggestion for crossing, but I do not think our not so tall folk would like it."

"What is it, Ihoitae?" whispered a breathy Presaya.

"Dean, Ifem and I can carry Diane, Bodolf and Presaya across. Ifem, Aelle and I are elves, so this should be mere child's play to us and Dean has long, strong dragon legs. Faolan and Tian should be able to make it across themselves, provided they are good jumpers."

Bodolf amended his loud voice to as soft as a dwarf can be and spoke first, "Aye, lad, time is not nigh for foolish dwarven pride. Dean, you should carry me, though. You are the strongest to carry a stout dwarf like me. The elven lads can carry a waif like Diane across easily enough."

Dean did not like the idea, but he also conceded that this was a trial of loyalty and love, pride must be swallowed and he would have to trust Ifem or Ihoitae to carry his love and unborn across safely. He nodded his ascent and grabbed Bodolf and began to navigate the jumping puzzle as quietly as a draconian could.

Ihoitae took charge and whispered as loudly as he dared his commands. "Faolan, you should go next and Aelle you follow. If Faolan gets in trouble, try to help him as best you can. Tian, you follow Aelle. Again, Aelle I ask that you wait for Tian so you can assist him as best you can should he also have issues. You are farmers first and foremost, so let the rock tell you how to jump just as the soil tells you how to till.

And you are warriors secondly, so keep that balance and sure footedness."

Faolan, Tian and Aelle all nodded their heads in understanding and went into the unknown after Dean.

"Ifem," began Ihoitae still being as soft as a mouse, "I will trust Diane in your hands. I know you can carry her safely across."

Both Diane and Ifem nodded their ascent. "My lady?" Ifem quietly inquired as he lowered down to allow Diane to piggy back and adjust her dress for the goal they needed to achieve.

Ihoitae looked towards Presaya. "That leaves just us, my young one," Presaya said to Ihoitae quietly. "I am glad that you chose me to usher over the pillars. I am honored."

Ihoitae blushed. "I don't know why, but ever since I met you, I feel like I have known you my whole life. I feel as if you are like a .......oh geez, father ...... to me. Please no offense."

Presaya giggled ever so softly and replied, "No, my young one, none taken. Now let's blow this sauna!"

With that, Ihoitae picked up Presaya and he began to navigate the pillar jumping puzzle that the trial provided. It did not seem that anyone fell or failed as no one heard any screaming and the stalagmites stayed intact. There was an occasional grunt or two as people jumped, but alas at the end of the trying pillars, the whole party found itself on a platform that led into a cave.

The cave mouth was dark and ominous. The party was not sure just exactly what to do next, but all knew that they could not go back. Almost as if in answer to that collective thought, the platform gently shook and a wall came up behind them, completely cutting them off from the previous jumping puzzle. Then the cave began to grow lighter as torches began to flare up one by one around the cave mouth and interior. The cave room itself seemed pretty simplistic. There was a door on the opposite end that was closed over by a bright, blazing light. The teams' guess was that this light would disappear once the party solved the puzzle and made it to the other side. There was a pedestal in the middle of the room that held a book on its top. There were statues of dragons and fairies and elves and demons and other demonic looking creatures that lined the walls. They looked as though they had been carved out of the caves walls and were in a never ending battle of good and evil. The floor was smooth and had tiles upon the floor with a design on each tile. The designs were that of a rose, arrow, horn and claw.

"Ah ok, so we have some traps here I would wager," Dean concurred as he glanced over the room. "This one would appear to be our engineer, sneak thieves abilities. Presaya......Aelle........if you will."

Presaya took one side and Aelle the other and together they checked the floors from one wall to the center. They did this step by step as they moved into the room trying to check for any traps. Their hope was to either trigger anything prior to their arrival or to dismantle it. Presaya and Aelle found that there was indeed one safe path around the room to the pedestal that held the book. The pattern was to step only on the rose and horn. If you stepped on the arrow, one would be promptly shot your way through the walls. These arrows would disappear into the walls and there seemed to be a never ending supply of them. Presaya and Alle also wagered that these arrows were probably also very much poisoned. If you stepped on the claw, part of the floor would fall away into a pit that was filled with deadly spikes at the bottom. Upon accidentally opening up a few holes, they saw skeletons that had been previously impaled on those spikes. Weary travelers that had gone treasure seeking never to come back alive. However, the floor must magically reset itself somehow at some point. The tiles were large and it was hard to jump from one shape to the next due to the distance, but it was the only way safely across.

They motioned for Ihoitae to come first. Although the tiles were large, they would not hold the entire party and if too many of them tried to jump the puzzle at once, then the whole floor would begin to rattle as if the whole thing would cave in from weight. So, Presaya helped Ihoitae to the pedestal and Aelle went back to wait until the signal was made for her to start assisting people across.

When Presaya and Ihoitae got to the pedestal, Ihoitae looked upon the book. Ihoitae made a frown and furrowed his eyebrows.

"Well……..," inquired Presaya.

Ihoitae looked down at her and his look was not good. "I believe that Ifem would be more suited for it than me. It is not magic. I believe it to be a history book. This is a very ancient tome."

So, Ihoitae went back and helped Ifem across the tiles. Ifem looked at the book and his face instantly lit up with joy. "Yes, you were right to come for me, Ihoitae. This is one of the lost books of the Mystics. It is the very beginning of Kelnaria's history written in Their own hand before the wars." Ifem gently began to pick up the book slowly and as he did so the light on the door on the other side of the room began to fade. Unfortunately, the floor also began to shake violently and parts of the tiles began to break away. Ifem quickly put the book back down and the light returned and the floor stopped shaking violently. "But I do not think we can take it with us as much as I would like too."

"Hmmm," said Presaya who was now frowning. "I think you are right. Now that I get a good look at this pedestal, if we remove the book, the whole room will collapse and with it, all of us. But, did you not also notice that the light also began to wane from the door. It appears this is our death and our salvation."

"This is most unacceptable," replied Ihoitae. "It's a waste, but I guess a necessary one."

"What do you mean?" asked Ifem.

"Someone is going to have to sacrifice themselves in order to save the party." Ihoitae stated flatly.

Presaya and Ifem both clasped their hands over their mouths. "Oh I see," replied Presaya.

After a few moments of silence and a stern yell from Dean, Presaya spoke first. "Ok, I will do it."

"What?" Ihoitae questioned emphatically. "No!"

Presaya nodded, "Yes, it has to be me. I am the only one that can and survive."

Ifem and Ihoitae looked at each other utterly confused. She intended to survive? It was madness.

She looked at them at smiled and laughed. "Oh stop that, you two! Just trust me. I am a tinker thinker, remember. Trust me, I will survive. Now go get the team across so we can blow this popsicle stand."

With even more confusion on their faces, Ifem and Ihoitae knew that they would just have to trust the crazy gnome to her fate and get everyone across. After getting back to the party on the cave entrance, they quickly explained what was about to happen and began to assist everyone across the floor.

"Is she crazy?" Dean stated flatly.

"Do you really need an answer?" replied Aelle sticking out her tongue in jest.

It seemed like ages to get the entire team across since they could only go a couple at a time and Aelle, Ifem and Ihoitae would come back across to assist someone else. But finally, everyone made it to the glowing door with only having a few stray arrows fly off and one or two tiles fall to the doom below. Otherwise everyone else was intact and ready to move out of the room.

Dean nodded to Presaya and said, "Don't die on me now. I just started to like you!"

Presaya laughed and nodded, but said nothing in return. Then she turned her full attention to the mechanism of the room and pedestal. She walked around it. Looked at the whole pedestal and looked over at the walls and ceiling. She scratched her head a few times, rubbed her chin and then it seemed as if a dazzling light went off in the room. It blinded the entire party. They felt the entire room shake violently and could hear the floor crumble where the tiles had once stood. Then the light faded and they were in complete darkness. No one moved for fear of falling off the little ledge they had towards their salvation.

"Well, move on already," spoke an agitated little gnome from the dark. "The door is unblocked; let's go before I fall to my doom! I Only have my big toes on this ledge!"

That snapped the team out of their reverie and they all moved single file through the door into the next room using the wall as a guide lest they fall off.

The next room was actually outside the caves mouth and into a forest area. Once all nine members had reached outside, the opening rumbled and closed up behind them.

"What a waste," Ifem said shaking his head lamenting the loss of the ancient tome.

"You mean this," Presaya said, holding out the book, which looked enormous in her small little hands, out to Ifem. "I would never let anything so valuable ever be destroyed. What kind of treasure hunter would that make me?"

"Oh my abyssal! Presaya, I could kiss you!" exclaimed Ifem as he gently took the tome with such reverence and care.

Presaya looked grotesquely at Ifem and advised, "I would prefer that you not, my sweet priest. Just seeing your happiness and knowing that this invaluable lore is in good hands is thanks enough for me."

Ifem looked dubiously over at the gnome and asked, "But won't your employer be upset with you for giving up such an artifact?"

Presaya giggled, "Quite the contrary, they would be ecstatic to know that this tome has been found and is now in the hands of the Head Priest of the Zadian Order. They will know it is where it belongs and will be well cared for. Assuming we all live through this, that is. That was a close one."

Dean nodded his head in agreement. "Well, now that is settled, it appears we are not done yet."

"I wonder how many challenges we have left," Faolan pondered.

The disembodied voice of Princess Radon came floating through to answer Faolan's question. "This is the last challenge, but it is a challenge of three parts. Up ahead you will find a grand tourney area. In this tourney, three of you will have to battle three challengers to single combat. The winner of the tourney will decide the fate of the stone. Two out of three wins the challenge. If you win, then you will receive the stone. If you lose, then you will die as there is no other escape from this realm."

"Well, that's a bit harsh," Diane spoke.

"Can we know the challenges?" Dean asked.

"Yes, one will be a magic duel, one will be a duel of wits and one will be a duel of power. It will be in that order. Choose wisely."

The party huddled and pondered this matter on whom to choose. After a little debate and much speculation, it was decided that Ihoitae would battle the magic battle since Diane was not privy to most arcane arts and Ifem did not do a lot of combat casting. Ifem preferred melee to magic. The next battle would go to Faolan. A duel of wits could be anything, but Faolan had convinced them that he just felt that this was his battle to face and he did not know why, but he needed to do it. Dean had his reservations, but if his feelings were this strong, then the weavers must be calling to him. The last battle would be Bodolf's to fight. After a bitter and furious debate between Bodolf and Dean, the decision came down to a rock, paper, scissors game and Bodolf won with rock crushing scissors.

The party walked down the road to the ethereal realm they were in tourney area. As they arrived, they were greeted by a male fairy. His wings and hair were the color of sapphires and his eyes glittered the same gemstone blue. His pale skin reflected the shininess of his wings and eyes. He wore only a leather loin cloth and a leather sash over his chest. Belted on his side was a slender sword favored by the fae folk. As he walked, his wings seemed to shimmer a glitter that trailed behind them. He assisted the three combatants to where they needed to go first to prepare. Then he took the rest of the party to their seats so that they could watch. He explained to them that this was a Fairy Tourney and that this one was specially to be held this day, this time for this reason as this is what was decreed by the weavers. Humanoids and Fae very rarely ever mixed and this was truly a once in a lifetime event for the entire group.

The tourney started without delay, and as Princess Radon advised, the first match was between

Ihoitae and a member of the Fairy Folk. It was a female and she was eerily beautiful. She was dressed similarly to her male counterparts except that she also had a leather bra for her chest to match the leather loin cloth and sash across her chest. Her wings, hair and eyes were a brilliant ruby red color and burned a blazing color. The area was much like any other coliseum with a pit in the middle and the sitting stands all around. There was one area of the coliseum that was clearly a royal stand for the Fae Queen and her entourage.

Their Queen was splendid and much more dressed and adorned more elaborately than most of her subjects, though her attire would still be considered inappropriate in the "mortal" world. The Queen's hair, eyes and wings shimmered with multiple colors, almost as if they were made of bubbles shining in the light. Her dress was a thin spaghetti strapped tunic that came down to her knees. It was the darkest ebony which contrasted with her porcelain skin. She was stunning in her full array of color and brilliance as it all intertwined beautifully.

An announcer spoke as Ihoitae and the Fairy woman took their places on the floor of the pit. "Welcome one and all to the Fae Tourney of Wind and Air. As had been pre-ordained, please welcome our guests sitting in the center of the stands. Our guests are most welcome and revered, come to answer the call of the Great Scrolls Prophecy from our cousins the Mystics. Welcome, Diane Moonstone, last noble daughter of the Telestics, Dean Moonstone, General of the Draconic Army and Leader of the Light Bringers, Princess Aelle Oakhaven, twin sister of Princess Safiyyah Oakhaven, last daughters of Lord and Lady Oakhaven and heiress apparent, Tian Farmson of Dioness Village, last surviving son, Presaya Lightfoot, esteemed Tinker Thinker of the Clinker Society and surefooted Treasure Hunter now of the Light Bringers, Sir Ifem Balasi, Head Priest to the Zadian Priests and most honored revered one to our cousins.

"Today our matches will be one of magic, one of wits and one of power. The magic duel will begin first and the combatants are Tianariallis of the Fire Clan and Prince Ihoitae Mahadeva Arabus, son to Queen Mylayeriannia of the Sylvan Elves and heir apparent, and son to Lord Mordecai General to the Demon Armies, second heir apparent.

"All three duels are to the death. Rules are simple, there are no rules other than the combatants cannot leave the pit arena. They cannot seek assistance from outside the pit arena and they are not to harm anyone that is a spectator. If any of these rules are broken, then offending party forfeits the duel and their life. Our fair Queen will decide the fate of the offender.

"Let the duel of the mages begin."

With that, Ihoitae and Tianariallis, who had reached the center of the pit by this time, immediately began casting different spells. Ihoitae's first spell was to place the ancient Sylvan Elf protection spell on himself. Having had no real prior time to prepare, he did not have time to previously cast protection spells and power boosting spells on himself. He was sure his opponent, however, had ample time to prepare for this battle and was already re-powered up after having previously placed all her protection spells and fighting boons.

Ihoitae had donned only regular traveling clothes for this battle knowing that armor would only hinder his spell casting. He also decided to belt a dagger just in case it came to melee blows as often happened when both mages reserves were spent. In what little time he had before the battle, he had placed himself in deep meditation so that he could preserve his magic reserves and he could fully concentrate on casting spells as quickly and efficiently as possible while still being fully aware of his surroundings. When he found out that this was a duel to the death, he knew he had to have all his wits about him and focus on this fight. All magic users were tricky and Fairies were the worst.

Ihoitae had just finished casting his protection spell when Tianariallis let off her first spell and it was a fire ball. He did not have time to dodge and would have been incinerated had it not been for his protection spell. The Sylvan protection spell would last a long time and would absorb almost all magical blows unless they were supremely powerful, but it was little protection against weapons. He would not have time to cast that protection spell.

"So, Tianariallis, are you only a fire mage?" Ihoitae spoke as they both were trying to figure out their next spells.

She smiled a very devilish smile and replied, "Wouldn't you like to know? I fear I hold all the advantages as I know everything you can cast and you know nothing I can."

"Well, this may be true as you have probably had time to prepare and I have not. However," he grinned a devilish smile right back, "I do know a thing or two about Fairies and I know that Fairies can only use elemental magic such as land, wind, air and water magics. I also know that the color of their wings, eyes and hair signify which magic it is that they can use. Some rare fairies can use more than one and even rarer still some fairies can use all four. However, you are too young to have been able to master all four."

She looked surprised at this as it was not known among her people that an outsider would know such details. This was not acceptable. In her anger, she quickly casted a fire bolt towards her enemy. It was a powerful one, but one easily dodged as it was not well controlled due to her anger.

"Oh, I see you did not think someone such as me would know anything about your race," Ihoitae laughed as he came out of his dodge. "But if you truly know about me then you know I have had a very long life and a very unusual history. And demons always make it a point to know everything they can about every enemy and potential enemy. This would also include Fairies."

She composed herself. Ihoitae definitely knew she was a Fairy of Fire born and bred. Her temper flared bright as flames and danced upon her features. She gave herself away in her anger and this was ok with Ihoitae. He had tried to goad her into it and it worked. Now he knew to use water or ice magic and could be spared wasting precious magic trying to figure out how to defeat her. It was a shame he was going to have to kill her. She had very strong magic. He hoped she was totally a Fairy of Fire. He just couldn't understand why they would pick someone so young and inexperienced for a duel to the death.

She backed up a bit. She had been casting imperceptive spells to test the strength of his protection spell. She knew that since he did not detect these little minor spells that he had not been able to cast a detect magic spell. He was unaware of her testing his shield strength and so she knew that she could cast an extraordinarily large fire spell called Blaze. This would drain her, but it would be powerful enough to wipe away his shield and incinerate him in the process. The spell had a pretty wide radius, so there would be little chance for him to dodge completely out of the way. Should he live through it, he would be severely wounded at the least and then she could use her dagger to finish him. She smiled in glee.

Ihoitae took all this in as he had casted his next spell with supreme quiet. It was a minor time spell that allowed him to slow time down for a moment. It would make her casting slower and would provide him a little more time to complete his own. She was deep in concentration on her spell so obviously she was casting a large and powerful spell. She meant to finish him. He knew this would be the last round of spells. So, likewise, he was going to cast a very dangerous, but a very effective ice spell. It would freeze her completely and then upon warming up, the ice would crack and she would crack along with it. It should be powerful enough to wipe any protection spells she had out of the way. She would not feel it as the ice would instantly freeze everything in her body and her being of the fire fairy variety, this would also extinguish her flame within.

She had completed her cast and sent her blaze forth towards Ihoitae. He stood there waiting for it. He knew his protection spell would not be able to dissipate the spell, but he had yet another trick up his sleeve that obviously one so young could not know about him. The blaze swept over him and he felt the fire keenly as it sucked away his protection spell and burned his clothes. The heat was intense as it went through, around, over and beside him.

Tianariallis cackled wickedly, "Stupid elf! He knew it was coming too and he didn't even try to move! I win!"

Diane had looked away as she could not watch Ihoitae get burned to dust. Ifem, Aelle, Bodolf and Tian stared in utter disbelief that he could be dispatched so easily. Presaya, however, looked at the group and laughed. They all looked at her as if she were a two headed troglodyte.

"Just what  is sooooo funny?" Aelle snapped at her.

"Silly people, you don't know much about demons, do you?" Presaya responded with that laughter still in her voice and on her face. "If Dean were here, he would be laughing too."

The rest of the team was about to get into words with the little gnome when Diane moved her head to look in the direction where Ihoitae had stood. The blaze had burnt out but the area was still filled with dust and nothing could be seen, but Diane still felt Ihoitae's life force and it was strong. She pointed to the area where the dust was slowly dying away.

The entire audience gasped in complete disbelief as the dust settled and the elf's form began to reappear. The form was standing tall and strong and morphed. His body was naked as his clothes had not been protected from the fire blaze. Even his dagger had melted away showing just how powerful the fire blaze had been. Ihoitae's true form stood there with his beautiful angelic wings shining bright albeit a little sooty and his red eyes blazing as he brought up one clawed hand and finished speaking his spell and the blue ice magic reached out towards his opponent. Tianariallis suddenly stopped laughing caught completely off guard. She had just a moment to realize her doom before the ice blast hit her full force and froze her in a crouched, terrified position.

The entire audience looked upon their Queen for surely this was some sort of trickery against the rules. But the Queen nearly nodded towards Ihoitae accepting him as the winner of the duel. Ihoitae bowed back and then, as if just now realizing that he was naked, walked out of the arena with as mush dignity as he could. He regretted that he had to kill the Fairy woman.

The announcer spoke. "Per her Majesties final judgment, the match was fair and was won rightfully by the half elf, half demon within the rules supplied. Demons are able to absorb fire and brimstone as they are created from the abyssal of lava. Apparently, Ihoitae's half demon heritage also allows him to absorb such incendiary fire as well. Just not his clothes, apparently." The announcer laughed at his jest. "I guess that was one for the ladies.

"Now, for our next battle, this is a battle of wits. The game will be of riddles. Each party will get to provide a riddle in which the other party will have exactly three guesses. The first one to fail at guessing will lose the battle. The only rules and limits on the riddles is that they be spoken in common so that all may understand. So, if a riddle cannot be said in common, it cannot be used. The party that loses will forfeit their life at the Queen's discretion.

"Please welcome Faolan Marduu of Dioness Village, last son and lost son of the Queen Lyra Wetton-Dagmar and King Roland Dagmar of Cardinia of the noble Dagmar line and his opponent Freonandiar of the Water Clan." Faolan looked startled at the announcement of him being the lost son. What did that mean? He had no time to ponder this; he had to concentrate as riddles were never his strong point when he would play with the other village kids. Tian would have been a better choice for this battle, but what's done is done and he would have to wing it. Something had told him he needed to do this battle and so now he must.

By this time, the arena had magically been cleaned to remove the frozen Tianariallis and smooth the scorch marks that had been placed when the fire spell on Ihoitae had been made. There also was now placed a table and chairs in the middle of the pit and a spell had been cast to allow ease for hearing the opponents and their riddles and answers. Faolan and

Freonandiar took their places opposite one another. Freonandiar had blue wings, eyes and hair much like the gentleman that had brought them to their designated spots had. Freonandiar was a male Fairy also dressed similarly to the door greeter. He, however, was much younger. He was also much more cordial than Tianariallis had been to Ihoitae.

Freonandiar looked over to Faolan and held out his hand. "Shall we shake? No hard feelings to you, young sir, should I lose to you and vice versa?"

Faolan reached out and took the fairy's hand and shook it. "Aye, I will die well should I lose to your honor and I hope that you will in mine should the weavers' pattern flow that way."

The two young men sat down. "I can see the king in you," stated Freonandiar. "If you live, it will be my honor to die under such as yourself."

Faolan nodded and he waited on his first riddle to solve. Freonandiar had won the coin toss that had been completed prior to the entry into the pit arena by the stage hands.

Freonandiar cleared his throat and began loudly and clearly, "Let us start off with an easy one. A man is lying drowned in a dead forest, far from water. How did this happen?"

Faolan pondered this a moment then replied, "Yes, I think this one was an easy one, but I must confess, I have never been good at these. So, I am not overly confident that this is the correct answer."

"Please answer," requested Freonandiar.

"Very well," began Faolan, "I believe the answer is that there was a duel between two very powerful mages and one cast a water spell and drowned the other and left the scene."

"Correct. Now, please challenge me."

Faolan took up his pondering position again with his hand on his chin as he rubbed it looking over towards the scorched area, thinking. He was looking but not really looking. After what seemed like ages, Faolan finally spoke clearly and confidently, "Violet, indigo, blue and green, yellow, orange and red; these are the colors you have seen after the storm has fled. What am I?"

Freonandiar took on a similar thinking stance as Faolan had previously just had and after a few moments responded with pure confidence, "I am a Raindow."

"Yes, that is correct, your turn."

"Look at me. I can bring a smile to your face, a tear to your eye, or a thought to your mind. But, I can't be seen. What am I?" replied the blue Fairy.

"Aha, I know that one! Your memories!" Faolan's smile took him ear to ear.

Freonandiar also smiled likewise. "You are better than you thought you were. I thought that one pretty tough. However, you are correct."

"Ok, I hope to really challenge you with this one," began Faolan, starting to grow a little at ease with this game. He had tuned out the audience and just focused on himself and his opponent. He liked this Fairy and did not want him to lose, but he knew that he could not lose either. "When John was six years old he hammered a nail into his favorite tree to mark his height. Ten years later at age sixteen, John returned to see how much higher the nail was. If the tree grew by five centimeters each year, how much higher would the nail be?"

Freonandiar laughed and clapped his hands together. "Oh my dear Faolan, that is an easy one for the fae folk. The answer is the nail would be at the same height since trees grow at their tops!"

"Oh how silly of me," Faolan laughed as well. "Of course the fae would know that one being from the forests! Correct."

"Ok then, let me give you another 'What am I?' one. Let me think," stated Freonandiar. After a moment, he said his riddle. "When you stop and look, you can always see me. If you try to touch you cannot feel me. I cannot move, but as you near me, I will move away from you. What am I?"

"Oh geez, that's a stumper, let me think," Faolan thought long and hard. "The only thing I can come up with is that I am a horizon?"

The blue fairy tinkled with laughter and nodded his head. "Yes, that is correct. You are much better at this than I thought. I will have to come up with a better one should I get another round."

"Ok, here is my best," Faolan advised. "I can be found where anything cannot; dead men eat me all the time, but if a living man eats me, he'll die. What am I?"

Freonandiar's laughter died. He pondered and pondered for what seemed like ages. He could not fathom what the answer could be. Finally he looked up at the Queen and she nodded her head. He then responded, "Well, my friend, you have stumped me. Please, I ask that you enlighten me before my death as to the answer so I shall not go to my death wanting."

Faolan frowned. The answer was too easy and was usually guessed by the small children in his village within a heartbeat. He could not understand why a Fae could not guess it. He slumped his shoulders and replied, "The answer is I am nothing."

"Then nothing is what I shall become. My Queen," the blue fairy bowed towards his Queen, awaiting her decision.

She stood up and looked at everyone in attendance then down at the two combatants and addressed them. "It is the will of the Queen that Faolan should dispatch Freonandiar in the way he seems fit since he is the winner of this challenge. I will abide by his decision and it should be completed here and now. What say you young prince?"

Faolan looked towards his friends in the stands and then he turned to the Queen. He pondered a moment and then decided that he would need to show utter confidence. They thought him a king and so a king he would show them. He bowed to the Queen and then stood as straight as he could. Then he addressed her and the entire audience. "My Majesty and esteemed Fae Folk. I am honored and humbled by your request of me. However, in what little time I have been here and have had to know your court and my opponent, I cannot take his life. I would ask that he be allowed to live so that he may challenge me in the future to another duel of wits."

The Queen looked at Faolan sternly. "Let me be clear since you are human and do not know the way of the Fae. If you spare his life, he cannot stay in the land of the fae as his life is now forfeit here. He cannot be killed by any hand but your own. Should you choose to stay that hand, then know that he owes to you a blood debt that he must redeem some day in order to regain his honor and remove the forfeiture. He may not live long enough outside our realm to pay your blood debt back. Every Fae knows the price and so no one enters these tournaments lightly. It's our way. So, your death of him would be an act of mercy. Knowing the rules, what say you young prince?"

Faolan bowed again and pondered her words. "Once again, my Queen, I cannot do this deed. Freonandiar has done nothing to warrant a death to the eyes of the humans. If he cannot stay with you, then I would honor his presence with me, though at the moment I have no home to stay in. I would be honor bound to take him as a pledge, though I wager he is probably a little older than me."

The Queen nodded and continued with her indifferent attitude, though her eyes seemed to gleam a bit more through their shifting translucence. "I see the wisdom in your eyes beyond your years, young king, and I know there is a reason for you to spare his life. Although I must abide by the rules of court and banish Freonandiar from court, I am glad that you spared his life. For you see, Freonandiar is my son. I am the one honored to have him join your court. Mayhap the Fairies and the humans can find a treaty in the future. He will be your pledge now and always to treat as you will....... It is done." With that the Queen sat back down and Freonandiar sighed a bit of relief. He had not wanted to die but knew it was a possibility. Faolan spared his life and for that he was grateful. He would owe allegiance to this young man without question for he could see Faolan's future and he could see the man he would grow to be.

"That was a most interesting battle with a most interesting outcome. I wish Freonandiar, our blessed Queen's son, well in the hands of his new found comrades. Mayhaps our futures will intertwine again as our great Queen has requested.

"Now, on to our last battle, the battle of melee. This is to be fought by Bodolf Horsetamer of Clan

Stonehammer and Second Commander of the Light Bringers; and Mileswalliae of the Turquoise Clan. This is a battle to the death. The rules are once again simple. There are no rules except that the melee must stay within the confines of the pit arena and the audience cannot be hurt. The only armor allowed was light leather armor to allow for maximum maneuverability. All manners of weapon and martial art skills are welcomed and can be switched at will between the combatants. Should either rule be broken, then the Queen will determine the offending party and it will be her will to their fate.

"Let the final battle begin."

By this time Bodolf and Mileswalliae had reached the center of the pit arena. It had been further cleaned of the previous two battles "debris" and was now completely bare of anything except the floor. Boldolf had chosen to wear only a loin cloth with a tasseted war skirt over it, leather bracers, greaves and cuirass. For weapons, he chose his two handed battle axe and a smaller single bladed axe as his second.

Mileswalliae looked similar to that of the other males mode of dress they had seen so far with the leather loin cloth and leather sash across his chest. For his weapons, he had chosen a spear and bastard sword.

They readied their weapons and took up their fighting stances. These two opponents appeared hideously mismatched as the Fairy stood a full human's height and Bodolf on his stubby little dwarven legs. Bodolf was stout while Mileswalliae was waif like. The Fairy had his long spear while the dwarf had his short axe. Unlike the previous two Fairy Folk combatants, Mileswalliae was older and had the appearance of a seasoned warrior. Maybe not as seasoned as the thick dwarf, but certainly not a greenhorn. This would be the most definitive battle of them all. However, Bodolf had one pressure off of him, he knew he did not have to win in order for the group to win, at least if the stinking fairies keep their word, he thought. But, why then, did this battle have to complete?

The Queen stood up and addressed the audience and the combatants, once again in her aloof tone of voice. "Her Majesty realizes that the battles were to be won best out of three. It appears that the first two battles were won by the Light Bringers. However, this battle must be completed as only its completion will break the spell that binds the stone in which you seek. Two hearts must be stopped on the same side in order for the spell to be broken and only one has stopped as one was spared. Someone must lose this match.........That is all." She sat back down.

Bodolf quickly tipped his head to the Queen in acquiesce so that he showed he understood. He could not spare this warrior no matter the cost and nor could this warrior spare his life. This one was a true battle to the death. Well, he was a battle hardened dwarf, so one more warrior to slay.........the fairy started the battle and charged Bodolf. Bodolf had been taken slightly off guard seeing as he had been thinking, but he quickly fell into melee mode and instantly dodged the oncoming attack.

The dwarf quickly fell in warrior mode shutting out everything but the opponent before him and the field of battle. Out of the corners of his eyes, his mind took in the scene while he focused front and center on the shimmery blue-green fairy. This fairy was good too as he pressed the attacked. Bodolf was having to dodge the spear but was unable to get inside due to the length of the spear and the arms of the wielder. Smaller than most humanoids as dwarves often are, he had the disadvantage. But a true dwarf never let that stop him from defending and stopping his prey. Bodolf would do what most dwarves did, he would let this fairy tire himself. Mileswalliae's disadvantage was that he was wielding a spear which was long and ungainly and would tire his arms with every thrust and swing. In time, Mileswalliae would have to drop it and switch to his bastard sword and then Bodolf would have the upper hand with his twin bladed axe.

The battle went on for what seemed like ages with Mileswalliae pressing his attack and Bodolf fending it off. It seemed as if the dwarf was losing as with every swing, he lost ground. But to the team, they all knew the strategy and knew this to be a feint on the dwarf's part. He was biding his time until the fairy grew weary.

And so, as Bodolf predicted, the spear fell to the ground and the fairy ran back to gain some space. Mileswalliae's arm had tired from the constant swinging and thrusting.

"It seems that you have excellent stamina and fantastic parrying abilities," Mileswalliae remarked jovially as he switched to his sword. He acted is if they were merely sparring partners practicing at swordplay, though there was a husk in his tone as if he were winded. "I applaud you."

Bodolf bowed, though never taking his eyes off his opponent, "Me preciates your kind words, lad. Aye and you as well."

"I fear that stamina is not on my side," simply stated Mileswalliae. "But I have a little bit to go yet. Shall we show them a true match?" He unsheathed his sword and prepared to renew the fight once more changing his stance to one that was familiar with his bastard sword.

"Aye, that we shall, laddie," replied Bodolf, maintaining his stance with his two handed double bladed axe.

They circled each other for a moment, neither one wanting to strike first. Each one wanting to continue to measure the other and both knowing that each were their equals with their weapons. Finally, Mileswalliae made the first move not wanting to prolong the inevitable any longer. He lifted his sword in the air and made a battle cry and charged the dwarf.

Bodolf was ready for him, grunted and waited for the blade to descend into whatever strike Mileswalliae was going to attempt to make. Mileswalliae made three quick strikes and nicked Bodolf on the arm and leg. However, Bodolf being a thick skinned dwarf accepted the cuts in stride and brushed them off as nothing more than flesh wounds and parried Mileswalliae's renewed attacks.

They went back and forth for several moments, thrust parry dodge, thrust parry dodge, but Mileswalliae's tiredness was seriously beginning to show and he was slowing down considerably. Bodolf just continued to let the Fairy wear himself down. Then Mileswalliae attempted a feint that Bodolf was well all too familiar with and he struck the killing blow. Mileswalliae fell to the ground, blood spreading quickly down his chest where the axe had bit in deep. It had severed the artery to the fairies heart and he was dead before he hit the ground. Bodolf bowed deeply at Mileswalliae's body and then turned to the Queen and bowed as well as the gladiator code would dictate.

The Queen stood up and likewise bowed. It appeared that she had a tear in her eye. "It is done. Though my heart is sad at the loss of our brave ones, I am well aware of the prophecy and its goals and I am glad that the Light Bringers won the tourney. All of you will meet me in the royal quarters in the back of the tourney halls." With that, she floated with her entourage away, presumably towards the royal quarters.

The team members that had been up in the stands were led by the same male fairy that greeted them at the gate, while Freonandiar led the combatants there. Freonandiar looked very sad and had his eyes downcast as they walked.

"Why so glum?," Faolan asked. "I mean, I know you lost two comrades, but you seem a bit more upset than a comrade would be. Were they friends?" The boy asked in as solemnly and as respectfully as he could. He knew that Freonandiar lost a lot today and he wanted the fairy to like him since they were apparently going to be lifelong companions.

"Oh, um," Freonandiar began a bit hazily. "They were my younger sister and oldest brother." Bodolf, Ihoitae and Faolan all gasped. "It had been our required duty upon the very hour of births that we were to fight you this day. Had mother had more children, then there would have been more battles. She effectively has lost all three of her children in as little as a few hours."

"That is very sad, Freonandiar, my sympathies," Ihoitae replied, placing a gentle hand upon the young fairy's shoulder. "I can truly understand how you feel."

"Thank you, Prince Ihoitae," Freonandiar replied. "I know of your history as well. Mother thought it prudent for us to know our enemy. And I know you lost your entire mother's side of people in one fell swoop. I cannot imagine."

"It seems more like this was a curse for your race," Faolan began thinking out loud. "How could the Mystics have asked that of your mother?"

Freonandiar smiled wanely, "Yes, it actually was a curse placed on the Fae Folk, but not by the Mystics. For you see, Kahlrab had twisted the strings of the prophecy as much as He could before He was vanquished. And this is one of those ways He twisted it. Another was when the Fates stole Prince Brandon, whom you know as Faolan Marduu, away from his parents at birth. The prophecy would not allow them to kill you, Faolan, but they were able to change your identity in hopes that you would never know who you are, thus stopping the prophecy in its tracks. I see it did not work."

Faolan looked a bit startled at Freonandiar. "But you see, it did work to some degree. I heard the announcer say that I was Faolan Marduu of Dioness Village, last son and lost son of the Queen Lyra Wetton-Dagmar and King Roland Dagmar of Cardinia of the noble Dagmar line and that really threw me off my game, but I ignored it so I could concentrate on my battle. To be honest, this is truly the first time I have heard of this. I am no prince. Just a farmer."

Ihoitae cleared his throat and said, "No, not technically. Zaire told us too. He told the king and queen that you had been found, but he did not elaborate. I should have guessed when he looked directly at you what he meant! Can I see your arm?"

Faolan lifted up his tunic sleeve to show Ihoitae first one arm all the way up to his shoulder blade and then his second. On his left arm, on the bicep, there was the birthmark of the red dragon, the one little Prince Brandon had.

"Ah ha!" exclaimed Ihoitae, "You are the lost prince. This proves it."

"But how?" asked Faolan.

Ihoitae began, but Freonandiar broke in wanting to make himself useful with his new comrades. "Only the royal house and the servants of the castle knew of your unusual birthmark. However, since it appeared you had been murdered most foully by the Fates, word was not spread about the birthmark to look for you. Your adoptive parents, nor the soldiers that found you, nor your village elders had any idea who you were. You were just another orphan found by the Cardinia soldiers. And to your biological parents, you were dead and lost."

Faolan looked at the birthmark on his bicep. He had always hated the ugly thing and been teased a lot as a kid, so he had made it a point to always hide it. "So, if I am this prince, then that means……"

"You are the heir apparent as you are the first son," Ihoitae answered.

Faolan sighed, "But I don't want to be the heir apparent! I just want to find my sister Fea and I want Tian, Fea and Tian's sister Tala to try and rebuild Dioness. I can't be this prince."

Ihoitae and Freonandiar both chuckled and clasped their hands on either shoulder. Ihoitae tried to give some reassurance and advised, "Trust me, it is not a duty anyone truly wants. A good ruler understands that duty is thrust upon his shoulders and he must take up the mantle to lead his people with wisdom, kindness and justice. Only an evil ruler thinks that this duty is a gods given right and privilege that he is required to have. I think in some way, Kahlrab messed up when he attempted to twist this string. For although your birth parents are righteous rulers and truly do the Dagmar line justice, that does not always mean that the children follow suit. Your birth brother is not the man to rule, in my humble opinion, for example, as he is a bit pompous because of his station. He may destroy Cardinia if he ever gets to lead it. But because of your humble beginings, I see a fine king in you. You are a good soul, Faolan, and I could think of no one more worthy of the title."

Then Freonandiar offered, "It will take time, my patron, to get used to this title. But title is all it is, albeit with a bit more responsibility. However, you do not have to let the title rule you. I truly meant what I said in our battle. You will make a good king."

"Can Fae see the future?" Faolan tentavily asked.

"Oh aye," Freonandiar's eyes glimmered.

Ihoitae looked stunned for a moment and then he had a question to ask. "Freonandiar, does this mean that your sister and brother knew that they were to die?"

Freonandiar solemnly nodded his head. "They did. And they chose to die because they wanted Kelnaria to be saved. But they had to pretend."

"Did you know I would save you?" pondered Faolan, curious.

Freonandiar's eyes twinkled again. "Aye, I did. Every Fae knows their own destiny and their own death. However, no other Fae can know another Fae's destiny and death, except the most powerful Fairy which is –"

"The Queen!" Faolan exclaimed. "Oh how sad, she already knew!"

"And accepted, except for my fate. You see, originally you would have had me killed too, but something changed and I knew at the start of the battle, but she did not. Pray, please tell me why you decided to spare my life?"

Faolan shrugged. "I don't know. You just seemed too much like me and I knew that if I were in your place, I would not want to die. And I don't think anyone should be killed without a valid reason. And well, I think just because you couldn't think of nothing as the answer, that just didn't warrant death. It seemed so silly to me. Sorry to balk your traditions."

"No, I am glad you think the way you do. Another trait of an excellent king. And this day you have repaired much damage Kahlrab did. The Fae Folk have hated the humans for centuries because they knew this day would come." Freonandiar stopped walking, "Well, we are here."

Bodolf, Faolan and Ihoitae stepped in. All three noticed that Freonandiar stayed outside the door. They guessed that since he was now considered dead among the fairies, he was no longer welcome in the royal rooms.

The Queen was already seated in what appeared to be a throne on a dais in the back of the audience chamber in which they now stood. She continued to have her stern countenance although it was apparent that she had shed a tear or two as she had approached the room. "The stone you seek is here. The chest that it has been kept in for the last few centuries is being brought forth along with its key. Freonandiar will be granted a few moments to collect his things so that he may have what he needs to take to his new home. He will be waiting for you outside this realm.

"Faolan, when you are of age and are in your birthright role as king, I will send an emissary to you. Mayhap in that time we can forge a treaty. As for now, my heart must needs to heal. Though I am happy for your victory, I am saddened by loss."

The entire team bowed and spoke words of condolences.

The Queen continued to speak. "Once you receive your prize, your welcome in Fairy will be at its end and you will be driven back to where Princess Radon and Queen Zinc await your corpses or your living persons. You have had a long journey so far and have learned much, but still have much more to learn. Despite the trials of this stone, I wish you well in saving the world of Kelnaria. We are as much a part of it as you are. Our realm lies in the fabric of its being and should it fail, then we, too shall fail." She waved her hand dismissively as the box approached. The female fairy that carried it looked a lot like the Queen having the multi colored hair, wings and eyes of translucent bubbles. She was very young, though.

Bodolf, Ihoitae and Faolan looked at her strangely. The Queen, noticing their inquisitiveness decided to provide an answer. "This is my last living child and the heir apparent to the throne and always has been. See, Freonandiar told you that had I had more children there would have been more battles, and he did not lie. For you see, this one is not one of my making. Heirs in our world can come from anyone. We know them by their color of wing, eye and hair. She will be as powerful as I am with all the elements and so she will be the next Queen when my time has come. Only one Queen shall be born to us at a time. So, she became my daughter upon the hour of her birth so that I may raise her to be the Fairy Queen."

The queen raised her hand to stop any retorts as she could see them coming from the mortal folk. They did not understand Fairy ways, but she felt it prudent to enlighten them. Maybe if these few knew, then it would help ease the path for the Fae to join the waking world. The Queen felt that the only way for the Fae to survive was to join in with the waking world and stop the dreamers. "Her parents are still very much a part of her life and always will be. Our ways seem strange to you, but I feel the need to express to you that the weavers choose our rulers, not just a happy coincidence of birth because your patron and matron were the previous rulers. Thus, it is my job to teach her how to rule. It is her parents' job to teach her how to love. She was made for this task where as my children may or may not have been. So, the Weavers chose this girl because she has the qualities that will lead the Fairy in the way we must be led. Do you understand?"

Faolan nodded and spoke for the party with a new confidence he did not seem to have before. "I do understand and I think, perhaps, the Weavers provide a better fate for your people than perhaps some of our own ways since we are born to privilege. I would prefer your way."

"Good," The Queen nodded. "I am glad to hear it. But, now it is time for you all to leave. Walk back to the arena pit and Freonandiar will be waiting for you there. You will hold hands and close your eyes and you will all be returned to the chamber from whence you came."

So, the party walked quietly back to meet Freonandiar and go back to the dragon cave with their hard fought stone in hand.

# Chapter Eighteen

HIS PREY HAD disappeared again. This must be a new trick of his and he was not happy that this trick existed. Could his prey have learned that he was around? No, not in all these years that he had been following his prey for his mistress had he ever once scented him. No, this was magic and a very powerful magic at that. A translocation spell of the highest magnitude not used as far back as he could remember. He didn't even think the dragons had anything that powerful. His prey had gained some pretty powerful allies. Gods maybe. If that were true, then his mistress being a minor demi-god herself, would be no match for the ones protecting and aiding his prey. It was time he went back to his mistress. This mission was done and a new objective would need to be found.

*** 

The party had met, held hands and closed their eyes as instructed in the middle of the pit arena. However, when they opened their eyes, they were not back in the chasm with Queen Zinc and Princess Radon. They opened their eyes and they were surrounded by spears pointing at them in a complete circle even as they stood. The spears were held by strange creatures that had the bodies of a horse and the torsos and heads of humans. This effectively gave them a horses tail and four powerfully, quick legs with hooves and two arms. The party had never seen the likes of them before. But Freonandiar, Ifem and Ihoitae both had an inkling as to what they were, the fabled Centaurs.

As the party dropped from holding their hands to holding them up in the air, one of the creatures pushed passed some of his comrades and moved into the circle of spears to address the group. At first he spoke in a guttural language that crossed the borders of some kind of neighing with speech and effectively completed his words with a finger point at the group. It sounded as if he had asked them a question. Dean, being the leader, decided that he would be the first to respond.

"I…..am…..Dean…..Moonstone," he intoned slowly and as clearly as he could. He hoped beyond hope that maybe one of these creatures could speak common.

"We…..are….not….here….to…..hurt…..you."

The male that had come forward groaned and replied in a gruff, but very understandable voice, "Ugh, outlanders. I speak your common tongue. What you here for? You trespass upon ancient Centaurian land."

Freonandiar, Ifem and Ihoitae exchanged glances. They all knew of the lore, but none had met one. Even Faolan and Tian seemed to be faintly aware of their myth from the wide eyes they gave the horsemen.

Dean continued to maintain his leadership status seeing that everyone else chose to be tight lipped. He knew nothing of the Centaurs and, being of dragon decent, cared little for them. He had never come across this race of beings before and immediately assumed it was because they never left their ancestrial home, wherever that was. "We come in peace, sir, wherever this is. We are on a mission for the crown of Cardinia. We did not meant to disturb you and your people."

The centaur grunted and said something in his guttural language to his people. A few of them spoke and then the one representing himself as the leader replied back in common. "We decide take you chieften. Chief and council will know what do with you. You come willingly?"

Dean nodded and everyone in the party also nodded and dropped arms to show no resistance. Then Dean said, "Can we have your word that no harm will come to any of us as long as we cooperate?"

The leader thought a moment then nodded his head and spoke to his group. "Yes, dragon kin, we will not harm unless you try be bad. We even let you retain your weapons until we get to chieftain. Then you must give weapons."

"Deal." Dean replied. With that, the entire group of centaurs and Light Bringers began to move off towards the city or camp or wherever this chieften was. Apparently, they had arrived near where the centaurs had a home, which is probably why they had immediately been surrounded, once the spell allowed them to open their eyes. This had been a scouting party, probably on patrol to protect the camp.

As they walked towards the camp, they had become somewhat a spectacle. Apparently, some younger ones had been doing a patrol of their own and saw the group approaching. They had sent some of their own back to report the strangers and from there the camp had been bursting with excitement. These were not only strangers; these were outlanders from the mainlands. Rarely, if ever, were they seen on their island. Usually the ones that were seen were only seen by the patrolling warriors and then either sent back the way they came or removed from the island permanently.

As Dean and the party walked through the camp they could see that these were nomadic people and probably travelled from place to place on this land. The land itself was warm and grassy with plains as far as they could see. It was a welcome change from the cold they had just come from with the White Dragons, despite that the warmth of the cave was warm enough.; the land was not. They could also sense that these people must also have different tribes or clans and were probably constantly at war with one another.

As the group speculated, they reached the middle of the camp where a large bonfire had been placed in a large, round fire pit. Then there was a wide, open space between the fire pit and the tentlike structures presumed to be as housing. This large open space looked like it would be for dancing or ceremony. One of the tentlike structures was rather larger than the rest and this is where the warriors seemed to be talking the group. They stopped outside. The warriors took up positions to guard the group while the leader went inside to speak with what the party assumed was the chieftain.

The leader came back outside and walked up to Dean. "Chieftain. will see two of you. He will not see lizard man. He knows your kind well. He say he see long eared thing with white hair and pretty lady with the black hair." He pointed at Ihoitae and Diane. "You give weapons to Karklic. White haired one leave armor. Lady may keep on her clothes. You follow me."

Ihoitae and Diane both slowly took off any weapons they carried in order to show they meant no aggression. Ihoitae removed his dragon armor curaiss, arms and leg armor and left only his light padding that he wore under his armor. They proceeded to follow the leader into the tent.

Inside the tent it was smoky from a pipe that was being puffed. It was being passed around between several centaurs that were in a semi circle around the room with one older one in the middle. He motioned for them to sit, doing so as they were sitting, to complete the circle. Ihoitae and Diane did as they were bid. They were small in comparison to the centaurs with their horse bodies sitting around the circle.

The chieftain spoke a few words to the leader and then motioned for the leader to speak. Ihoitae guessed that the chieftain most likely spoke common as well, but didn't want the "outlanders" to know it, so Ihoitae played along. "I am Mehawkin, chieftain's son, and I am leader of patrol group what found you. We do not have many strangers of mainland here. You are not welcome, but we would know why you here. You live for now."

Diane and Ihoitae looked at each other a bit alarmed but both quickly relaxed. Silently, Diane motioned for Ihoitae to talk since he was more worldly than her and she guessed knew something of the myth of the centuars. Ihoitae nodded and bowed to the chieftain and, in turn, to each member of what he presumed was the council to which Mehawkin referred too. "Good chieftain and council members. My name is Ihoitae Arabus and this is my patrol comrade Diane Moonstone. We did not mean to trespass upon your lands. We were with the White

Dragons and then a spell transported us here. We are on a mission for the human crown called Cardinia. Please ask anything and we will parlay the truth for you noble sirs. We wish honor, not death."

The chieftain listened as Mihawkin relayed the words in their harsh toungue and then the chieftain nodded and looked at each council member and then spoke a few words to Mehawkin. He then translated, "This is great Chieftain Barsillic. He hears your words and will honor a parlay with you. We not wish bloodshed either and would wish wisdom of the outside world.

"Chieftain Barsillic and the great council have heard that war has ravaged the mainlands for many seasons and they see great flying beasts above. Some have come to shore, none have lived. But we feel we no longer ignore what happen outside our island. Chieftain would hear what you say."

So, between Diane and Ihoitae, they were provided the floor and between the two of them, they managed to truncate the war, the prophecy and their mission as best they could in hopes that, as it was translated, it would be understood. The council members and cheiften nodded as Mehawkin translated as Ihoitae and Diane went along with their tales. The chieftain asked about the party, the two human kingdoms and the mission that the Light Bringers were on. The meeting took a long time and the party members outside were growing nervous and weary of what may be transpiring inside. But, to their credit, they stayed strong and did as they were told by the warriors. They were brought water and food and the warriors had them sit down while they waited.

Towards the end of the parlay the chieftain decided that he would acknowledge that he spoke the common words and began to speak directly to Ihoitae and Diane. "I see good souls in you. I believe your words as does the council." The members all nodded their heads in agreement. "We will let you live. But trust you yet, we do not. Trust must be earned, you agree?"

"Yes, great chieftain," Diane answered.

"Aye, what are your terms and conditions?" Ihoitae asked.

"Smart one," Chieftain laughed and pointed at Ihoitae. "There is water man here, we captured. We think trying to take our fish. He say he is medicine man of water people tribe and he knew you coming. He try tell me that you seek stones. We think he is lying, but now appear his story may have truth to it. We test."

With the admission that these once thought of myths knew of the stones that the party was seeking, Diane and Ihoitae gasped in utter shock. "You know of the stones?" Ihoitae asked.

"Yes, chieftain have one. Pretty green," and he pulled out a necklace that had been hidden in his leather jerkin. There was a leather thong that had birds feathers and bones adorned on it. At the end, in what looked like an eagle's talon, was clutched a green emerald. "Been handed down from father to son since time unknown to Centaur. We told by Great Ones, that we to protect it and only give it to the correct outlander. We never believe story though we revere our ancient ones. Now, perhaps, ancients tell truth. We test."

Ihoitae bowed again and Diane followed suit. She knew that these were ancient and honorable people. While the council and chieftain had been conferring after Ihoitae and Diane's tale, Ihoitae explained to her what little knowledge he knew of the mysterious island. He told her that the Centaurs were rumored to be the first race of Kelnaria, having been created by the Mystics themselves. They were placed on this island, which is charted as "unknown" on the maps, but mythed to be Centauria Island. Anyone who came here, never returned, so no one could confirm or deny it. The island was given to the Centaurs by the Mystics and was protected by the gods to keep this race pure. It was rumored that the Centaurs were warlike people, ferocious but honorable. They were also known to have the body of a horse and, where the neck and head of a horse would be, was the torso, arms and head of a human. He surmised that they must have learned their common from one of the many visitors that came to the island looking for fortune and glory. They must also have kept somewhat in the loop with the mainlands by what little news they could discern from their unwanted guests.

The chieftain, after a few minutes of reflection, began to speak again. "Great Ones tell ancient ones that you come one day. Told ancient ones that we were only to talk to white haired, pointy eared one and beautiful lady with long raven black hair. They tell ancients that lady is from long dead race Telestics. We once allied with Telestics. We believe you are one of them as you have the mark. We have gift for you." The chieftain made a motion with his hands and one of the council members got up and left the tent. "Markusic will get gift."

Diane looked confused and dared to ask a question. "Chieftain, please forgive my ignorance. How do you know? I just recently found out myself and I am so lost."

"Not be lost for long child of Telestics. Gift will show you. You have the bodily mark. It surrounds you as it surrounds everyone, but all life has specific marks."

"Do you mean an aura?" Ihoitae asked, a little uncertain.

"I have heard of beings calling colors around body that. So, yes."

"You are far seers!" Ihoitae exclaimed. "They were thought destroyed during the Gods War. It was rumored your people fought in those."

"Ancients did. Then Great Ones placed us here, told us we be safe, not to leave island. We have not since. We have everything we need here. We told to make sure mainlanders not leave our island if any should come. So, we kill or make them part of tribe. Rare to make part of tribes, depends on clan leaders. We told that when time was right and the true champion came, we would leave again to join world. We think time had been coming soon by stars tell us. Then you arrive."

The chief got up and walked outside the tent motioning for the others to follow. His horse body was a dappled gray under the blanket that had been covering it. His human torso showed the normal wrinkles and chubbiness of the elder moving out of their prime. He wore a light leather tunic over his chest with an intricate bone neckplace that resembled a breastplate of sorts. It had beads, feathers and patterns intricately and beautifully woven throughout its length. It was his medal to show his rank among his peoples. Ihotae noticed that his son had one similar, but not as long on the chest as his father's. Ihoitae's guess was that Chief Barsillic was not only the clan leader of this tribe, but was probably the head tribal leader of all the clans when they would meet together.

Ihoitae and Diane were gently pushed to follow the chieftain and the council out of the tent back into the circle where the unlit bonfire was. There they say that the other centaurian warriors were still standing guard over their friends, but that their friends had been allowed to sit and given some water and food. They were being treated fairly and honorably as Mehawkin agreed they would be.

The chief walked around the group, examining each and every member. First he looked Dean and Aelle up and down and simply shook his head. Then he gleaned over Ifem and Tian and Bodolf and had much the same reaction. He stopped when he saw Presaya and Faolan.

He pointed at Faolan and asked, "Please get up. I would look upon you."

Faolan complied and held his arms out to show that he meant no aggression.

"Lift up shirt on arm, you have birthmark?"

Faolan looked stunned, but nodded and complied. There on his arm was the birthmark of the dragon. The very birthmark that marked him as the missing prince of Cardinia.

The chief grunted and spoke in his harsh language to his people. Then the tribe erupted in shouts and cheers and whoops. Some of the tribe raised their spears and began to whoop into the air what sounded like a cheer of triumph. The party just looked to and from one another. Each and everyone of them just as lost as the other, except Presaya, whom was smirking. The chief looked down at the little gnome then and asked her to stand as well.

Presaya did as she was bid, but with an easier and less unsure gait than the rest of the group.

"I know You, Revered One. You are one of the Great Ones. I would know You were I blind." Then the chief bowed to Presaya. Once the rest of the tribe saw their chieftain bowing to the little gnome, they too bowed realizing this was one of their creators.

The rest of the party, confused before, were all now just down right flabbergasted. Presaya smiled and answered, "It is time. I can longer hide my identity now that I walk among my children." With that, Presaya began to glow a red color and was engulfed by it. The light grew taller and after reaching a height of about seven feet it grew a bit wider in girth and then it faded away. Presaya no longer stood there. A man stood there who looked every much like a warrior from out of time. He was tall and muscle bounded. He wore a leather plaited skirt studded in brass and leather fur lined boots. His chest was naked except for the scars that he carried and for the crisscrossing straps that held his two swords across his back. At his belt he had an enormous twin bladed axe. He wore leather vembrances on his arms that were studded with brass. His head held no helmet and was bald with a strange tattoo on the back of his skull. His skin was tanned and his eyes blazed blood red. He wore a gruff beard and mustache.

The tribe shouted even greater whoops and hollars as they all realized what their chieftain had known. The rest of the party just continued to look shocked and stunned. Presaya turned man looked around and raised his hands in an attempt to request everyone to quiet down and listen to him.

First, the Presaya-man looked at the party and addressed them first, knowing that the centaurs would wait until he bid them to action. "Guess I have some explaining to do, huh?" He laughed reminiscient to the way the little gnome had.

Ihoitae was the first to recover because he recognized the voice from when he was dying in Waren's Tower. "You are the one that has been watching over me." It was not a question, though Ihoitae did not sound sure of himself. "Are you......are you a God?"

The Presaya-man shrugged, "I was once."

Dean now a lot more annoyed and not so dazed anymore responded. "Not good enough. I demand an explanation!" He stepped towards the Presaya-man and was rewarded with a few spears at his throat.

"I know. Enough of these bloddy riddles!" the Presaya-man answered, clearly agreeing with Dean. "My brothers and sister were ever the fans of them. Thinking it would be a fun game. I told them it was stupid. They should just be straight forward."

Ifem glared at this warrior and then realization dawned on him. Then he too bowed and spoke so as to clear things up, "You are a Mystic. The God of War, Khalon, I would presume."

"Aye and I created the Centaurs," Khalon confirmed. "So, stand down, my children. Dean will not harm me. He is just angry and confused. He has every right to be." The centaur warriors stood down at their Father's request. "I survived somehow when all my other brothers and my sister were slaughtered. I went into hiding after I knew the seed of the prophecy had been planted. And then, when Ihotae was born, I deemed to watch and protect him. I feel as if he is sort of my child as well, though he is not the seed of my creation."

Ihoitae stared at him and then thoughts of past friends and animals and every living soul that had treated him with kindness that was not his mother and half sister flooded through his mind. They all had a kind of twinkle in their eye and the elf or human ones had the same laugh.

"Yes, you know me now, my young one," and Khalon smiled kindly at Ihoitae. "I have surely grown soft after all these millennia!" He laughed heartily. "Especially being that I am a God of War!"

Diane looked up at the now God of War. "I understand now why Princess Radon said she would keep your secret. You have taken a big risk this day. You are the last Mystic when all have thought that the Mystics were completely extinct."

"Yes, daughter of the wise ones, I have indeed taken a big risk," began Khalon, "But as I said before, I would not have been able to hide myself from the Centaurs even had I wanted to. They have true sight and sound and not even the power of the Gods can be hidden from their eyes. It was the gift that We bestowed upon them, among other things. What Ihoitae referred to as Far Seers. Centaurs were created by my brothers and my sister and I. They were originally to be the guardians of Kelnaria, which is why they are such a fierce peoples. But when the Onae came and the God Wars began, we knew things had to be different and so we safeguarded Our children here on this island until their talents were needed for the final battle. We did not want them marked extinct the way the Onae tried to obliterate the Telestics and our other allies, the Sylvans, whom the demons effectively destroyed."

Diane looked over at the chief and over all the Centaurs, then replied, "So, this means that they can see our true selves no matter what our outward appearance is. Can they also understand everything we say even if it's not in their own language?"

Khalon nodded.

"That means they knew us from the minute we teleported here," grunted Dean.

Khalon nodded again. "But they had to be sure it was not some trick. We warned them that tricks could happen and so they had to be sure. When they saw me with you, they knew that either I was somehow captured or you were the true ones of the prophecy."

The chieftain spoke up now. "We know you not enemy now. Our Father is with you of His free will. We help you and now it time for us to join the rest of world. We believe Cardinia is side we are to fight on from what pointy ear and raven hair have told us.

"Daughter of wise ones, Markusic comes with gift. He will give to you to look when ready. It was left to our care by your father and brother. We told they will find you in Cardinia once battle with devil demon done." The chief waved to Markusic for him to give her the leather bound journal.

Khalon turned to the chief and asked, "Are your people ready for this?"

The chieftain nodded and whoops were shouted from several of the warriors around the spectacle. "We ready. Built boats as stars foretold. Trained warriors as told. Last matter is of stone........and fish man."

"Ah yes, they will complete the trials as required by the quest," Khalon began. "I believe your test was strongest of your warriors must be bested by the strongest of their warriors?'

The chieften nodded.

"Very well, prepare him or her and we will prepare ours. I cannot compete as it would be a tad lopsided. After this battle, we will see to the fish man dilemma and then you will send your envoy to Cardinia." Then Khalon turned to the party. "Once we leave this island, I will be Presaya once more. I am protected by the mists my brothers and I placed on this island, but once I leave, I will be open again to powers like the Djinn.

"The rules for this battle for the stone are simple, your strongest warrior against their strongest warrior. It is not a battle to the death, but that it is a possibility as with all battles. It is a battle to the yield. I think that you would be wise to choose someone of true heart and whom is untested in battle."

Ifem looked directly at Dean and spoke the words of the riddle, "Seek out the green jewel which is the heart of Kelnaria But you must prove your worth to all of Centauria This is done by words of trust From someone whose people where once thought dust. Dean, you are going to be angry, but I think this one goes to Diane."

Dean growled, "What?!?! NO!!!!!! She cannot. She is.......she is......."

"I am what?," Diane broke in a little upset. "Pregnant? Yes, but I do believe that Ifem is right. I am the daughter of the wise ones and until recently, we all thought the Telestics, my people, were extinct.....dust."

Dean sighed. "So be it, though I do not condone it."

"Your words are marked," Diane replied with dignity. "But the match is not to the death, so at least the worst that could happen is I would get badly beaten up."

Or lose our baby, Dean thought but did not reply. Instead he just nodded his ascent. Diane went to Aelle to see if she could borrow some female armor that would be a little more suited to the task.

*   *   *

While the Centaurs simultaneously prepared to convey to all the tribes across Centuaria Island that the time was here as well as to prepare for the battle for the stone, Ifem and Ihoitae decided to sneak away and see if they could approach the "fish man" before anyone else did. Ifem could not get this feeling that the "fish man's" appearance at this time was not just mere coincidence. Especially since the passage that was between the white stone and the green one was about a fish of man.

Travel to the crystal waters for the jewel blue
Only can a fish of man rescue it from the dune
Let it be known that trust must be gained
From a duel that is a king's bane

Ihoitae and Ifem discussed this as they searched this camp for where enemies would be caged. They discovered a small hut made of wood rather than the tents. This hut had a thick wooden door that had slots in it that resembled placed for lookouts and food plates. It was also guarded by warriors on all 4 sides. Off to the side of this hut was another tent that appeared to be a sort of barracks for the warriors that served as guards. Four on and four off and two commanding officers, one for each shift, which ran messages from the chief to the hut. One of these commanders was currently in the process of explaining the commotion in the camp as Ihoitae and Ifem approached. Ifem indicated that Ihoitae should speak since most likely he would be more "recognized" due to the story that had been passed down for generatons among their people.

Upon their approach, the commander abruptly stopped speaking and all three warriors on that side turned their attention on the two elves. The commander spoke first in a demanding tone of voice, "Chieftain know you here? If not, you leave or we place you in hut."

Ihoitae began to respond as he and Ifem both held out their arms wide and bowed their heads to show that they were not a threat and meant no harm. "I am Prince Ihoitae Mahadeva Arabus of the Sylvan Elves. We heard rumor that you held a wonder for us. A fish man. Neither of us have ever seen one before and we were curious. We mean no disrespect and will leave upon your request."

The commander looked the two elves up and down and thought for a moment. "Alright," he relented, "I will let you see fish man." With that he turned around and motioned for the two guards to open the door and give the elves a candle so they can see the fish man. "You even talk to him. Maybe he talk to you. If you can, get him tell why he here."

Ihoitae and Ifem both nodded and bowed with respect. Then Ihoitae accepted the candle that was given to him by one of the warriors. It was unlit. They stepped inside the hut and were immediately locked inside. There was some light coming through the cracks in the walls and the areas where the slots were for looking in and placing food plates, but the sliders were closed, so it was not much. Ihoitae used his magic and caused the candle to catch flame.

In the back of the hut was tied a very sad looking humanoid. It was definitely male as the Centaurs had left him naked. His skin was a pale blue color that faintly shimmered as if it were scaled and he had eyes that were large round, dark saphires. His face was very elfin like with the sharp chiseled features of an elf of nose and high cheekbones as well and long pointy ears. His head was bald, though it appeared as if fins were aligned on his head, arms and legs. His cheeks had slits in them almost as a fish would where its gills would be located. If Ifem and Ihoitae could see his feet and hands, they would notice that they had a think web membrane linking all the joints together.

"You came!" the fish man exclaimed quietly and with much pain. "I feared I would die before you arrived."

"You know of us?" Ifem asked.

The fish man vigioursly nodded his head, though this caused him some pain. "Indeed I have. I saw the currents shift so I surfaced from my city under Lilos Lake Island to read the stars. Finally, the prophecy was coming to an end. So, I stole the blue stone from the king and came here because I had to give it to you. There was no other way for you to get it."

Ifem and Ihoitae both looked extraordinarily astonished at one another. Then Ifem continued, "Yes, we are on a quest for Cardinia, nay, all of Kelnaria, to find the five sacred stones and the two halves of the sword, so we can reforge Tremblount to defeat Khalrab. Where is the stone now?"

"It is here, inside me. I didn't want anyone to find it, so I cut open my side, placed it inside and sewed myself back up." He shrugged when he saw the looks of disgust on the two elves faces. "My life is forfeit anyway. I can never go back because of my actions and we merfolk can only live on land for a limited amount of time. Mine is running short.

"My name is Esmarlen. I am what you land dwellers would refer to as a shaman among my people. I was honored among my people as one of the most powerful known in recent times until I fought with the king of the merfolk over the very stone you seek. However, I knew what was right, so I became a thief in the night and stole it from the king's crown. I knew you would come to the Centaurs first and so I came here. I was early much to my chagrin since my time on land is limited. I tried to explain to their chieftain why I was here and what needed to be done. I knew they also had a stone. I also knew that their shaman had also seen the same signs, but none of them listened to me and placed me in here to die."

"That is terrible!" Ihoitae stated. "But there must be a way to save you. Magic? Water? What?"

Esmarlen laughed gently. "Oh aye, if you restore me to water, I still have time to be refreshed for life. But, when I said my life is forfeit, I meant that I could never go back home and, if sighted, I would be killed. And with the naga that live in the ocean, I could never survive on my own. The ocean is vast, but merfolk only survive because we live in numbers as a school of fish do. Lone merfelk tend to die quickly in the sea, especially if the naga capture you. I would rather die here than in the centaurs' hands than the nagas'."

"Ah, I see your dilemma," Ifem responded though greatly dismayed.

"I see it as well, but I see its folly," began Ihoitae. "If I could save your life, would you be willing to go with the Centaurs to Cardinia, to be my personal messanger? I would also ask for the stone, but it seems you are already willing to give me that, correct?"

Esmarlen nodded his head. "I am only here to give you the stone as I have already fought for you to have it. Although I am willing to hear you out, I fear there is nothing you can do for me."

"I can. How much longer do you have to live?"

Esmarlan tilted his head and thought a moment. "I came the night of the last full moon. I have until the light of the next before I will completely wilt and die as though a – well – fish out of water. The enchantment only lasts that long."

"Enchantment?" Ifem inquired. "Can't it be recast?"

Ihoitae motioned for the merman to be quiet and spoke this time so Esmarlen could save his strength. Ihoitae shook his head now and stated, "No, the enchanment he speaks of can only be granted once in a merfolk's life so that they can know what its like to be on land for one month. Some save it for the end of their lives, some use it in their wild and reckful youths. Esmarlen apparently saved his for an emergency. He must return to the water or he won't be able to breathe any longer. But I know another way."

Now it was Esmarlen's turn to look startled and he glared at Ihoitae. "You do?!?!!?"

"Yes, I do," Ihoitae became silent a moment as he made a quick calculation in his head and then advised, "I need to speak with the chieftain as soon as Diane finishes her task. Esmarlen has roughly three days before the full moon shines once more upon us. I need to have him freed before then because I will need him to be able to bathe in the ocean waters one more time."

"But I cannot return," Esmarlen lamented.

"You will not return home, Esmarlen. If you are banished and a land dweller you must become, then you will need to forsake your merfolk condition. I learned of it when I was in my father's camp. Demons do this sort of thing all the time. It's how they get around banishments from ill trained wizards, and the like, that summon them. I see no reason why it won't work for a magical creature such as a merfolk."

"I see," Esmarlen and Ifem almost replied exactly at the same time. However, Ifem's voice was a bit more reflective while Esmarlen's held hope.

"Ifem, would you stay with our new friend? I am going to untie him. Please give him some food and let him regain some strength. His new ordeal to come will not be an easy one." Ihoitae asked.

Ifem nodded in ascent. "Of course."

Ihoitae untied the fish man and left him with Ifem for ministrations. Then, he told the commander to accompany him to the chieftain so that he could hear what was requested after the battle for the green stone.

***

The "battle" was already underway when Ihoitae and the guard commander had approached to speak with the chieftain. It turns out that the battle was indeed meant for Diane as the warrior that the Centaurs had chosen was also a woman and they were locked in some sort of mental confrontation. To Ihoitae this made perfect sense. Being as the Centaurs were Far Seers, their most powerful warrior would have been with magic not brawn and a female would most likely be the strongest of this ability since the males were stronger in physical prowess. Also, the verses that related to this stone stated:

Seek out the green jewel which is the heart of Kelnaria

But you must prove your worth to all of Centauria

This is done by words of trust

From someone whose people where once thought dust

Diane is from a people that where once thought dust as Telestics were thought to be extinct and only she would be the best at providing words of trust, especially to that of the powers of the Far Seers. The two "warriors" were standing in a circle surrounded by Centaurs and party members alike. They stood in front of each other faced eye to eye, their hands locked in a sort of mock arm wrestle. Sweat poured down each of their faces and their arms. There was no sound or action other than the occasional grunt or grimace that crossed one of their faces from time to time. This battle was internal.

The commander motioned for Ihoiate to approach the chieftain so they could discuss the terms of the fish man's captivity while the women fought. Though neither woman moved very much, Ihoitae could tell that the "fighting" was intense and that they were locked in a mental game of wits in which only peoples of their talents could see. Ihoitae knew that the Centaurs could see and hear everything in which Diane and their chosen warrior were doing. He also knew that it would be driving Dean crazy with worry that he couldn't. Ihoitae tried to place this in the back of his mind so he could have all his wits about him when he approached the chieftain about his request.

"Hail, Great Chieftain," bowed the commander, "Prince Ihoitae would like speak about fish man."

The chieftain sighed and looked from the combatants to the commander and Ihoitae. Thought a moment and then nodded his head. "We go to chieftain hut and speak freely. Bring my son and honored counselor Karlmanick."

The commander went off to locate the two Centaurs the chieftain requested and motioned for Ihoitae to follow him into the hut. Ihoitae did and sat patiently with the chieftain. Neither speaking, just waiting. The chieftain had started up a pipe and offered it to Ihoitae while they waited. Ihoitae was not a big smoker of anything, but felt it would be rude to disregard the offer and so he gingerly puffed and coughed for his efforts. The chieftain found this amusing and nodded his head to Ihoitae to encourage him to take a bigger, longer puff. He did and coughed less.

After a few moments, Mehawkin and Karlmanick entered into the hut. Each one went on either side of the chieftain and folded their horse legs under them to sit next to the chief. The chief also passed the pipe to each one and they also smoked as was the custom of their people before a discussion.

"Speak now, pointy eared one," Chief Barsillic began. "Speak plainly and truthfully."

Ihoitae nodded to the chief and then to Karlmanick and then to Mehawkin, thinking that Karlmanick would have more seniority as an elder counselor over the younger chieftain's son. "I, Prince Ihoitae Mahadeva Arabus, would request to take custody of the one you call fish man. I have spoken with him. Your commander was gracious enough to let me see him and speak with him. I believe he tells the truth and came to you at great peril to himself because he is a shaman, or as what you would call a medicine man among your people. He will die at the next full moon unless you release him into my custody. This is all I have to request."

Karlmanick, Mehawkin and Chief Barsillic all looked at each other a moment and then spoke in their guttural language while Ihoitae patiently sat and waited for their questions or their response. He did not have to wait long before he was asked a question. Chief Barsillic continued to speak.

"Where stone he say he has? We could not find. So, we don't believe his story, though he speak with truth behind his words. It.........confused us."

"Ah, I see the dilemma now," Ihoitae began, "But perhaps it was good that you delayed. Otherwise you may have thrown him back into the ocean and then he would have died anyway. You see, he stole the stone from his chieftain because he knew the time was right for the stone to be given to us. He came to the Centaurs in hopes that you would help him where his people did not. He says your races have had a somewhat uneasy truce over the years. But he understands your caution. He hid the stone inside his abdomen for protection."

All three centaurs gasped at that. But the chieftain recovered first and nodded his head without counsel of the other two. "Request granted. But if did steal from chieftain, his life is forfeit as is centaur custom too. He no return to sea or he will die. How you save him?"

Ihoitae smiled and bowed his head. "I thank you for your great deed this day. I know his life is forfeit, he explained this to Ifem and I. This is why my request was that you release him into my custody. I would care for him until he can survive on his own on this strange land to him. I can save his life by a special demonic spell I learned when I was conscripted into my father's army. Demons have a special magic to.......shall we say........get around banishments. I think this will work for our friend Esmarlin as well because this magic that afforded him the ability to walk on land is similar to the demons avoiding banishment."

Mehawkin was fascinated and asked in wonder, "Will work?" He did not want to see the merman killed as he had grown fond of the blue skinned half elflike, half fishlike creature.

Ihoitae turned to look at Mehawkin and shrugged. "I truly, honestly don't know. It may fail, but I feel strongly that it can succeed. Esmarlin has agreed to allow me to try."

Karlmanick looked to his chieftain and received a nod that he had permission to speak. "I agree with chieftain that fish man be placed in your care, but I think after cure, he should stay with Centaur until pointy ear can truly care for him." Then Karlmanick looked directly at Ihoitae and said, "Prince Ihoitae, no dishonor, but you still have prophecy of Great Ones to complete."

Once again all three centaurs looked at one another and nodded, then spoke once more in their own language. Then Chief Barsillic addressed the floor once more. "Karlmanick speak great truth. I granted custody to you. I will also grant amnesty to fish man until time comes you can care for him or any member of your party. Agreed?"

"As long as he is treated fairly, then I see no reason why he could not stay with you. I feel that this would be a great boon to both your peoples and so I accept these terms. I hope as well that he can accompany you to Cardinia, as an emissary for his people as well as yours. But I must try the spell immediately."

Then all three centaurs stood up, nodded and all said together, "Agreed." With that, they walked out and Ihoitae knew his meeting went well. When he stepped outside, he could see Mehawkin already speaking to the commander about the new agreement in regards to Esmarlen. The commander and Ihoitae walked back to the prisoner hut so that preparations could immediately begin.

*** 

As Ihoitae and the commander walked back to the fish man, the trial had ended and with it, Diane was victorious holding the green stone in her hand. The female centaur was on the ground, laying down breathing heavily. She was weak, but she would recover. Later, when any of the party members would ask her what happened, all she would say is "It is not something that I would relive, nor could I explain it. Please, let us leave it as it is."

Aelle went to go assist Diane into getting a bath and changing as Aelle knew she would also be exhausted after such a strenuous mind battle, probably even more so because Diane was with child. Dean knew that Diane was in good care with Aelle, so he went to discuss with the chieftain about allowing them to stay the night and rest.

"Of course you stay," Chief Barsillic laughed. "You are honored guests. We celebrate tonight!" Then he grunted some orders in his language to a couple of his women and a couple of his men. Dean assumed it was to prepare shelters for the party and to begin preparations for this celebration it would seem that they would have to attend.

After this issue was cleared up, Dean then went to go find his missing in action elves, Ifem and Ihoitae. He told Freonandiar, Faolan, Tian, Bodolf and the once God of War, now back to Presaya, to stay and help preparations or be useful wherever they could be so as to show that they were indeed grateful for the hospitality they would be provided. He also instructed them that once Aelle was done and Diane did not need her anymore, to see if Aelle could help as well. But he wanted Aelle to play nursemaid to his wife for as long as it was needed. He knew Aelle would not hesitate to care for Diane as long as was needed.

Dean found the prisoner hut and heard Ifem and Ihoitae inside with another voice that sounded a bit watery. Dean assumed this one was coming from the "fish man". He walked inside and saw a hospital scene that had recently been completed. There was a blue stone in Ihoitae's hands as Ifem finished stitching up Esmarlin's side. Ihoitae turned to see Dean in the doorway and greeted him.

"What is going on?" Dean asked firmly.

Ihoitae quickly took Dean back outside and motioned for the commander to come over and confer with Dean to confirm all that Ihoitae had to say. Ihoitae filled him in quickly with the story of Esmarlin and everything that had happened while Diane and the centaur warrior had their fight. The commander nodded and let Dean know that all was agreed upon and was true. Then Ihoitae told him that Ifem and he had to remove the stone from his abdomen first before Ihoiate could perform the banishment spell on Esmarlin. This would be done tonight at the water's edge before the waxing moon. Removing the stone now would allow Esmarlin time to heal up and gain some strength back before the spell attempt. It would also provide Ihoitae the best time for his magical abilities to be used since the Elfin Moon Goddess favored his people. Sylvans were always more powerful at night and, especially, during full moons. But, Ihoitae could not wait for a full moon to remove the stone. That would have to be done tonight before the full moon in order to save Esmarlin's life.

"I just hope it works," Ihoitae wondered with a bit of doubt. "Esmarlin will stay with the Centaurs as a sort of emissary between his people, the Lightbringers and the Centaurs until I can return for him. Or, as the chieftain suggested, anyone in our party."

Dean nodded his agreement. "This was fair, I think. I am glad you and Ifem were able to get him freed and I will hope that your demon banishment spell will work."

\*\*\*

Later that evening, there was a lot of celebrating going on as the centaurs danced around the great bonfire and ate heartily. The rest of the party joined in with eating and some tried to dance with the centuars too. The women spoke together and many rubbed Diane's belly where a very small baby bump was forming. The centaurian women wished her well in the carry and birth of her unborn.

Ihoitae, Mehawkin and Karlmanick all assisted Esmarlin down to the beach with a small group of warriors for protection from other tribes. The beach was not very far from the main Chief's clan, so they were able to reach it in about an hour. However, they were well out of sight and sound from the celebration going on at the centaur camp.

Ihoitae and Ifem wore light clothing as they would go into the ocean with Esmarlin. Mehawkin stayed at the waters edge in case something should attempt to attack them. Karlmanick stayed well back to observe but not to intrude on the ritual that would be performed. Per Ihoitae, Esmarlin would need to return to the sea in order to meet the obligations of his one time ability to walk on land. Then once he was a full merman again, then Ihoitae could perform the banishment spell on Esmarlin making him a full time land dweller. Esmarlin would most likely crave salt water from time to time, but otherwise, he could dwell on land for the rest of his days safe from retribution of his people. Ihoitae also felt that Esmarlin would probably be able to still swim better, faster and hold his breath better under water than any other land dweller. Ihoitae could not promise he would remain looking as he did now.

Esmarlin, though still weak from his capture and removal of the stone, walked of his own accord and completely submersed himself in the water, moving past Ifem and Ihoitae whom only went in as far as their waists. In order for him to complete the land spell, he would have to completely go into the water and breathe in the ocean once more. Once that was completed, then he would come as close to Ihoitae and Ifem as he could without loosing his ability to breathe underwater. It would be challenging due to the waves, but the sea was calm tonight.

After about twenty minutes, Ihoitae motioned for Ifem to move further into the water, up to their chests. Once they were this far in, Esmarlin swam to them and gently grabbed their arms. Ihoitae grabbed Ifems to complete a circle. Then, Ihoitae began to chant. It was very guttural and almost sounded as if he were between howls and growls and grunts. It was the magical language of the demons. As he spoke, the water began to glow an ugly blood red around the three of them. Ifem and Esmarlin closed their eyes so they would not be distracted by the color and kept all thoughts on Ihoitae and what this spell was supposed to accomplish.

The blood red glow gleamed brightly against the night sky and the dark waters around them. It began to bubble as if it were boiling, though no heat was being produced. Suddenly, Esmarlin began to feel a twinge in his limbs and it radiated inwards to his very core. The pain intensified as the light grew brighter and brighter around them. He began to jerk and tug against the strong grasp of Ihoitae and Ifem and then, he could no longer breathe. His lungs hurt. His limbs ached and he desparately tried to get away from them. He was no longer thinking clearly and all he could think was that the spell had failed and he was dying. Then he knew no more.

Ihoitae stopped speaking and motioned for Ifem to grab the thrashing merman and drag him onto shore. Ihoitae was too weak himself and Mehawkin grabbed the elf to assist him to shore. Mehawkin was in total wonder and awe as he saw the magic that had been performed. He had never seen it before. For while the Centaurs had a special type of magic, they never performed magic; he was exhilarated.

Ifem was able to half carry, half drag Esmarlin to shore and let the spell finish its transformation. Ihoitae had warned them all ahead of time what could or would happen and so, Esmarlin was indeed changing. His body maintained its blue sheen, but he lost his webbed hands and feet and the scaling on his skin was gone. The gills that were on his cheeks were gone and replaced by smooth skin. His eyes were still a beautiful saphire in color, but were no longer bulbous like a fish and resembled more of a human's eyes. Lastly, he was changed to resemble more of a humanoid male in the lower regions where before he had been smooth because of the nature of fish reproduction. Once the twitching had stopped and Esmarlin fell into a peaceful slumber, Ifem wrapped him up in the blanket that they brought with them.

"It is done," Ihoitae said weakly. "The demon spell of banishment changed him from a merman into a hybrid of human as nature saw fit. He is truly unique." Then Ihoitae passed out, but before he could hit the ground, Mehawkin caught him and swung him up to carry him.

Karlmanick walked over to the once fish man and gently picked him up as if he were cradling a new born baby and looked at Ifem. "Are you able to walk? I can carry this one."

Ifem smiled and responded, "Yes, I am fine. A little worn out from carrying him thrashing from the sea, but the magic was all Ihoitae's. I had no idea the spell was so strong, nor would wipe him out so completely."

Mehawkin looked at the warriors that had accompanied them and grunted a few commands and they formed up a circle around the last standing elf and two Centaurs. "It was amazing!"

"Yes, it was," Ifem laughed.

The whole troop walked back to the campsite. They were greeted by a much more subdued celebration than when they had left. Many had worn themselves out and went to sleep. Many lay where they had passed out from too much fun. Mehawkin and Karlmanick went with Ifem to find the Lightbringers tent and there they placed the sleeping Ihoitae and Esmarlin.

Ifem looked at Dean who was not asleep, but was laying beside his wife, who was fast asleep. "It went well, I think."

"Good," Dean said. "Now, please rest and we can hear all about it in the morning. We still have one stone to go and the blade pieces."

Ifem nodded and took a sleeping mat that Dean had indicated and fell immiditaely to sleep. He was much more tired than he realized.

# Chapter Nineteen

THE PARTY WOKE to find the Centaur camp extremely busy. During the night, many of the different tribal clans had arrived. They were being given orders and organized into the army that would join the Cardinian troops. This camp was also being broken down to store away what would not be used while the warriors were away and the elders and women and children were given shelters and food stores to assist them with the coming months in which they would be left alone. Some warriors would stay behind to protect the clans' homes, but most would be going to war. Chief Barsillic would also stay behind with his people since he was no longer hale enough to fight. Mehawkin would take his place, but would not command the armies. He would serve as emissary and would battle with his clan's troop, but he was not experienced enough in the ways of battle, so it was decided one of the other more seasoned warriors would lead the command. Centaurs were going to the beach where the ships were being loaded with supplies for the journey.

As the Lightbringers also broke camp, ate some food to break their fast and prepare for the next part of their journey, Faolan took Freonandiar aside to speak with him.

"Freonandiar," he began. "I would ask that you go with the centaurs to Cardinia Castle. I need for you to act as emissary on my behalf for them. I also need for you to advise my......um.......parents that their son has found himself and he will join them soon. They have every right to know who their son is. Tell them of my birthmark and tell them the story of how I was found. They know I am with the Lightbringers and Ifem.

"Ask them if they would grant you amnesty on my behalf and I will prove myself to them upon my arrival to the castle."

Freonandiar nodded.

"I have nothing to give you to provide to them except faith. But I would wager that since Zaire mentioned it the night Ifem was named the new Head Zadian priest, they may grant you a boon on my behalf. Also, make sure you tell them you are the Fairy Prince. I know you have your family ring to prove that. They should treat you as a dignitary."

Freonandiar once again nodded.

"And lastly," Faolan sighed, "If you can, see if my......um, well I guess you would call her my foster sister now, Fea, please let her know Tian and I are alive and well."

"Aye, my foster brother, I will do as you ask," Freonandiar replied. He picked up his pack and went to find out where he should go to accompany the Centaurs to Cardinia Castle.

Dean nodded his agreement that Faolan did the right thing and then added, "I know the King and

Queen fairly well. I believe they will treat him well enough just on his princely status as Fairy Prince. But, being that he knows their long lost son, I truly believe they will be beyond grateful. He knows of the birthmark so they will know he is speaking the truth. No one really knew about it except the royal house and the midwives and nursemaids. It never left the castle steps."

"Thank you, Dean. I do need to hear that. It is still tough to understand that I am a prince."

"You will honor your family, Faolan. You are a wonderful person. Prince is just a title. But your honor is all yours to make or break." Dean advised.

Ifem stepped up to Dean and Faolan and asked, "So, where to? The last verse in regards to the stones says The last of the jewels can only be found in ruins
Yellow is the soul where an extinct race once has been To test ones heart is the only way to win Or all the world will falter to his unforgiven sin."

Ihoitae looked at them all and spoke, "Isn't that one obvious? We need to go back to the Onae ruins."

"WHAT!?!?!?!" Dean and Ifem almost yelled together. Then Ifem carried on, "We were just there when this all began. Are you sure?"

Ihoitae sighed solmnely. "I am sure. At first I thought it referred to the Telestics, but since we now know that they are not truly extinct, just, shall we say translucent, then it has to be the Onae."

Diane spoke up, "I agree with Ihoitae. We all felt something while we were there. For something that has been dead for so long to still have so much dread........it is the only place that makes sense."

"Well, what does everyone else think?" Dean asked of everyone.

"Aye, the laddie is right," Bodolf agreed. "I sensed it too."

Faolan, Tian, Aelle and Presaya also nodded in agreement.

"Alright, Ihoitae, are you recovered enough to use your translocation spell to port us back?" Dean began as the commander attitude took over.

Ihoitae nodded.

"Great. We will leave in one hour so everyone has enough to pack up and get some grub. Ihoitae," Dean motioned towards Esmarlin. "Please also provide instructions to your ward to accompany the Centaurs with Freonandiar."

"Yes, sir," Ihoitae responded and went off to go find Esmarlin to see how he was faring in his new body.

When Ihoitae found Esmarlin, he was eating voraciously as well as admiring his new feet and hands in between mouthfuls. He would also take in huge gulpfuls of air relishing in the fact that he would never need to breathe underwater again. He saw Ihoitae approach and he smiled a very large grin that spread from ear to ear.

"Well met!" exclaimed Esmarlin to Ihoitae.

Ihoitae could not help but smile back and responded likewise, "Well met, my friend. How do you fare?"

Esmarlin's voice was now deep and resounding and did not resemble the same watery voice as it once had. "I am well! Re-energized. A bit strange as I am getting used to the subtle changes, but otherwise, well. Thank you so much!"

"Oh you are very welcomed," Ihoitae chuckled. "The hardest thing for you to get used to will be the male reproductive parts, I wager, as they are much different from fish reproduction, but I suggest you do not learn from the Centaurs. When you get to Cardinia, please seek out a physician or a Zadian priest that is of a more human nature to help you."

"I will. So, I am to go to Cardinia now?"

"Sadly, yes," Ihoitae sighed. "As I am sure you are aware from the stars, time grows nigh."

"Aye, yes," Esmarlin lamented, "I am happy to know that I still have my shamanic abilities, except instead of waves and water currents, I now read wind and air currents. I knew I was going with Freonandiar before you approached. I just hoped I was wrong." The former merman chuckled.

"No, you are not. But after this quest is done, we will have to return to Cardinia to forge the blade, Tremblount. We can spend some time together then."

Esmarlin nodded in agreement. "It is done. But, I have a warning for you. The air tells me something foul is creeping after you. It has attempted once already to destroy you. Its next attempt will not fail in your capture, so please keep it at bay."

Ihoitae looked stunned.

The former fish man shrugged and stated "I told you. I am one of the most powerful shamans of my time. It seems that with the banishment spell, my powers were enhanced and not lessened."

"I will heed your words then, my friend. Until we meet again." Ihoitae held out his hand to shake farewell to Esmarlin and was pulled into a hug instead.

"As my former people used to say, May the current speed you on your way."

Ihoitae left his new friend in the care of the parting Centaurs and headed back to the party's tent to clean up any last needed items and gather his fellows to travel back to the Onae ruins known as Onari.

# Chapter Twenty

HIS MISTRESS WAS not happy with his news, but it was news she needed to know regardless of whether it displeased her or not. She was angry, but surprisingly did not take her anger out on him. She instead decided that there was another way to dispose of her rival, her enemy, her half brother. She wanted their father's undivided attention and to stop focusing on his bastard son begotten from a slutty elf. She sent him back to the ruins in which he came from and told him that when the time was right, he would have Berdinian soldiers there and they would claim her half brother. It was time for Kahlrab to be resurrected.

\*\*\*

As before, the spell was instantaneous. It brought the party to the exact spot that they left before they went to go visit the White Dragons in Lahrtden. It was night time, however, when they arrived as this place was halfway around Kelnaria. The ruins seemed to glow an eerie yellow color and the atmosphere had definitely changed. It was almost as if the land had expected them.

Once they were able to gather their wits, they saw that one of the ruins was that of a temple and was what was causing the eerie yellow glow. It was no longer a ruin as it had been the first time they were here. It was intact and it was beckoning to them. They approached the entrance because none of them could deny that call. All nine of them were caught up in the prophecy and the prophecy would not be denied.

After they reached the entrance, they all stopped as if compelled to do so. A voice spoke to them. It was male, deep, loud, booming.

"Stop travellers of another time," it started. "You are here because you seek that which is mine to give. The stone of the soul."

All nine party members looked from one to another. None knew what to do, so Ihoitae decided to take the lead. Afterall, it seemed most of everything stemmed around him anyway.

The voice continued. "I know who all of you are. I know what you have faced and I know what you will face. However, this trial is for one of you alone as have previous trials. The one known as Ihoitae will be tested. Should he win, the stone will go to the boy king. Should he lose, then all will fail. Know now that the boy king is to wield Tremblount, but only the demon elf can defeat Kahlrab."

"But, if I can't wield the sword, how do I defeat him?" Ihoitae asked, more to himself, but the voice responded anyway.

"The sword is not the slayer of demons and gods. It is the uniter of nations. There is another way to defeat Khalrab as you will learn in time."

"Fair enough," Ihoitae began. "So, if I am to be tested, shall we begin?"

"Very well," the voice stated flatly and suddenly all around Ihoitae his comrades began to cry out in pain, fall to their knees and disappear. Ihoitae was rendered motionless and could do nothing to help them.

"What is happening to them?!," Ihoitae demanded to know.

"I am the Crystal Cave of Wonders. I am older than everything else on Kelnaria as Kelnaria was created around me. I was the first home of the Mystics until the Onae came and drove them away. I was where the Mystics created the Great Scrolls and the prophecy and.......well.........you. I have been warped from my true purpose as a temple of peacefulness to one of power and benevolence. I house the soul stone and only one of true heart and soul can retrieve it from my halls. If that is you, then you will succeed. If not, then you will fail and everything the Mystics ever worked for will fail with you.

"I am an easy test, for I have one question for you. If truth be provided, you will walk into my entrance hall and receive your reward. If not, then your friends and you will wander my halls for all eternity while Kahlrab reigns over the mundane world above you. Is this made clear to you?"

"Crystal clear," Ihoitae said extraoridinarily flatly. "Speak your question and I will provide you my truth or falsehood."

"Your unforgiven sin. Ihoitae, are you willing to forgive yourself of your unforgiven sin?"

Ihoitae flustered. Sin? What sin?, he pondered. What is this thing talking about?

Then he said out loud. "I am mortal. I have committed many sins over the years to be sure. I know some I have readily forgiven myself for. Some I have sought forgiveness from others for. But I truly cannot think of one that I should pay an ultimate price for. I would relinquish everything that I am to save my friends, please tell me of my sin so I can save them." Ihoitae begged to the entrance way that began to grow brighter and brighter.

"You do not know yet, do you, child?"

"Know what?," Ihoitae flabbergasted. "What am I supposed to know?"

"I see that you do not," the voice continued almost as if Ihoitae had not spoken. "Very well, I will not tell you this truth at this time. Your mother must tell you. But I do see in your heart that you speak the truth of your friends and your life. You would gladly give that to spare them. Be careful what you wish for son of unknown origins. I will grant you a boon. The stone is yours. Step inside and take it."

Ihoitae was utterly confused. It could not be this easy. Something was wrong. But the feeling that had compelled him and the rest of the team earlier also compelled him now and he could not refuse. He entered the temple and lying in an altar in the middle of the room was the yellow stone of the soul. It was what was glowing so brightly that had caused the eerie yellow glow.

When Ihoitae walked out of the temple it suddenly disappeared and the world snapped back into place. Ihoitae suddenly realized what had happened to his friends. It was not the temple at all. He was surrounded by Berdinian soldiers and his friends were all lying on the ground out cold. The stone that had once been in his hands now disappeared. The soldiers quickly took advantage of Ihoitae's distraction and knocked him out cold. The world went dark.

***

When the party woke up, Faolan found the yellow stone in his tunic pocket along with the other stones. However, neither the temple nor Ihoitae were anyhere to be found. The soldiers' boots were a telltale sign of just what had happened as the thief and scout of the group put together the events of the night.

"Berdinia has him!" shouted Presaya. "By the gods, how did I let this happen!"

"Calm down, Presaya," Diane attempted to intervene. "We will figure it out."

"No, we won't. They have him! We have to rescue him!" Presaya was pacing at a mad dash back and forth as the party slowly recovered their wits. "You don't understand!"

Dean grunted. "I agree, Presaya, we should find him and rescue him as it does look as though he was captured. But, Berdinians? Here? The Djinns more like.......or his father. We are back on the island flooded with demons."

"NO!" shouted Presaya. "It was the Berdinians. Look at the boot marks!"

Aelle and Dean inspected the footprints left all over the ground. They did note that they had more of a human appeal to them rather than a demon and Djinns would have just floated as they refuse to touch the ground. However, Bodolf was the one to notice something strange in the chaos of all the prints in the ground. He pointed them out to Presaya and Aelle.

"What do you make of these lassies?" Bodolf asked.

Presaya and Aelle and Dean all three examined the prints that were mixed with the soldiers' prints. These were clearly demon or draconic prints as they were scaled and clawed. They ruled out Dean's prints because Dean was a rare Draconian that actually wore boots. So, they decided to follow the prints and noticed that they led off and away from the soldiers' prints shortly past the camp. Then, without any warning, a creature as dark as midnight jumped up and ran lighting fast past them. All three were caught off guard. But Faolan, whom had been watching the three intently, noticed the movement from behind the ruined block the creature was hiding behind and he threw a rock at the creature's head. It hit the creature just right on the temple and knocked him out cold. Ifem and Tian immediately went to the creature and tied him up.

"Yep, definitely demon tracks!" exclaimed and excited little gnome. "Now, we wait for him to tell us what happened so we can go rescue our friend."

They did not need to wait long. This demon had a strong constitution and he awoke quickly. He realized immediately what had happened and hissed. He received a sword tip at the edge of his throat for his efforts. Dean held the sword and looked menacingly at the little demon.

Dean started the interrogation. "I do not like your kind and I would not hesitate to run you through. You are only alive because our little gnome friend here believes you can tell us who took our elfin friend. So, talk or die."

The demon glared at Dean and showed his yellow canine teeth. His blood red eyes sparking hate from him showing nothing but contempt. His mistress would revive him, he was certain, so he would let the draconian run him through.

"He no gonna talk!" Bodolf stated. "Canni try? Me thinks he needs some dwarven persuasion."

Dean sheathed his sword, shrugged and stepped back.

Bodolf chuckled wickledly and drew a very tiny dagger from his belt. He approached the little demon and sliced its arm. The creature winced, but refused to cry out. Then Bodolf spoke, "Little one, this dagger be tiny cause it be very deadly now. It has a rare poison not evern your kind can withstand. I have the fix if you talk, or else you die."

At first he did not believe the dwarf, but within a few moments the world began to swim and he felt hot and befuddled. His stomach heaved and felt as if he would puke. He then knew that the dwarf was not lying and knew that these people would let him die without a thought. His doubts about his mistress saving him suddenly leapt into play. Maybe she wouldn't resurrect him. She was finicky and he had displeased her recently.

"I reckon you have about ten more minutes before even my fix canno fix you." Bodolf looked off as he spoke as if the little creature's life was of no consequence. As if on queue, the other party members began to break up and pack up.

The little demon squealed, "The gnome is right!," it hissed. "The Berdinians came and took him. Knocked you all out while he was in some sort of invisible bubble. Once the yellow bubble popped, they took their chance and seized him. I stayed to make sure you would not find him."

Bodolf slowly moved towards the little demon and fumbled with his belt looking for the "fix" as he called it. While he did so, Presaya walked right up into the demon's face and demanded, "Why do they want him? What was he captured for and no the rest of us?"

The demon laughed. "Give me the antidote and I will tell you."

"Give it to him," Dean commanded.

Bodolf went up to him and poured a small vile down the creatures throat. It attempted to bite him, but he was too quick and moved his chubby little dwarf fingers back lighting quick. "Dwarves are fast for their stubby limbs," remarked the little demon. "He is to be the sacrifice to awaken Kahlrab." The demon laughed again a menacing growl like laugh. Then he continued. "You see, while the Mystics made their prophecy, The Great Scrolls, the demons also made a prophecy to circumvent – or as the druids love so much – balance the scrolls. We call ours the Prophetic Vision.

"The Berdinians found our scrolls and fanatically adopted its faith. They have been working to resurrect Kahlrab for many decades now. They recentlty stumbled upon the way to do so and they needed the mixed blood of an elvin and demon prince. Your precious Ihoitae."

"Ugh, this is not good," Faolan stated flatly. "I think things just went from being ok to very bad."

"Agreed," Dean commented at Faoaln, then looked at the creature. "If this were true, though, why did not Lord Mordecai sacrifice his own son to raise his Lord God?"

"Simple," it replied in hissing snakelike fashion. "Lord Mordecai hates Kahlrab as he thinks Kahlrab is too chaotic and too out of control with bloodlust and power. But without bloodlust and power, what else is there?"

"So, if you don't work for Lord Mordecai, who do you work for?" Faolan asked.

The creature paused a moment and thought about the consequences of telling them and decided that his mistress would approve. She wanted to come out of the shadows. "My master, or rather mistress, is Princess Aillenia Arabus, Ihoitae's half sister on his father's side. She would have her brother killed so that she was the next in line for the demon throne. Many demons think that Mordecai is too soft. She will rule them into their next great era. She will enslave all the races on this puny planet and do so with Kahlrab as her king."

"So, she will kill Lord Mordecai and her grandfather, Arabus, to banish them to the nine Abyssals. She will kill Ihoitae to resurrect a fanatical tyrant all so she can rule the demon kingdom and Kelnaria?" Faolan surmised, more to himself rather than to ask the foul little creature any more questions.

Presaya pulled her fist up and punched the little demon out of pure anger. Then she grabbed its scaly black head and looked deep into its blood red eyes. "I will not let that happen! Your kind has destroyed enough of this planet. You will not destroy it utterly!"

The creature merely laughed. "We shall see. Both sides, I will admit, have a good chance at this point. But the tides will turn once Kahlrab is reborn. And that time fast approaches."

With that, Presaya had heard enough. She took her sword and she chopped the little demon imp's head off. Then she cleaned her weapon on its little tunic and stalked off muttering, "Damn demons. Shoulda never let them come through the gates! Too soft hearted my sister was!"

Dean looked at the creature's body one last time and then looked at the party and barked his commands. "Ok, time to head to Berdinia's castle province. We know that is where they keep the sarcophagus of Kahlrab thanks to many accounts of spies and reconnsaiance over the years, but we never knew why. Now we do."

Ifem cleared his throat to gain attention. "Two things. One, should we do anything with its body? Two, without the transportation spell, it will take us at least a week or more to reach Berdinia. The soldiers probably have at least five or six hours ahead of us and they may have even used teleportation spells. At the very least, they would already have had boats and they won't be going through hostile territory. We will never reach him in time."

Everyone in the group looked up and over at Ifem and suddenly all were in dismay. Ifem was right. Even if the ceremony wasn't for a month, as it was most likely going to have to be done around a full moon and the most recent full moon cycle was occurring tonight, they still would never make it on time.

Aelle suddenly had an idea and looked over at Presaya. "Um, Presaya.......I hate to ask you this, especially given our need for discretion but....well......um, can't you.....just this once........exert some, well, you know – godly intervention?"

The entire party looked at Presaya with pure desperation in their eyes.

Aelle spoke again, purely begging, "It is a good cause. I know what a great risk it would be to you, to us, but it's the desperate hour, is it not?"

"It is not," a strange voice came to them out of the air. They looked around in different directions trying to find the voice that spoke. It was clear, strong and feminine. "But it will be soon. So, I will help as I was bid by my mistress to assist you." The figure materialized into view.

"Shyaralia!.," everyone but Faolan and Tian exclaimed. Dean, Aelle, Bodolf and Diane all bowed in reverence to their client's avatar.

Presaya scoffed and scowled, "So, she finally decides to help! A bit overdue, isn't it?"

Shyaralia shrugged. "I understand your mirth, revered one. But I have no control over my mistress anymore than you do."

"Is she aware that her precious boy is about to be murdered to resurrect a lunatic god that we all fought so hard to destroy? Is she aware that her Mordecai had another child whom wants to see the world end? Tell me, is she aware of anything?" Presaya snapped back.

"I cannot answer that for you," Shyaralia said without any emotion at all. "You know that. Perhaps she heard you. Perhaps she listens now. But regardless, I was sent to grant you a boon so that you......oh dear, um, Presaya is it?.............you could maintain your identity. She recognizes the need for that. She also recognizes your urgency now."

"Fine. It is accepted," Presaya remarked curtly. "But only because my discretion is imperative at this time. How far are you able to grant this boon?"

Shyaralia nodded her ascquiescence and advised, "I am allowed to teleport you within a day's reach of Berdinia. The reason for that amount of distance is due to the magic. The evil dragons that fly constantly over Berdinian lands will know of the ancient draconic magic being used and you will be captured or killed instantly. The safest but closest spot is within a day's reach. Will you accept?"

Presaya looked at Dean. Dean nodded his ascent, then everyone else nodded their ascent. Bags were gathered with military precision, Shyaralia had everyone stand in a circle, and hold hands as Ihoitae had done the last two times they used this spell.

Instantly they had been transported just south of a day's march of the castle proper of Berdinia. Presaya noted that they were placed exactly between Pofhon and Arthon and within a day's march north as Shyaralia had advised. However, when the party opened their eyes, the avatar was gone. And, without a word, the entire party began to move as swiftly and as cautiously as they could towards the capital of Berdinia, Berdinia Castle Proper.

\*\*\*

The party faired well and travelled swiftly. They only had two "run ins" with Berdinian troops. The first "run in" they were actually able to avoid. There was one set of patrol guards walking idly down the road making sure that the caravans passing by were unhindered by highwaymen. The party was very close to a set of wagons and passed themselves off as hired mercs for the caravan.

The second "run in" was a bit more involved as they stumbled accidentally into another small patrol group. This time they were nowhere near any travellers or caravans, but were still able to play it off as if they were travellers coming from one of the provinces to see the resurrection. This was a risk to mention, but seeing as the Berdinians now had Ihoitae; they hoped that this would confirm that they were not on a wild goose chase. The patrol guards turned out to be quite helpful and over confident that there wouldn't be any enemies anywhere near the sovereign of Berdinia. So, they assisted the Lightbringers in getting closer to the castle completely unhindered.

They had arrived just in time it seemed. The whole city was abuzz about the coming ceremony and the resurrection of the long lost god of the Prophetic Vision. The prince of Lord Mordecai had finally been captured and his blood would revive the banished god. The party had attempted to try and find shelter so they could make a base camp, but every inn and tavern was booked solid for the event. They learned that the Berdinians had actually arrived with Ihoitae about four days before they had arrived. That meant that the entire party had been knocked out cold for at least two and a half to three days before they travelled. Word had travelled fast, apparently.

The party was trying to effect any way they could to rescue Ihoitae from Berdinia's dungeons. As they walked around the city, they could see that there was not a way to do this. The town was too well fortified both inside and out as people were arriving from all over Berdinia to witness the resurrection. The security was not anywhere near as lacking as the one they had encountered when they rescued Faolan and Tian. The group began to despair and all they could think of was the death of Cardinia's hope.

Sneaking inside the city as pilgrims had been easy enough, but any attempt to rescue someone from the dungeons was entirely different and impractical. When they finally did locate the dungeons, Presaya had been the only one that could sneak down into the dungeons to do some reconnaissance. She was only able to do so because she took a risk at using some of her abilities as a god to do so. She very unhappily reported back just how even more fortified and guarded the dungeons were compared to the rest of the city. It did not bode well.

She also informed them of Ihoitae's condition. Poor. They had beaten him severely and stripped him completely so that he was naked and covered in his blood and flith and whatever prior "residents" filth was also in the dungeon. He appeared to have been tortured and his condition was such that he wasn't even able to use his shape shifting abilities. His wings were dirty and ripped. His claws had been torn and shredded. His normally stark white hair was encrusted with blood and mud. His wounds were infected and he was feverish.

"But seeing as he is to be sacrified on the morrow," Presaya completed her report, "I hardly think they care. He will not die from his infections before they can take his blood tomorrow."

"Damnit, is there nothing we can do?" Dean spit, slamming his fist into one of the walls of an alley the party had commandeered as their headquarters.

"No," replied Presaya. "He is in the third and final level of the lowest part of the dungeons. There are four guards posted at every entrance and exit and along the halls on every level every so many feet. And the halls leading down into the bowels have six guards. There is never a time when the posts are abandoned as the current watch cannot leave their posts until their new guard relieves them of their duty. And they always come together, so it would be like fighting a small army in and a small army out. Then........there are the traps.......I don't even want to get started on the traps........." She looked away in the direction of the dungeons and sighed.

"Can't we just go in like the Reeshane tribes do and stealthily get him out?" asked Aelle, hopeful.

"No, I do not need to explain how I was able to visit him," Presaya responded. "And since I am the only god among you, I would be the only one that could get in and back out. But I can only do this when I am in my godlike state and can be invisible to mortals. If I go in and get him out then all will be lost anyway. I would…..shall we say……let the Reeshane out of the bag. I don't think I need to explain the consequences that this would bring not only to Ihoitae and us, but also to the entire prophecy in general."

Dean shook his head. "No, we can' do that. But we cannot just sit idly by. Perhaps, we can bide our time and there will be a way to rescue him when they move him from one location to the platform we saw in the castle square. No matter how fortified this city is and how well the troops are disciplined, there is always a kink in the movement. As most of you know, that's how we rescue 99% of our jobs."

All nodded, especially Diane, Aelle and Bodolf remembering many past such jobs of extraction.

Dean continued, "We have no choice then at this time. We will have to attend this vile resurrection ceremony and if the chance presents itself to effect a rescue we shall. We will learn every inch of that platform tonight for anticipation of tomorrow's horror.

"But!," Dean stated sternly and with great lamantations, "I truly hate to utter these words; I don't think we will be able to snatch him from the Grim Reaper twice."

\*\*\*

The next day, they were able to attend the ceremony without issue as they still were under the guise as pilgrims come to see the resurrection of the Prophetic Vision's god, Kahlrab. The stage that this foul deed was to be done was large and semi circled so as to provide maximum view for all spectators. This was Berdinia's moment of triumph over Cardinia, or so they believed, and they wanted to celebrate as long and as loudly as they could.

In the center of the platform lay the shrine to Kahlrab where His sarcophagus was raised upright and was as black as midnight, much like His pets, The Fates. His image was embossed on the cover. The table that was to be the sacrificial altar was in front of Kahlrab's tomb lengthwise so there would be as much view of the sacrifice as possible.

Off to one side of the platform was the booth that would house the Royal Family and its entourage. The other side contained a booth for the priests and chaplains of the Prophetic Vision pantheon. There was another smaller table near the sacrificial altar that held the tools to be used.

The commoners and lesser nobles whom did not warrant a seat in either of the booths were allowed to seat first. This was so that they could view all the pomp and circumstance and the glory that was to be Berdinia's new found power. The Fates were lined all along the stage both for show and for crowd control.

Normally these vile creatures could not be controlled by anyone, but They knew Their true master was coming soon, so They were in rare obedience.

As the ceremony began, first marched in the priests and sages whom took their seats of prominence in their booth. Next came in the Royal Court, Royal House and any other notable nobles. They filed likewise into their booth. The head priest came in last. He was dark skinned with green eyes that resembled a lizard's with thick, black dreds for hair. He wore robes black as midnight on a moonless night with a ribbon of crimson red that tassled around his neck. He wore one solid gold chain around his neck that bore the symbol of Kahlrab at its crux and provided his credentials as the head of the order.

He approached the center of the stage and held up his arms. The crowd slowly went from loud, idle chit chat to soft murmured voices of excitement. The priest muttered a few words and then his voice was loud as the spell he had cast completely projected his voice throughout the province. The party watched all this with growing dismay. They were as close to the stage as they dared with the Fates there. They wanted to avoid being sniffed out. They held nothing but despair.

"Today is a glorious day," began the priest in a deep base voice that boomed from its magical enhancement. "Today the prophecy yields that we must arise our god," he paused as the crowd cheered and the party stared in utter disbelief.

"Today, the Fates and the magnificent Berdinian Army Soldiers of Troop A350 have brought to us our worst enemy. Today we have Prince Ihoitae Mahadeva Arabus in our capture," he paused as the crowed first cheered the capture and then booed and hissed at the mention of Ihoitae's name, then he began again, "and we can use the wayward son of our great ally and master Demon Lord Mordecai to resuurect our glorious god, the Demon God Lord High Kahlrab!"

Cheers erupted everywhere. The sound was a lot overwhelming and deafening as the peoples of Berdinia rejoiced. The priest smiled a wicked smile in pure satisfaction and the party cringed.

"Bring the prisoner!" The priest motioned towards the offstaged area. Two guards half carried, half dragged Ihoitae out onto the dias. He had been cleaned up and his skin and hair were clean, although his bruises and wounds were still visible. They had dressed him into a linen robe that was sheer to cover his nakedness. He was still shoeless and his hair was hanging. The evidence of his torture was still very present. He did not seem to be conscious, but even in his weakened state, Ihoitae still possessed a godly sheen. His hair gleamed pure white while the gold flecks in his now cleaned white wings picked up the glint of the sun. His demon heritage evident with his pointy ears and his claws for hands and feet versus nails. His porcelain skin, though flawed from his beatings, was radiant. The audience gasped at the sight. None had expected this Adonis type creature to be the evil son of Lord Mordecai.

The guards lifted him onto the altar, and although his barely conscious form struggled, in his weakened state he was no match for even a butterfly. Ihoitae cried out, "Father! Why?" But his voice was barely audible and his father was not there. In fact, his father had no idea that this ceremony was about to occur. If he had, he would have rescued his son from this folly that the Berdinians were about to commit. Both for love of his son and to keep the lunatic god of the demons right where he deserved to be. The demons did not want their ancient, evil, soulless, heartless, chaotic, horrible god re-awakened anymore than the goodly folk around Kelnaria did. Only the fanatics of the Prophetic Vision wanted him resurrected.

The priest moved over to Ihoitae and pulled out a jeweled encrusted, ceremonial dagger to commence the sacrifice. The priest whispered to him so no one could hear but Ihoitae, "Your father is oblivious to this, boy. His day on the throne is numbered as a new demoness will soon rise. One more fitting to wear the title of Lord Demon. Too bad you won't be around to see it. It's your half sister. Your father cannot save you."

The priest held up the dagger and smiled a wicked smile. He then began to chant the spell of resurrection in the horrible, guttural, grunting tongue of the demons. His chanting was once again loud having resumed the megaphone spell. He moved the dagger over Ihoitae's chest in a specified pattern. The guards moved to rip off the robe and to tie Ihoitae down so that they would no longer need to hold him down. One guard stayed at the foot of the altar with a vessel that would allow him to catch the blood that would flow down pre-carved lines on the altar towards the bottom in rivulets.

Ihoitae lay there weak, naked and in terrible shock over the news he had just heard and he struggled none the less despite the futility of his efforts. While the priest chanted and was caught up in his spell, Ihoitae also chanted a very quiet spell under his breath. He knew that he was very weak and they had placed wards, so any attempt to use magic may even be a waste of the last of his energy, but since he was about to die anyway, he would take the risk. His chanting done and last hope of a spell of protection to aid him, with his final breaths he prayed to the Sylvan goddess of the Moon, Sohalia.

Then the priest's chanting ceased. He opened his lizard like emerald eyes and with that wicked grin on his face brought the knife to bear. He sliced down Ihoitae's chest, starting from the neck and sliced down to his navel. He needed Ihoitae to stay alive as long as possible so his heart would pump out his life blood. Then the priest continued by slicing each arm from wrist to elbow. Next he sliced down Ihoitae's inner thighs from groin to knee. He allowed the blood to flow freely and swiftly for a few moments then finished by slicing Ihoitae's neck open from ear to ear.

Ihoitae groaned as each cut was delivered and his blood flowed faster. He began to grow colder and colder and began to lose consciousness. Finally, the world blacked out and Ihoitae knew no more.

"I cannot watch, " cried Diane to her husband, tears flowing freely down her face. She did not care if they were found out at this time. Aelle was grimfaced and was determined not to cry even as she heard her sister's echoes of wailing in her mind. All Aelle wanted to do was to go to her sister and comfort her. Ifem and Bodolf both hung their heads in reverence and hoplessness. Dean watched, sternfaced and determined to etch every moment on his memory for revenge he would exact at a later date. He seethed with anger. Faolan and Tian just looked lost.

Presaya had a tear in her eye and her hands were bleeding from where she had been clenching her nails into her hands so very tightly, but became the voice of reason, "Come, we must leave! There is no more we can do here and our very lives are in utter danger!" She gently nudged everyone to start them moving, hoping no one else in the crowd would take notice. Fortunately, the fantatics were so swept up in the events of the resurrection that they did not notice the little party moving out.

# About the Author

TERESA K CONRADO was born in Greensboro, NC. She began writing when she was twelve, creating wonderful tales of different worlds and different creatures. She now currently resides in the Tampa Bay area of Florida, where she lives with her wonderful husband and two children. She enjoys reading, as well as writing, gaming and playing with her family. Read Teresa's Smashwords Interview at https://www.smashwords.com/interview/TConrado.

# Other books by this author

Please visit your favorite ebook retailer to discover other books by Teresa K Conrado:

***The Maiden's Tale***
A short story, now available for download

***<u>The Kelnaria Chronicles</u>***
***Book One: The Great Scrolls***
***Book Two: The Demon Within****:* Book Two (Coming in Summer 2016)

## Connect with Teresa K Conrado

I really appreciate you reading my book! Here are my social media coordinates:

Friend me on Facebook:
https://www.facebook.com/teresa.conrado.92
Follow me on Twitter:
 https://twitter.com/Safiyyah713
Favorite my Smashwords author page:
https://www.smashwords.com/profile/view/TConrado
Visit my website:  http://worldofkelnaria.webs.com/
Email me at: tconrado713@gmail.com